Prologue

Two years ago . . .

As the darkness faded and the world came into focus, Beck Samson had time to process exactly three things.

The first was the body at his feet.

The second was the gun in his hand.

And the third was the flash of some very recognizable red and blue lights.

THE
HOSTAGE

Amazon bestselling author **Melinda Di Lorenzo** writes in her spare time – at soccer practices, when she should be doing laundry, and in place of sleep. She lives on the beautiful west coast of British Columbia, Canada, with her handsome husband and her noisy kids. When she's not writing, she can be found curled up with (someone else's) good book.

To find out more, follow her on
Twitter **@melindawrites** or Instagram **@melindadilorenzo**.

THE
HOSTAGE

MELINDA DI LORENZO

HEADLINE
ETERNAL

First published in 2022
by HEADLINE ETERNAL
An imprint of HEADLINE PUBLISHING GROUP

2

Cataloguing in Publication Data is available from the British Library

ISBN 978 1 4722 8650 5

Typeset in 11/14 pt Minion Pro by Jouve (UK), Milton Keynes

Printed and bound in Great Britain by Clays Ltd, Elcograf S.p.A.

Headline's policy is to use papers that are natural,
renewable and recyclable products and made from wood
grown in well-managed forests and other controlled sources.
The logging and manufacturing processes are expected to conform
to the environmental regulations of the country of origin.

HEADLINE PUBLISHING GROUP
An Hachette UK Company
Carmelite House
50 Victoria Embankment
London EC4Y 0DZ

www.headlineeternal.com
www.headline.co.uk
www.hachette.co.uk

With many thanks to Jo Watson

Chapter One

Joelle Diedrich splashed a little more water onto her face, then patted it dry with a disposable towel from the dispenser. The commercial-grade paper scratched at her skin, and she winced. If the sting wasn't a reminder that she was in an airport bathroom rather than the comfort of her own apartment, she didn't know what would be.

Which is the whole point, she said to herself as she tossed the paper towel neatly into the trash bin.

A change of scenery. A change of pace. It was exactly what she needed. In fact, it was the entire reason she'd accepted the sudden request. It kept her from having to face going back to her regular job—something she wasn't ready for. Not yet.

A sigh slipped through her lips anyway, and the redhead in the mirror—someone who looked an awful lot like a deflated, less shiny version of herself—sighed, too. Joelle wrinkled her nose, trying to find at least a piece of her former self in the reflection. The physical changes couldn't possibly be all *that* dramatic, and surely they were a normal part of grieving. Because three months of sadness and guilt would take a toll on anyone. Wouldn't they? Probably. But she struggled to find anything but fault in her appearance.

She studied herself, picking apart her present state.

Her hair was too long and too wavy. She usually kept it styled in a crisp bob, held in place by exactly four spritzes of finishing spray. At the moment, it touched her shoulders. Maybe even went past them a little. If she'd had an elastic, she might've been able to make a ponytail for the first time in a decade. And with the last-minute call to fill in for the medical escort who'd pulled a no-show, she hadn't had time to even think about getting it properly trimmed, let alone done it. The one thing that should've been a plus—the fact that the extra ten pounds she always complained about had evaporated—was actually a nuisance. Now that it was gone, her black dress pants hung a little too loose. Her cream-colored blouse was a tad big, too, and it kept trying to slide to one side. Even her feet had somehow narrowed. The casual flats she'd tried to put on first had fallen off when she started walking, and she'd been forced to trade them out for a pair of lace-up leather shoes. What really struck her, though, was the flatness in her green eyes. How long would it take for the sparkle to come back?

"C'mon," she said in a soft voice. "You're better than this, J.D. Get it together."

Of course, the mirror-her mouthed the words, too. And from Joelle's point of view, it looked like her reflection was mocking her. She rolled her eyes. But that only made things worse. So she let her lids sink shut instead, taking a second to block it all out.

She needed to get a hold of her professional self-assurance. And while she was at it, the personal insecurities had to be dropped. There were only five minutes left—give or take—before she had to meet with the rest of the Prisoner Transfer

Unit, and they'd be expecting someone competent. More than competent.

So far, her only interaction had been a quick check-in with the pre-flight Correctional Manager—a harried woman who'd scrutinized Joelle's credentials, reeled off a short list of instructions on how to get to the right terminal, then clacked away in her impractically high heels. It had left Joelle dazed. And to be honest . . . a little intimidated, too. What were the others in the unit like? Equally brusque? Even *less* congenial? Presumably, all of them had experience that exceeded hers. At least as far as prisoner transfers went. Her own decade of working as a nurse in corrections had been directly inside a facility. Stomach aches. Bruises and contusions. The odd cough or rash. Those were the ailments she attended to on a daily basis. Anything truly serious—or truly interesting, for that matter—got referred to the prison doctor. And she was left with the paperwork.

Again . . . she thought. *That's why I'm here. Something different.*

Despite the reassurance, nerves flitted through her. And with them came a hit of acute longing to be back in her bed. Maybe it was a mistake to believe that she was ready for a new challenge. She'd only been back at work once since taking her leave of absence. Just a brief meeting with the warden. Basically a glorified high five. But even the short visit in the familiar environment had been overwhelming. There'd been so many people. So much hustle and noise. Far too much of everything. And if Joelle was being honest, she still missed her mother every second of every day.

She lifted a hand to her chest, trying to press away the physical manifestation of the sadness. But her palm just barely met the spot above her heart before a throat-clear made her eyes fly open. She spun toward the sound, embarrassed to have been caught in the contemplative state. Her gaze landed on a blonde woman in her forties, who was standing in the doorframe of the bathroom, clad in an airline uniform, and looking far less awkward than Joelle felt.

"Sorry," said the woman. "Are you Joelle Diedrich?"

Automatically wary—and abruptly worried she might be about to be turned away—Joelle nodded. "I am. Is something wrong?"

"No, not at all. I just thought you might want to know that the Lead Transfer Escort just got back in from doing his inspection. He's a bit of a grump." The woman smiled as she said it, taking any unkindness out of the last statement. "I'm Wanda, by the way. I'll be your team's dedicated flight attendant today."

"Nice to meet you. And thanks for the heads up," Joelle replied, grabbing her jacket, then stepping away from the sink to follow the flight attendant out the door. "I take it you do this regularly?"

"I do," said Wanda. "Some of the flight attendants prefer not to get near the prisoners, but I grew up around that kind of thing—both my parents were involved in the law business—so I don't shy away from the bad guys. And the *good* guys like me because I don't come close to peeing my pants when a prisoner looks my way."

Joelle couldn't help but laugh. "I can see why that would be preferable."

"What about you?"

"Are you asking if I'm going to pee my pants?"

The flight attendant flashed another smile. "I guess I am. Is this your first run?"

"First prisoner transport, but not my first prisoner," Joelle said. "I'm just filling in for a colleague. Last minute, emergency thing. Hard to say no to the overtime."

All of the statements were true. They were also rehearsed. A miniature cover-up that she'd designed solely for keeping her emotion under wraps and repeated to herself in the car on the way from her apartment to the airport. Now, Joelle held her breath, waiting to see if the other woman showed any hint of seeing through it. But Wanda just smiled yet again.

"Totally get it," she told Joelle. "All money is good money."

They entered the pre-boarding area, walked past the meager number of passengers who were awaiting a crack-of-dawn flight, then headed for a set of frosted doors marked with the words "Executive Lounge". Wanda pulled open the door to reveal a trio of suit-clad men who stood in one corner. They all had their eyes on a shared binder, and none of them looked up at the silent intrusion.

"I take it those are my guys?" Joelle asked in a low voice.

"They sure are," said Wanda, her words equally quiet.

"Which one is the grump?"

The flight attendant laughed under her breath. "The tall one with the perma-frown. His name's Darby O'Toole."

Joelle's eyes sought the man in question, and she nodded. "Okay. Here goes nothing, right?"

"I'm sure it won't be nothing," replied Wanda with another laugh. "And if it is, I'll give you an extra package of snacks on the house."

"Deal. See you onboard?"

"You bet."

"Thanks again." Joelle inhaled and stepped toward the group, schooling a professionally cool smile onto her face as she joined their circle. "Hi, all. Sorry I'm a bit behind. Last-minute addition. I just got the call an hour ago."

Darby O'Toole turned a puzzled look her way. "And you are . . .?"

"Joelle," she replied. "Diedrich. A lot of people call me J.D."

He shared a glance with one of the other men—a shorter, stockier guy with steely gray hair, and whose pants were cinched with a steer-head buckle—then met her eyes and spoke slowly. "Jo. Elle."

"Yes. That's right."

"Not *Joel*?"

Her cheeks warmed, but she answered smoothly. "Nope. Not Joel. You'd be surprised how often people misread it, actually. But here I am, reporting for duty as the replacement Medical Escort."

He stared for another second before at last extending his hand and smiling a tight smile. "Apologies. You caught me off guard."

Sloughing off a trickle of unease, Joelle clasped his palm and shook. "You're the Lead Transport Escort? Darby O'Toole?"

"Indeed. It sounds like you're a step ahead of me despite your status as a last-minute addition, Ms. Diedrich." He sounded anything but impressed. "Do you need introductions to the rest of my unit, or have you got them pegged, too?"

The heat in her face crept up again. "No, sir. No other pegging going on."

"Well, then . . ." He swept an arm toward the short stocky man. "Let me introduce Shane Dreery, our Onboard Transfer Coordinator." He jerked a thumb at the third man, who was averagely built and had nondescript features. "And this is Win Redburn. He's our Onboard Correctional Manager. The guards will meet us onboard."

Joelle murmured a greeting and shook each of the men's hands before asking, "Do you guys know why the prisoner needs a Medical Escort? The conversation with my supervisor was a bit vague, and I'd like to be prepared."

"Allegedly, there was an issue with a seizure a few months back," O'Toole told her.

"Allegedly?" Joelle echoed.

"You know how these assholes are," Dreery interjected. "Maybe it happened, maybe it didn't, maybe they just want an extra buddy on the trip."

"Right," Joelle murmured, a bubble of concern sliding in.

"I take it you've already filled in the waiver, Ms. Diedrich?" O'Toole asked.

She redirected her attention his way. "Sorry?"

"The liability waiver." He didn't hide his impatience. "If you haven't filled it in, you'll need to do that before you join us on the plane."

He snapped his fingers, and Win Redburn yanked a piece of paper from the binder and held it out to her. A pen appeared in Dreery's fingers, too. Joelle took both and fought to keep from chewing the inside of her lip.

"Well," said O'Toole, "I've got a few things to check, so if you'll excuse me?"

"Sure," she replied. "Of course. Just let me know when you're ready for me."

"We're already ready for you, Ms. Diedrich. If you're not finished with the paperwork in five minutes, you can meet us on the tarmac." The tall man nodded at his counterparts. "Five minutes, gentlemen."

Then he spun and strode off toward the doors. Frowning a little, Joelle watched him go. Had he deliberately alienated her with his parting words, or was it an oversight? And as late as she was to join them, she'd still expected to hear at least a few more details.

A few more? *How about* any?

With a request for clarification poised on the tip of her

tongue, she turned back to Dreery and Redburn. But the two men had already moved on. Each of them was seated in one of the lounge's chairs, engrossed in their respective phones.

"Okay, then," Joelle said to herself.

She hovered where she was for another second, then gave in and sank down into one of the leather-backed chairs a few feet away from the other prisoner escorts. She balanced the paper on her knee and lifted the pen. But her fingers stalled, even before they could write her name in the blank space at the top of the form. Maybe she'd made a mistake in agreeing to do this. She certainly didn't feel welcome. Or anything close. Doubt surged and swirled and wouldn't settle. And under that feeling was another, stronger one. Disquiet.

*   *   *

Beck stared at the water-color painting that hung on the wall on the other side of the room. *Roses.* The vibrant shade of pink was the brightest, prettiest thing he'd seen in God knew how long.

Twenty-one months, sixteen days, said an obnoxious voice in his head.

"Shut up," he growled.

He let his eyes rest on the flowers for another few seconds before he dropped his gaze down to his hands. Sometimes, he didn't recognize them as his own. For fifteen years, his fingers had the luxury of working behind a desk. They hadn't been soft. Not exactly. Beck had still been a fisherman and a camper—a man who liked to get away from the city. A weekend warrior. Slightly more than that, maybe. A *long*-weekend warrior. Possibly even a *week-long* warrior. Now, though, there was nothing weekend or even week-long about the way his hands looked.

His palms were calloused. Roughened by the manual labor program that he'd opted to enroll in while incarcerated. Six months into his twenty-five-year sentence—six months of boredom mixed with anger and frustration—had made it seem like a good idea to be productive in some way. So he learned to build furniture. It was almost funny. It definitely served its purpose. Tiring his body to the point that his mind could rest. Feeling half-good about creating something. Even if he never saw the finished projects in the real world.

Sometimes, he lay awake at night wondering just where his latest piece of prison-crafted cabinetry had landed. If the person who'd bought it knew that it'd been crafted behind thick cement walls by a man like him. He hoped not. He liked the idea that somewhere, someone loved something he'd made without the stigma attached to his current life. Maybe the most recent piece—a simple coffee table with perfectly rounded corners—had been given as a gift to a couple of newlyweds.

Beck stifled a snort. *Right. Newlyweds. For all I know, it wound up in a place like this. Built in one goddamn institution, housed in another.*

His attention lifted back to the painting. He doubted that the artist who'd crafted it envisioned it hanging in an airport security room. Hell. He couldn't even come up with a good reason for someone putting it there in the first place. Did they think one random decorative piece would add something warm and fuzzy to the atmosphere? It wasn't as though there was any denying the room's purpose. Between the two-way mirror, the camera in one corner of the ceiling, and the not-so-fashionable bracelets that held Beck to the table in front of his uncomfortable chair, it was clear that the spot had a specific and limited function. A painting did nothing to change it.

Beck sighed and shifted in his seat, making his chains clink together. "How the hell much longer do they expect me to sit here, anyway?"

As if on cue, the door rattled, then came flying open with more force than necessary. The rose painting shuddered, and two guards appeared. One—who stayed in the doorframe to act as a sentry—was an older man with a paunch, and Beck didn't know him on any personal level. Marty-something, maybe. The other, though, was a distastefully familiar face and a polished-to-a-shine bald head. He was Beck's least favorite guard at the penitentiary, and he'd just *happened* to be assigned as his primary escort.

He stalked into the room, a smirk on his face. "C'mon, Samson. It's time to play dead man walking."

Beck grimaced, but he also went ahead and took the bait. "You know, Allan, I really feel like it's a big part of your job to be familiar with the fact that we don't have the death penalty here in Canada."

"A guy can dream." The guard leaned in to unlock the cuffs from the table. "Besides which, who said anything about the death penalty? You're about to take a nice little trip in a tin can, thirty thousand feet up. Chances aren't terrible that I won't get my wish."

Beck stiffened, but this time, he didn't bite. It was a fact that he hated flying. It was also a fact that the warden at the prison had denied his request for another mode of transportation. That didn't mean the smarmy guard needed the satisfaction of hearing it.

"Aren't you forgetting something, Allan?" he said instead.
"What's that?"
"If I go down on the plane, you go down with me."
"Fuck you, Samson."
Wordlessly smiling to himself, Beck waited for the other

man to pull the chains from the table, then refasten them to the bonds at his ankles. He held still as Allan gave the shackles a onceover and tugged on all the points of closure to make sure each one was secure. Despite Beck's lack of reaction, the other man was still smirking when he was finished.

"On your feet," he said.

Beck's eyes narrowed. "The plan was to meet up with Dr. Karim before we left."

"Sometimes, plans have to be changed." Allan gave the manacles a sharp tug. "Don't worry, muffin. You'll still get your special medical escort."

Suspicion crept up. It settled in Beck's chest. It burned. He stood, though, and fell in line. What other option did he have? Fighting back would only get him tased. Or worse. So—with Allan in the front, the other guard in the rear, and Beck practically wedged between them—he let them lead him out to the empty hall. Their pace was purposeful. But the longer they walked, the more the unease strengthened. He was sure he'd heard someone say they were only about thirty seconds away from the boarding zone, yet they didn't slow down at any of the closest doors. They took a left at a T in the passageway, and a right at another and another. More than a few minutes definitely went by, and finally, the only thing in sight was the emergency exit. Beck realized it had to be their destination. There was nowhere left to go. In response, his feet stalled, immediately prompting a grunt from the man behind him. Allan turned back to face him, too.

"What now, Samson?" he said. "You see something shiny?"

"Other than your head?" Beck replied. "No. I'd like to know where the hell we're going, though."

"Pretty sure you should *already* know the answer to that, babycakes."

Allan smirked. Then he turned away again. The other guard gave Beck a small shove, and he had no choice but to move. The gap between them and the emergency exit closed far too quickly, and the step through them was jarring. It was technically morning, but the dawn hadn't broken, and the dark closed in, barely pierced by the runway lights. The air was crisp to the point of icy. Windier there at the airport than it had been near the prison. Beck shivered. His prison-supplied clothing—jeans and a long-sleeve shirt, designed to look as unobtrusive and "normal" as possible—was nowhere near adequate against the temperature.

"Go ahead," said Allan, pointing into the dimness.

Beck squinted. Just ahead of them, a black SUV sat on the pavement, somehow managing to look *not* out of place. It wasn't the same vehicle they'd used to bring him from the correctional facility to the airport, and nothing about it screamed prisoner transport. Yet one of the rear doors hung open, and Beck knew what it meant.

"You expect me to get in there?" The question came out before he could stop it, and he regretted it right away.

The guard's smirk became a grin that flashed in the dark. "What I expect is for you to do exactly what the fuck I say, exactly when the fuck I say it. But I'm happy to provide you with some motivation if need be."

This isn't how this is supposed to go, Beck thought.

They'd told him, step by step, what the exchange would look like. Prison. Plane. Meeting spot. Drop. Notably, not one of those steps had involved driving over the tarmac in an SUV. He had a strong feeling that once he climbed into the backseat, his fate was going to take him in a very different direction than he'd hoped. Not in a good way, either.

Briefly, he debated fighting the situation for real. He could start with flinging his chained arms around Allan's neck. Then move onto taking the man hostage until he freed Beck. Finally, he could end with zipping away in the SUV on his own terms.

"Now or . . . well, just *now*, Samson," said Allan.

Beck tossed him a glare. He wanted to opt for the crazy escape attempt—he really did—but people were counting on him. He'd given them his word. He needed to keep toeing the line until he'd kept it. With a grimace, he ducked his head, folded his tall frame into the backseat, and waited for something to happen. Nothing did. Or at least nothing extraordinary. The two guards climbed into the front seats. A tinted glass shield rose up between them and Beck. The engine came to life, and the vehicle rolled to a start.

If it's all so banal, then why do I still feel like something's off? he wondered.

On high alert, Beck kept his eyes on the passing scenery. Not that there was much to see. Just stretches of mostly dark airport, slowly gliding by. The only thing he did note was that they seemed to be getting farther and farther away from the main terminal, which triggered more unease.

At last, though, the SUV took a turn and coasted to a stop on the edge of a much smaller tarmac. There, Beck's two guards got out, leaving him alone in the vehicle. He didn't care. Maybe it was even a bit of a relief. It gave him some time to study his new surroundings through the window. The first thing he spied was a small plane. *Quite* small. The hull was still emblazoned with a commercial logo, but it certainly didn't come close to being the 747 he'd been told they were taking. His gut churned.

He dragged his attention from the plane to the people around it. Shrouded in the pre-dawn shadows, they moved around the exterior of the aircraft, some appearing to be loading luggage, some performing tasks Beck couldn't distinguish.

He was about to lean back into his seat again when a solitary figure caught and held his eye.

She—*definitely a 'she'*—hurried across the tarmac. Her motions seemed urgent, but she still stopped halfway to the plane and stood there, looking like she wasn't quite sure what to do. As she did, the light from one of the luggage carts gave Beck a much better view of her features. And for a moment he forgot his concerns over what was going on. He also took back what he'd thought about the painted roses being the brightest, prettiest thing he'd seen in God knew how long. That award most definitely went to the woman standing in the middle of the tarmac with her hands on her hips and her auburn hair whipping around her face.

Chapter Two

Ignoring the way the air bit at her skin and sent her hair flying into her face, Joelle frowned at the plane. Ordinarily, she might've been annoyed that she'd been left out in the cold. She *hated* being cold. And she was already irritated by the fact that being forced to sign the waiver had separated her from O'Toole and the others. Add the chill to that, and it was a recipe for prime crankiness. But right then, she was too distracted by the size—or lack thereof—of the aircraft to think about it beyond pulling her jacket a little tighter. The polyester blend wasn't designed to ward off this kind of weather, and it only helped marginally as she stared at the plane.

She hadn't consciously envisioned their mode of transport. And if she had, she was sure she would've imagined something bigger. Maybe something like the one that had flown her and her college roommate to Greece for Spring Break seven years earlier. Definitely, her brain hadn't suggested that this assignment would involve boarding via removable stairs. Although to be fair, she'd also kind of assumed that the details of the job would be slightly more fleshed out by now as well. Her brow wrinkled even more, and her fingers tapped her thigh. Her lips puckered, too.

Keep making that face, missy, and it will freeze like that, said her mom's voice in her head.

Her heart panged. But she also automatically obeyed, relaxing her forehead and jaw as she studied the plane for another few seconds before starting to move toward it. She got only a few more steps before O'Toole appeared at the top of the wheeled staircase. His eyes landed on her, right away.

"Hang tight, Ms. Diedrich!" he called, his words somehow managing to carry over the wind. "Just making a seating arrangement adjustment up here. When we're done, I'll send Wanda to let you know."

He didn't wait for an answer before slipping back into the plane. How many times was the man going to stall her? And why? They'd requested her presence here, not the other way around.

Joelle gritted her teeth. For the most part, she felt well-respected in her usual role. More often than not, the guards—male or female—were inclusive. And they were definitely happy to turn over anything remotely medical to her. But right now, she felt as though she was being deliberately cut off from the proceedings, quite possibly because O'Toole had a misogynistic streak. And she hadn't even met the patient yet.

"And that's kind of critical, isn't it?" she grumbled.

"What is?" said a smooth, male voice.

Joelle jumped at the unexpected response. She spun to her left, startled to see that she'd stopped beside a black SUV that blended in with the shadows. The rear window was open, and through it, a man was looking at her expectantly. Curiously. Her face heated. And for a second, her tongue refused to cooperate and form a reply. Part of the protracted silence was sheer surprise. But part of it was the speaker himself. His dark hair and blue eyes were striking to the point of distraction. His full lips and the line of his jaw gave him double-take good looks that Joelle was embarrassed to note made her want to gawk a little. She tried to rein it in. But diverting her attention only made things worse. Her eyes followed the hint of stubble down his chin to his Adam's apple then landed on his collarbone, which peeked out over the top of the buttons on his black Henley.

"So?" the man prodded.

She cleared her throat. "I, uh. Nothing."

A dark eyebrow lifted. "Nothing is critical?"

"Yes. I mean, no." The heat in her cheeks crept higher. "Sorry. It's nothing. I'm just having a moment."

"Because of O'Toole?" he asked, inclining his head in the general direction of the plane.

"You know him?"

"Sadly, I do." The man smiled, revealing a set of perfect teeth. "I take it you don't? Or at least not very well."

"We're newly acquainted as of today," Joelle said.

"Ah. Well, if he hasn't already ruined your first impression of him on his own, I guess *I* probably did just now."

Joelle felt her mouth curve up, and for the first time since walking out of the airport bathroom, her body relaxed ever so slightly. "I think I can overlook it."

"No, don't," he said. "I want to *keep* ruining it. So I'll add to my earlier comments and tell you that he's kind of a . . . well, his name says it all."

Joelle couldn't quite stifle a laugh. "I won't tell him you said that."

"You can. I might enjoy seeing the expression on his face." The man offered a wink, drawing attention to his unfairly long, thick lashes.

She forced herself not to stare, clearing her throat a second time. "Are you a part of the transport, too?"

"Unfortunately."

"You don't sound very excited about it."

His eyes flicked toward the plane. They darkened almost imperceptibly before he brought his attention back to Joelle. And though he smiled again, it was a little tighter and a little less genuine now.

"I'm not particularly excited, no," he said.

He grimaced after speaking, and a silence followed, hanging pensively in the air. Joelle bit her lip. Clinical connection was her thing. Personal connection on the other hand . . . not so much. And this definitely felt personal. Which meant that it was probably a good moment to segue out of the conversation. But when her mouth opened, it wasn't to excuse herself at all.

"Is it flying itself you don't like?" she asked. "Or just doing it with O'Toole?"

"How about I tell you a story, and you can choose the answer?" he replied.

"Seriously?"

"Yep."

"Okay. Fine. Why not?"

"Good," he said. "So here it is. A couple of years back, I had this whole romantic thing set up. Tandem paragliders. A ring. My girlfriend. Me. So it starts out smoothly. We're up there in the sky, I pull out the velvet box, and I'm ready to pop the question. But out of nowhere, this seagull swoops in. Steals the ring. Ruins the proposal, and my relationship is over, just like that. Hated getting above sea level ever since."

"I . . ." Joelle trailed off, wondering if she'd just had the weirdest auditory hallucination of her life.

The man's expression remained flat for a moment more, and then a grin cracked through. "I can only assume that he couldn't afford his own ring. Not sure how much salary seagulls collect in two months. And it's probably measured in fish, anyway."

She groaned. "You just made all of that up, didn't you?"

"Or maybe the gull pawned it to buy some sardines. Impossible to say."

"So I take it that it's not the flying itself you hate?"

His smile morphed into another grimace. "Bit of both today. Not the head of O'Toole's fan club, and this plane seems a little . . . I dunno what."

"A little *little*?" she suggested.

He let out a chuckle—a pleasant, rich sound that made Joelle want to hear it again. "Yes, exactly. A little little."

"I was having the same thought," she admitted. "I guess when I heard we'd be on a commercial flight, I imagined something bigger."

"Something *commercial* commercial?" he joked.

She smiled. "Yes. That."

"Well, the good news is that it's a short trip—just an hour over the Rockies—so we won't be on the plane for long."

"That's true."

"Always a silver lining."

For no good reason, his statement made Joelle warm a little from the inside out.

She cleared her throat. "Do you know why the prisoner is being moved?"

"Don't you?" the man countered with a half-smile.

"They weren't exactly forthcoming about it," she admitted.

He studied her for a second, his eyes slightly narrowed. "Do you think that's odd?"

She had a strange feeling that he was fishing for something. She wasn't sure what. And she didn't think the intention was nefarious in any way. But she still refused to take the bait.

"Just an oversight, I think," she said. "You know how these things are sometimes."

"Yes, I do." He paused. "If it makes you feel any better, the transport is on the books as a routine facility change."

"Good to know. Thanks."

"Delighted to be able to help."

He dropped a wink, and that all-over heat came back. It was pleasant. But startling. And when Wanda appeared at the top of the stairs just then, motioning her hand in a "come here" gesture, Joelle wasn't sure if she was relieved or disappointed.

"I guess that's your cue to go," said the man.

"I guess it is," she agreed. "What about you?"

"Not quite my turn yet. I'll see you onboard?"

"Yes, you bet."

"Looking forward to it," he told her.

"Me, too," Joelle replied.

As she turned and walked away, she realized she really meant it. Possibly more than she should, actually. She also realized something else—she hadn't asked the man's name. And she wanted to. So much so that she almost swung back around to do it. At the very least, she could ask him what part of the transport he was involved in. It was a totally reasonable excuse. And maybe she would've done it if not for the fact that O'Toole himself stepped out of the plane and glared down at her. His presence and expression drove away the pleasant afterglow of the interaction with the unknown man, and Joelle stepped a little quicker, hurrying to the stairs then up them, two at a time.

Remind me never to take on an assignment for a change of pace again, she said to herself as she entered the plane.

Aloud, she greeted O'Toole with as much cheer as she could muster. "Are we almost ready for me to meet my patient?"

He didn't smile. "We're talking about a murderer, Ms. Diedrich. You might not want to be so eager."

Joelle bit down to keep from responding with an equally snarky reply. Maybe he hated women, maybe he hated his job. Maybe both. Either way, she refused to stoop to his level and be so unprofessional. When she said nothing, O'Toole let out an impatient sigh.

"All right," he said, swinging an arm out. "You can see that this plane is equipped with a small First-Class section. The team—you included—will be seated there. The prisoner and his guard will have the front row on the left, while Dreery and Redburn will take a spot right behind them. The first row on the right will remain vacant, and I'll be in row two on that side. You and the spare guard will be in the one behind me."

"Got it," Joelle replied, marking off each seat assignment with her eyes.

"Good." O'Toole gave her a single crisp incline of his head. "Mr. Samson will join us momentarily."

He added something more about the fact that there were no civilian passengers sitting in the rear portion of the plane, but she missed it all as she blew out a small, startled breath. *Mr. Samson.* Her charge was a man. No wonder O'Toole and his workmates had been surprised to learn that she was Joelle rather than Joel. She wanted to smack her hand to her forehead. She made herself nod instead, and she opened her mouth to reply. She was cut off, though, by the arrival of three figures darkening the plane's doorframe.

Right away, she recognized the man from the SUV. It was a relief to see him, actually. A friendly face was more than welcome. She started to smile at him, but she stopped halfway. Her lips froze in an awkward position as her gaze landed on his accoutrements. Chains. Threaded through handcuffs. Leading down to shackles, secured at the ankle. And her brain moved in slow motion, telling her in an overly slow, overly simplistic way what was happening. Not only was her patient a man, he was *the* man. The stranger from the SUV. The ridiculously good-looking one with whom she'd just shared the most pleasant conversation she'd had since forever. *He* was the prisoner.

The murderer.

*   *   *

Amusement pricked at Beck as he paused just inside the entrance and watched the redhead's eyes—such a pretty shade of green, even in the shitty lighting—widen in near caricature fashion. She'd been pleased to see him just a moment earlier. There was no doubt about the smile she'd started to direct his way. It still hung there now.

He lifted an eyebrow and directed a silent question her way. *Not what you were expecting, I guess?*

Her gaze narrowed. Her mouth closed, and her lips pressed into a thin line, her irritation shining through the slight pink of embarrassment in her cheeks.

Not impressed, said her expression. *Not in the slightest. Jerk.*

Or maybe a word that was stronger than jerk. If she was the stronger-word type.

A hint of guilt tried to fight its way past Beck's mirth. Truthfully, he hadn't set out to deceive the woman. Hell, he hadn't even expected the window to come down when he'd reached out and pressed the button. It'd startled him. He nearly rolled the damn thing up again before the redhead's mutter had caught his attention. Her voice was throaty. Almost seductive. As attractive as her looks. It'd prompted him to speak without thinking. He'd immediately braced for her to put him in his place. Very quickly, he'd realized she had no clue who he was.

Then it'd been on. Sticking it to the so-called good guys. For two or three minutes, Beck had operated under the guise of a normal man talking to a normal woman. Flirting. Possibly enjoying it more than just as a simple ruse.

Now, of course, the jig was up. The only enjoyment to be had was knowing that his cleverness had put him on top for a few minutes. In reality, Beck had precious little normalcy in his life. And just then—as if to drive that fact home even more—O'Toole leaned closer and said something to the redhead in a voice too low for Beck to hear.

It irked him. That closeness. The way she looked at Darby and nodded. She'd said she didn't know him. Beck had believed her. He *still* believed her. After all, what reason did she have to lie? Yet the other man somehow had the privilege of being able to whisper in her ear.

There was a line between Beck and these men, and the redhead was on the wrong side of it.

Are you jealous, Samson? What for? It's not like she was going to jump over here and join you in the depths of your criminal existence based on a conversation that lasted less than five minutes. Mile high club? Hardly a possibility.

Allan gave him a nudge from behind, stopping his sardonic thoughts from going any further. "You really *are* trying to drag this out, aren't you, Samson? Three rows up, very front. I know you can do it if you try hard enough."

Beck flashed him an over-the-shoulder smirk. "I just want to spend as much time with you as possible, darling."

The guard rolled his eyes. "How about you take a seat instead, and enjoy this one and only chance to ride in First Class?"

"Perfect. I like my champagne just below room temperature."

"And *I* like my nights spent in a warm bed with a warmer woman. But we can't always get what we want. Move, Samson."

Allan nudged him again, harder this time, and Beck complied with the command. Dragging his chains with him and rattling louder than the ghost of Jacob Marley, he made his way up the short aisle, then pushed himself into the seat with as much force as he could.

He fired a grin toward the guard. "Care to join me?"

"One day, Samson, your jokes are going to get you hurt," Allan replied.

"Well, at least I'll die laughing."

"I'm going to the bathroom before we take off. Try to be a good boy while I'm gone."

"You trust me here all alone?" Beck said. "That's so sweet."

"I don't trust you anywhere, alone or otherwise." Allan's tone was flat. "But don't worry. The other guys will keep an eye on you. And in case that fails, I'll let the stewardess know she can hit you with a food cart if you try anything."

"Flight attendant."

"What?"

"They stopped calling them 'stewardesses' a few decades ago, numbskull."

"Whatever, Samson."

"Whatever indeed, Allan."

The other man turned away, and a voice crackled through the overhead speakers, making an announcement about final boarding and providing a few flight details, including a warning about some expected turbulence. Beck's tension revved higher. The tin can would soon be getting ready to take off. They'd be at the mercy of the pilot and the sky. He clenched his teeth, wondering sarcastically why he'd wasted his free weekends learning how to turn tree branches into feasible shelters when what he really needed were parachute skills.

Relax. It's less than an hour, he told himself. *Fifty-four more minutes after takeoff. I can tolerate that. Hell, maybe I can sleep through the whole thing.*

A nap wouldn't be an entirely unwelcome venture.

He started to lean back and let his eyes sink shut before it struck him—abruptly and belatedly—that there was a key person missing from the group on the plane. His contact, Dr. Karim. The man had been Beck's main focus since leaving the prison. Since before that. The man was the real reason for this trip. The one who'd set up this exchange and who would ensure Beck's safe delivery on the other end of the flight. How the hell had he managed to let the doctor's absence slip by him?

Shit.

Maybe there was a simple explanation. Maybe he'd been so involved in staring at the redhead that he hadn't noticed Karim. Maybe his dislike of soaring over mountains inside a hunk of metal had slowed his brain. Or maybe the doctor just hadn't boarded yet. Beck straightened up and tried to swing a surreptitious look behind his seat. He didn't get any farther than turning his head. The distracting woman was standing right there, her green eyes zeroed in on him.

Startled, Beck inhaled sharply. The breath brought an intangible scent with it—light, buttery, and definitely emanating from the redhead. He barely had time to adjust to that before she plunked herself in the seat beside him. The doctor fled his mind again as she leaned in.

"Well, hello there," he greeted her, trying to cover the lightning bolt of attraction that struck as she got closer. "I didn't think you'd be quite so eager to chat again."

"I'm just here to do my job, Mr. Samson," she replied, her tone even. "And I'm not sure what you hoped to gain by tricking me back there."

"It wasn't a trick. I was being friendly."

"You deliberately led me to believe you were with the transport."

"I *am* with the transport."

"No," she corrected. "You *are* the transport."

The statement got under his skin, and he gritted his teeth. "Forgive me for wanting to be a person rather than a thing."

"That's not what I meant."

"Oh, really? Then I guess you're the only one in this bunch who doesn't see me as either a number or as a commodity. Or maybe both."

"It doesn't matter what they think. I'm not here for them."

"Who are you here for then?"

She gave him a dubious look—pursed lips, wrinkled nose, and fiery eyebrows bunched together. "I don't have time for more games and another seagull story, Mr. Samson. I'm here for *you*, obviously."

The claim genuinely caught him off guard. "Me?"

"I'm your nurse, Joelle Diedrich. The replacement Medical Escort," she said.

Now he was more than caught off guard. He was punched-in-the-stomach stunned. Worried questions slammed around in his head. Where the hell was Dr. Karim? What did the lack of his presence mean? Was this woman—*Joelle*—a proper replacement? How could he find out?

And what if she isn't with Dr. Karim? What then?

"Mr. Samson?" said Joelle, her voice full of concern. "Are you okay?"

He tried to roll his shoulders to ease away the prickle that slithered between them, but he only succeeded in making his shackles clang.

Damn, damn, damn.

Was his safety still guaranteed? Suddenly, the warden's

choice to send him on a plane rather than via bus or train seemed a lot more suspect.

"Mr. Samson?" Joelle's worry was even more audible now.

"I'm fine," Beck muttered. "Positively peachy."

She obviously didn't believe him because her hand—soft and warm, even through his long-sleeved shirt—landed on his forearm. The contact sent a jolt of electricity across his skin, and he jerked his eyes up to meet hers. He opened his mouth, but whatever bit of truth he'd been about to accidentally spill was stalled by Allan's reappearance.

"Ms. Diedrich?" the guard said, his voice as flat as his expression. "We're getting ready to take off. Darby wants us in our seats."

Joelle let out a small breath and offered the guard a forced-looking smile.

"Absolutely." She turned to Beck one more time, and she didn't move her hand away yet. "Are you sure you're all right?"

Beck met her eyes again. Her gaze reflected true compassion. Real caring. Or at least an excellent approximation of both. And neither that nor the gentle touch was something he'd experienced at all over the last two years. It made him want to speak up and say that he was most definitely *not* okay.

Maybe she really is *here for you,* he thought. *And if not . . . maybe she could be.*

It sounded good. In theory. The truth, though, was a whole other matter. He didn't know anything but what she'd told him, and there was no way to verify that it was true. Now, more than ever, he had to exercise caution. Dr. Karim was the only person he could trust, and without the other man there . . .

Beck gave himself an internal headshake, dialed back his moment of undeserved hope to zero, and offered Nurse Joelle Diedrich a smirk and a raised eyebrow.

"Did you want to come closer and feel my forehead to check?" he asked. "Maybe check me a few other places, too?"

She responded to his comments with a look that said she didn't quite buy his tone or his words.

"Ms. Diedrich?" Allan said again, his voice tinged with irritation.

Joelle didn't turn and reply, and for a second, Beck thought she might insist on staying where she was. She had a stubborn set to her mouth that made her appear as though she was considering arguing with the guard. Hell. Maybe Beck ought to do that himself. What did he have to lose? It's not like they were going to cut him free. At least being tased would be interesting. Another heartbeat passed, though, and Joelle's expression cleared. She squeezed Beck's arm and pushed to her feet.

"If you need me for anything medical, I'm just a couple of rows back," she said as she stepped into the aisle.

"I'll keep that in mind," he replied.

"Please do."

She nodded curtly at Allan, then left Beck to stew over what the hell was going on.

Chapter Three

Joelle sidled past her seatmate—a short, thick man with wiry gray hair, who barely grunted an acknowledgement of her arrival—and she glanced around the plane. O'Toole was nowhere to be seen. His spot in front of her was notably empty.

So much for sitting back down, she thought sarcastically.

Her fingers tapped her thigh, and she bit her lip. She considered getting up and searching out the man in question, but the pilot came onto the speaker, stopping her by turning on the seatbelt sign. Joelle barely heard him as he outlined the flight details. She did, however, hear the warning of some expected turbulence on the trip. Her apprehension thickened. But in truth, her focus kept straying to the chained man a few rows up. Even when Wanda began the standard safety demonstration, Joelle kept one eye on her new patient.

Samson.

What was his first name? For the second time, she hadn't thought to ask, and for the second time, she regretted it.

She stole a glance at the guard who sat beside her. Did he know? She was sure he must. Now that she thought of it, he might have quite a bit more information about their mutual charge. It was just a matter of asking him. And, she supposed, a matter of whether or not he'd be willing to share. So far, Joelle's experience hadn't filled her with warm fuzzy feelings, and there'd been no hint that any of the men was compelled to change that.

She fought a sigh and shifted her eyes back to Wanda, hoping to put her mind elsewhere, at least for a minute or two. But the flight attendant appeared to be done with her talk. She was already folding up the emergency card, and the demonstration seatbelt was nowhere to be seen. The uniformed woman offered the cabin a final friendly smile, tucked the pamphlet away, and disappeared into the staff seat compartment. Moments later, the plane began its taxi up the runway. The vibration and speed quickly increased. The roar of the engines kicked into high gear. The mechanical whir of the wheels lifting sounded, and the aircraft took wing. And Joelle went back to thinking about Samson.

When she'd told him that she was his Medical Escort, he hadn't just seemed surprised. He'd looked momentarily shell-shocked. So much so that Joelle had thought he might be about to have one of the seizures she was there to treat. But as he'd sat there in silence, she'd sensed that his reaction was an emotional one. *Fear.* That's what she'd felt emanating from him. And it begged the question of why. Why would a convicted murderer be *afraid* when he found out that his Medical Escort had been switched out?

And on the subject of murderers . . .

Joelle bit her lip and ordered herself not to look in Samson's direction. She'd met her share of killers, and they definitely came in all shapes and sizes. Often, it wasn't pleasant interacting with them, but it was part of her job. She was perfectly capable of putting aside judgement in order to administer treatment, even for the worst offenders. But every now and then, she encountered someone whom she was sure wasn't guilty as charged. She had that feeling now. Something about the man under her care—or sort of under her care, as the circumstances seemed to be—made her want to question it in this case.

Why? Are you looking for an excuse because of his pretty blue eyes?

She dismissed the thought. Yes, Samson was attractive. She wasn't going to deny it, and she wasn't going to beat herself up for acknowledging it. That would be worse than just admitting it and moving on. And that wasn't it, anyway. She wasn't looking for an excuse; she didn't need one. Something just felt . . . *off*.

Deciding to give in and dig for some info, she turned her attention to the man beside her and put a smile in her voice. "Hi, there. I don't think we've been properly introduced. I'm Joelle."

The guard blinked, as if it surprised him to be spoken to. "Yeah, I know. You're the lady doctor."

"Nurse," she said, careful not to sound like she was correcting him.

"Right."

"And I didn't catch your name."

"Marty Strom."

"Nice to meet you." She paused. "Hey. Can I ask you something?"

His shrug rode the line between irritated and indifferent, and he flicked a quick glance around before answering. "Go for it."

"You work at the prison where Mr. Samson is incarcerated?"

"Yeah. Been there for a few years now."

She leaned a bit closer and added a conspiratorial tone to her next question. "Do you really believe he has the seizure issue?"

Some indefinable emotion flashed across the man's face, then disappeared as quickly as it came. Joelle worked to keep herself from frowning. What did the look mean? Quickly, she filled the silence with a small laugh.

"Sorry," she said. "That was a weird-sounding question. I just asked because Darby O'Toole made a comment along those lines, and I honestly wasn't sure if he was kidding or not."

Marty didn't look in the slightest bit amused. "One thing I can tell you for sure is that Darby rarely kids."

"Oh, wow. So you guys really think he might be faking it? Why would he do that?"

"Beck Samson is a murderer. Who knows why the fuck these guys do anything that they do?"

Beck.

Mentally storing the name—and pleased to have learned it—Joelle pretended to think about the guard's other words for a second, then said, "Can I ask you something else?"

"Why not?" he replied. "Might as well get it all out of the way now."

"What kind of murder was it?"

"You got a strong stomach?"

"I work in a prison every day, too, Mr. Strom."

"Right." His eyes slid toward the front of the plane then came back to her. "Well, Samson was a white-collar guy. Accounting or some boring shit like that. Had a girlfriend. Had a business partner. Then his business partner *had* Samson's girlfriend, if you know what I mean."

Joelle ordered herself not to let the guard's darkly lascivious tone get under her skin, and she nodded her understanding.

"Crime of passion?" she said.

It added a layer of sense. In Joelle's experience, it was the thing that most commonly turned average people into murderers.

But Marty shook his head. "More like an execution and a, uh, very specific message. Two shots in the head, and one shot in the . . . well. I'm a gentleman, so I won't say it aloud."

She didn't think the man was anything close to a gentleman, but she understood what he meant. So vividly that even when she tried not to let the image of the described carnage fill her mind, she couldn't quite manage it. Her stomach—strong or not—churned. And her face must've given away her disquiet, because for the first time, Marty looked pleased.

"Yeah," he said. "Brutal shit, right?"

"Brutal," she agreed.

"I did try to warn you."

"Yes, you did."

He smiled in a stiff way that seemed forced. "Would you excuse me a second?"

Joelle nodded again, actually thankful to have a moment of reprieve. "Of course."

The guard unbuckled and pushed to his feet. And despite her relief at being alone, she watched him. She couldn't help it. Every instinct she had was alight with wrongness. She held her breath when he paused for the briefest second beside O'Toole, who'd obviously found his seat at some point without her noticing. It was impossible to tell what was said, but as Marty Strom continued past the front row and turned the corner toward the bathroom, O'Toole stood up and started down the aisle toward *her*.

Nerves sliced up her spine. The breath she was holding refused to expel, and her lungs burned. The closer Darby got, the surer Joelle became that it was about to become a fight or flight situation. And neither would end well up there in the sky. But then her fellow escort simply walked past. The air that Joelle had been involuntarily retaining let itself out, and her eyes followed O'Toole as he headed for the general seating area.

What's he doing? There's no one back there.

Joelle couldn't even guess at an answer. But the sense that something was off grew stronger, overriding her trepidation and fueling her with a need to figure it out. She reached for the latch on her seatbelt and unhooked it. It was as far as she got before the plane shuddered hard enough to make her teeth hurt. Murmurs filled the cabin. Right away, the aircraft shook again.

Joelle ignored it all in favor of seeking out Beck Samson. Not just because he was supposed to be her patient, but also because something told her if she didn't get to him now, she was going to be forcibly stuck in her seat. And something even stronger told her that would be a bad thing.

* * *

Beck's eyes were closed. His hands were tight on the armrests. There was no doubt in his mind that Allan was entertained by both facts. The man had already made no less than three disparaging comments about Beck's apparent fear of flying. Beck didn't care. It was common—and entirely reasonable—to be nervous about sailing thirty thousand feet above the ground.. In all honesty, though, that wasn't his primary concern. He was worried about Dr. Karim. Tense about having no way of knowing what had happened to the man. To the plan. So the guard could mock him for the duration of the flight. Until Beck was on solid ground, standing in front of his pre-arranged contact on the other side of this whole thing, he wouldn't relax in the slightest.

Maybe not even then, he thought.

He squeezed his hands harder and inhaled. When he did, a hint of Joelle's buttery scent carried in, and Beck's eyes flew open. There she was, just coming to a stop beside his row. He opened his mouth, but she was looking at Allan rather than at him.

"Excuse me," she said, "but I'm going to need you to trade places with me."

The guard cleared his throat. "Er . . . what?"

Joelle gestured to Beck. "Mr. Samson is clearly under stress."

"He's a prisoner."

"That doesn't rob him of his rights."

"His stress isn't about his rights," said Allan. "It's just his natural state as a result of his incarceration."

The redhead's voice became authoritative and overly patient at the same time. "I realize that you likely aren't familiar with what may or may not trigger a seizure, but I can assure you that *I am* familiar with the triggers. And stress is most definitely one of them."

"You think Mr. Samson is going to have a seizure?"

"I *know* that the possibility is the whole reason I'm on this plane."

Her eyes—which Beck could swear got greener every time he saw them—finally found him. They contained a clear plea to back her up. His usual response to a request made by someone in a position of authority in the prison system was to argue against it. To prove, however vainly, that they didn't control him. This time, he didn't do it.

"I *have* been feeling a little light-headed," he stated instead. "That's how it started the last time."

"See?" said Joelle, stepping back in the aisle to make room for the guard's exit. "Unless you're planning on stopping me from doing my job?"

"Fine," Allan grumbled after another second. "Suit yourself. Not like I enjoy his goddamn company."

Beck waited until the other man was gone before addressing his undeniably pretty Medical Escort.

"Well, that was a fun ruse," he said.

She slid into the seat beside him and ignored his comment. "You've never really had a seizure, have you?"

"What makes you say that? Magical nursing powers?"

"Are you always this confrontational?"

"Mostly," he admitted.

"Why are you lying about having a medical condition?" she asked.

"Why are you asking why I am?" he countered.

"You know that there's no reason to be ashamed of having a fear of flying, right?"

He flashed her a dark smile. "Who says I'm a reasonable man?"

She rolled her eyes, which made him want to laugh. A chuckle actually built in his chest, but before it could make its way out, the plane listed to Beck's left. He didn't enjoy the disconcerting movement, but he had no complaints about the effect—Joelle was practically in his lap. Or she would've been, if not for the cumbersome chains in the way.

"I just mean that it's normal to be nervous about cruising thirty thousand feet above ground," she replied as she righted herself.

"Particularly when the hunk of metal is seeming less stable by the second, like this one?"

"That's not—"

The plane jerked once more, this time to the right. Again, Joelle slid with it. Her feet knocked against Beck's heavy-looking work boots, and his chains let out a light clang.

"Maybe you should buckle up," he said. "You know. Just in case I'm not completely insane."

"Maybe you should do the same," she replied, clicking her seatbelt firmly into place. "And does that mean you *are* afraid of flying?"

"I said insane. Not afraid." He lifted his handcuffs. "You don't think these are a good enough replacement for the safety measures provided by the airline?"

She eyed the bonds. "Are you suggesting it's overkill?"

"*Overkill*?" Beck countered, raising his eyebrow. "Interesting choice of words."

Joelle's face pinked and her mouth opened, but just then the speakers crackled, effectively cutting off whatever she might've been about to say.

"This is your captain speaking," announced a disembodied voice. "We're heading into some ongoing turbulence here, folks, so we're going to ask everyone to fasten their seatbelts, remain seated, and refrain from moving about the aisles until we let you know we're in the clear. Thanks for your cooperation and enjoy the rest of the flight."

The plane rocked again, this time seeming to go in both directions at once. The motion sent Beck's shoulder bumping against Joelle's, and his chains jingled noisily. He just barely managed to straighten himself up before they were bounced again.

"Couldn't send me on a train, could they?" he muttered.

"I'm sure we'll be fine," said Joelle.

"Will we, though?"

"You really don't like flying, do you?"

"No, Miss Diedrich," he said. "I really don't."

"Do you want to tell me why?"

"Not in the slightest."

"I can't help you if—"

The plane jerked forcefully, and despite the seatbelts they both wore, they were tossed forward. Beck brought his secured arms up in time to protect himself from impact, but Joelle wasn't so lucky. Her forehead smacked into the wall in front of them. She let out a cry, and when she pulled herself back, Beck saw that she'd earned a small split just above her left eyebrow. Blood was already hastening its way out of the wound.

"Dammit," he said. "Let me help you with that."

In a move that he wished didn't showcase just how accustomed he was to doing things in shackles, he pulled a napkin from the pocket beside his seat, reached over, and dabbed gently at the cut. Joelle winced, but she didn't pull away. In fact, she leaned into the touch a little, and after a moment, she brought her palm up and placed it on top of his hand.

"Thanks," she said. "That was a bit unexpected."

"Yet another reason to dislike flying," he replied.

"You still haven't told me the first reason," she reminded him.

The plane did its version of a jig, and Beck grimaced. With a stab of regret, he pulled his hand out from under hers and dropped it back to his lap.

"Loss of control," he said. "We're in the air. No way out. Something goes wrong, we're screwed, and there's nothing we can do about it because we're trapped."

"We're always trapped somewhere, aren't we? Even when we feel like we're in control."

"That's pretty deep, Miss Diedrich. You a psychologist *and* a nurse now? Am I getting a two-for-one deal here?"

It looked like she was trying to stop her mouth from quirking up. "Just drawing on my twenty-nine years of life experience, Mr. Samson."

He lifted an eyebrow. "And that experience hasn't taught you that things fall apart easily?"

Her half-smile disappeared, and he wondered what thought his words had drawn out.

"Statistically speaking," she said, "we're more likely to be struck by lightning than we are to die in a plane crash."

"You don't say."

"A fact is a fact."

"A *fact* fact?" he teased.

"A *fact* fact," she echoed, lowering the napkin from her head. "How does it look?"

He bent forward and studied the cut. With the blood wiped away, he could see that it was less serious than he would've thought. A small scrape.

"If you move your hair over, you won't even be able to see it," he said.

She smoothed an auburn lock in front of the injury. "How's that?"

"Perfect."

A strange sensation worked its way through Beck as Joelle smiled at him. It was warm. Personal.

Except it's not, his conscience reminded him. *You're locked up for murder. You have an endgame. And you have no idea where she sits in all of this.*

He was tempted to ask her outright. Was she a replacement for Dr. Karim? Or a *replacement* replacement? But another blast of turbulence stopped him from doing it, and this round of bouncing was followed by a noise—a high-pitched whistle—that zapped through the cabin. If that wasn't strange enough, as the sound cut off, a man in a flight-attendant uniform came scurrying past them, heading straight for the cockpit. For a second, Beck swore he recognized the guy from somewhere—not in a good way, either. His pulse danced an unsteady beat.

"What the *hell* is going on in here?" he said under his breath.

"I thought you might have a better idea about that than I do," Joelle replied, also quietly.

He met those green eyes of hers. They were devoid of any deception. Either she was as confused as he was, or she was a very good liar.

Why do I want it to be the latter so badly? Beck wondered.

"Not a clue," he said, answering both his own question and her statement.

Allan's voice cut into the conversation then, his tone grim. "Time to trade places again."

The guard stood next to their row, his face dark. An unexpected surge of protectiveness made Beck shake his head.

"Not happening," he said.

The guard tossed a look his way. "Someone put you in charge of something, Samson?"

Beck was saved from answering—and saying something he'd regret—by the arrival of their dedicated flight attendant.

"Sir, you need to return to your seat," she said to the guard, the epitome of calm firmness.

"This *is* my seat." Allan pointed to the spot where Joelle sat strapped in.

"Wherever you were a moment ago, sir," the flight attendant amended. "We can't have anyone standing in the aisles right now. *Anyone.*"

The guard narrowed his eyes, but he also spun on his heel and stalked away.

"Thank you, Wanda," said Joelle.

"Don't thank me yet," the flight attendant replied.

She spun away, too, but her quick steps took her in the

opposite direction as Allan. There was something ominous about her words and her exit, and a tense ball formed in Beck's stomach.

He dropped his voice as low as he could and tipped his mouth as close to Joelle's ear as space and decency would allow. "You should find a way to uncuff me."

Her reply was a gasp. "What?"

"Something is about to happen. I don't know what, but I'm damn sure I don't want to be all tied up when it does."

"Even if I were stupid or crazy enough to consider setting you free, I don't have the ability."

Once more, the speakers crackled. They whined with ear-piercing feedback before a voice carried into the cabin.

"Morning again, everyone. This is—" There was a pause and an audible cough. "This is your captain. Again." There was a pause. "Also. We're experiencing a few mechanical problems along with the turbulence, but they should be sorted out soon. Remember the safety instructions and enjoy your flight."

Beck met Joelle's gaze. "I don't think that was the captain this time."

Her eyes were wide, and her response was a whisper. "No. I don't think it was."

Automatically, he reached out to take her hand and offer some reassurance. But his fingers didn't quite find hers before the cabin simultaneously plunged into darkness, and the plane itself began to plummet.

Chapter Four

The next sequence of events happened so quickly that Joelle had almost no time to think about one before another followed.

First, darkness blinded her.

Then her body lifted from the seat.

That roller-coaster drop feeling—unpleasant but familiar—hit her stomach.

There were panicked screams and angry hollers, and under those sweat-inducing sounds, the disconcerting *clink-clink, clink-clink* of Beck's chains.

Then came the speed. The terrifying throttle of a nosediving plane, somehow seeming so much faster than an aircraft on its intended trajectory.

Every loose object made an airborne appearance.

A crash was coming. That much, Joelle knew.

Her mind blanked on how to react. How to brace.

What do I do?

She didn't know.

Give her a hand in need of stitches. A wound in need of inspection. A broken bone. Anything that involved blood. But this wild ride . . . it wasn't one she knew how to deal with.

In the end, it didn't matter. She didn't witness the crescendo. She *couldn't* witness it. Because something silver—a coffee carafe, she thought—came flying at her head. It struck her hairline with entirely more force than she would've believed possible. Her vision muddied. Her brain pointed out that there had to be some kind of irony in being knocked out just prior to dying a fiery death.

Half a heartbeat passed.

Then an abyss sucked her below its surface, and quite suddenly, the plane ceased to exist. In its place was a white room.

Confusion and panic slammed into Joelle even harder than the carafe had. If there had been nothing at all, it would've made sense. Or if her life had been flashing before her eyes like all the old adages promised, she'd have understood. But this? The white walls? The feel of something hard under her legs? And a smell that was both vague and familiar at the same time? None of it had a place. It was disconcerting. Almost disturbing.

She opened her mouth. Nothing came out. But a voice in her head answered her, nonetheless.

You're unconscious, it said. *Dreaming.*

It made sense. She acknowledged the silent explanation with a mental nod, and her heart rate slowed.

Yes, okay, she thought. *But where am I? Why this room?*

Not home. Not even close. Stark and cold and with no personal touches at all. But known, all the same.

This is the hospital, said that same voice in her head.

As soon as the suggestion came, Joelle's surroundings solidified. For a moment, she thought she might be the patient. That perhaps the accident had passed, and her subconscious was drawing on the things around her. But she quickly realized that it wasn't possible. She was sitting at the side of an adjustable bed rather than in it. The rail was up. A blue blanket had been tucked in tightly down the side. Tubes and wires rested on top of that, ruining any chance of making the setup appear to be anything but what it was—an ending. An ending she knew already. Because this wasn't a dream; it was a memory.

Mom. Joelle wanted to say it aloud, but her throat hurt far too much to even try. *Please don't leave me.*

It wouldn't have mattered anyway. The doctors had already told her that they'd done everything they could. The life-saving machines wouldn't be able to do their job much longer.

I'm sorry, Mom. I'm so sorry.

Joelle's eyes sank shut. She breathed in and out, and it burned hotter than the tears that trailed down her face. Her head hung low. Heavy. She had to force it to lift. Force her eyes to open, too. But when she did refocus, she found the bed empty. Panic slammed into her all over. This wasn't how the memory went.

She pushed to her feet. The bed wasn't just empty. It was stripped.

Mom?

She spun toward the door. But the door was gone.

She whipped back to the bed. And the voice rose up in her head once more.

This isn't real, it whispered. *It isn't a dream, either. Or even a memory.*

Joelle answered. *Am I dead?*

In response, her mother's gentle laugh filled her ears, and it was followed by her voice. *You're alive.*

The words were a splash of the coldest water, and Joelle's eyes flew open—this time for real—confirming the statement. Yes. She was definitely alive. But based on the state of the world around her, she wasn't sure how much longer that would last. Not so long as she stayed where she was.

An inferno brewed a mere six feet from where she lay on her

side. It spewed smoke and flames both up and out, and even through her haze, Joelle could see that it was making short work of the debris underneath it. Bits of who knew what crackled and snapped.

Not bits of who knows what, she thought. *Bits of plane.*

The recent memory poured back in. The transport job and Beck Samson. The turbulence and supposed mechanical failure. The crash. She hurt all over, but she'd survived. But what about everyone else?

"Oh God," she croaked.

She dragged her gaze around the immediate area, but there was nothing in her line of sight except the fire and its fallout. Her eyes came back to the flames. For another moment, the horror of the orange-and-red dance held her paralyzed. Then self-preservation kicked in. With the intention of getting to her feet, she shifted her arms. She put her palms out and pressed them flat. And she immediately stopped and pulled her hands back, startled. The ground was cold. Almost icy. Completely at odds with the hot display in front of her. Her eyes lowered. Snow dusted the dirt rocks in front of her.

It doesn't matter, she told herself. *The weather isn't what's important at the moment.*

She flattened her hands again and tried to push up. Something held her back. Joelle tried harder. Her body didn't budge. She wiggled, trying to free herself. Her movements earned her nothing. Her pulse rocketed. She was trapped. How was she going to get away from the fire? How was she going to—

The seatbelt.

She dropped her hands to her hips. *Yes.* There it was, the nylon band pulled tight across her lap and still secured to what was left of the seat itself. She almost laughed. But there was no time for hysterical amusement. She slid her fingers along until she located the clasp. Her near-giggle became a near-sob, and she lifted the lever. When it released without protest, a choked noise made its way out of her throat, but it quickly dissolved into a cough, reminding Joelle that she had to move or be consumed by smoke and fire.

Her hands found the ground again, and this time she was successful in sitting up. The transition to her feet didn't go quite as smoothly. Her new position made the world spin. The push to her knees sent a wave of nausea through her so fiercely that she nearly sat right back down again. But she made herself power through it. She crawled away, putting a reasonable amount of space between herself and the burning wreckage, then collapsed to the ground again. She closed her eyes and counted to thirty before opening them once more.

The dizziness diminished slightly, and Joelle took another slow look around. The destruction went beyond anything she'd ever seen. Broken metal. Charred plastic spewing acrid smoke. Shattered trees. A few hundred feet away, the back half of the plane, cracked open like a discarded eggshell. But closer than that was something far worse. A man's body.

"You don't know that it's a body," Joelle whispered to herself. "He could be alive."

Her mind repeated the sentiment. *He could be alive.* And it propelled her to try to find out. Nausea and dizziness momentarily forgotten, she at last stood up. Pain shot through her leg. She ignored it, limping toward the man, cataloging the details as she did.

He wore gray pants. One patent leather shoe, one black sock. His shirt was a white button-up—the kind that Joelle associated with needing a tie. But if he'd had one on, it wasn't in evidence now. A glint of gold flashed on his left hand. *A wedding band.* That little fact made Joelle's heart constrict. If he *was* dead—if any of them were—they'd all have people at home who'd miss them.

Her feet slowed. Her mind went to her mother. To the half-dream, half-memory she'd been yanked from just minutes ago.

Who will miss me? she wondered.

The question sounded self-centered, even in her own head. But it was also true. Her circle was so small that it was almost non-existent. A bereft feeling swept through her, augmented by a blast of snow-tinged wind.

Ordering herself to focus on the things she could control—or at least possibly influence—Joelle closed the gap between herself and the man on the ground. As she neared him, she realized who he was. Or at least recognized him for his role. The white shirt wasn't as plain as she'd thought. Instead, it was marked with epaulets on the shoulder. This man was the pilot.

She reached his still form and dropped to her knees, intending to check his vitals. But she no sooner got down beside him than she saw it was hopeless. The pilot's neck had been punctured. Blood pooled around the side of his body that Joelle hadn't been able to see before, and the cause of death was apparent.

Exsanguination.

As Joelle pushed to her feet, she blew out a breath and prayed that it'd been quick. With any luck, he'd been unconscious before meeting his demise.

"I'm sorry I couldn't help you," she said softly.

She couldn't dwell on it. Not now. There might be other survivors.

Swallowing back the sadness, she turned in search of someone she might actually be able to assist. It didn't go well.

She spied Wanda first. The flight attendant's legs stuck out from under a piece of the plane's wing, and there was absolutely no chance she was still breathing.

Joelle's eyes landed on Marty Strom next. He was strapped to his seat, just as Joelle had been. Dirt and soot marked his uniform, but aside from that he looked almost perfect. *Almost.* Because his head . . . *his head.*

"Oh God," Joelle whispered.

His skull was crushed in on one side. Things were visible that just ought not be seen. Bile rose up, and she turned away and closed her eyes at the same time. Her throat burned with sickness over the violence and sorrow for the loss of life. She couldn't be the only one who'd made it off the plane alive, could she?

Dizziness encroached, and Joelle fumbled for something to help her stay upright. But as her hand flailed, a groan came from her left, and she shifted her attention. Someone *was* alive. Trying not to let her hopes get too high, she spun toward the sound. She didn't immediately spy the source. Her heart dropped. Then the groan came again, and she realized that whoever it was, they were obscured by a thick, hip-high patch of leafless bushes.

Please be okay, please be okay, please be okay, she willed as she fought the dizziness and hurried over.

She paused. Took a breath. Gathered her professional composure. Then rounded the bushes, where she immediately paused again. It was Darby O'Toole. He was a dozen feet away, curled up on his side. And the recognition threw her for a second. But she quickly grabbed a hold of sense. While he might not be her favorite person, the fact that he was definitely breathing filled her with relief. She adjusted her jacket, inhaled again, then headed toward him. Except she only made it three steps before a hand landed on her shoulder and yanked her backward.

And then a low, newly familiar voice spoke directly into her ear. "Move even an inch, and we'll both regret it."

Beck.

Fear likely should've been Joelle's initial reaction, given the man's history, his apparent freedom, and his current actions. But what actually swooped in was surprise. Why was he grabbing her? What did his threat mean? She didn't get a chance to posit an answer—or to question why she wasn't afraid—before her eyes offered her an explanation. One that *did* send a spike of alarm through her.

Across the clearing from where she and Beck stood was the man who'd rushed by them just before the plane began its untimely plummet. He was still clad in the flight attendant's uniform, though the garments were now visibly singed and torn. But it was neither the recognition nor the damaged clothing that made Joelle's pulse trip. It was the fact he had a gun in his hands, and that it was trained right on *them*.

* * *

Beck had no intention of using Joelle as a shield. None at all. That didn't mean that the man standing across from them had to know it.

"What are you going to do?" Beck said. "Fire at me and risk shooting an innocent woman?"

"Of course not," the other man replied.

"Then I guess you'd better just let us walk away."

"I'm afraid you're misreading the situation, Mr. Samson."

"How's that?"

"Two ways, really."

"Fascinating. Two entire ways?" Beck filled the reply with sarcasm, but in truth, he was just stalling to keep the man talking.

His real attention was on his surroundings as he flicked a look around in search of an escape.

C'mon, he willed silently. *Give me something. Anything.*

Aloud he said, "I guess you think I should be happy that it's only two things."

"You should let the girl go, Mr. Samson," replied the gunman.

"And give up my leverage? I don't think so."

"See? That right there is your first misread. She isn't leverage at all. I'm not worried about hitting her by mistake."

Beck's eyes landed on a boulder that might provide sufficient cover if they could get to it. "That confident in your shooting abilities, huh?"

"I do happen to be a *very* good shot," replied the phony flight attendant. "But this has more to do with your second misread than it does with my marksmanship."

Beck brought his gaze back to the man. "I can tell how much you're dying to tell me about it. So why don't you just go ahead?"

"Happy to oblige that request. Your second misjudgement, Mr. Samson, is the assumption that I *care* if I hit her. I only need one of you alive, and I'm afraid it isn't Ms. Diedrich."

Beck's stomach dropped. *Shit.* He *had* misread the situation. The other man wasn't hesitating because of the stalling. He had no intention of letting Joelle live. He just wanted to show off his power. His perceived cleverness.

The man smiled. "Now you get it, Mr. Samson. I can see it in your eyes."

He lifted his weapon an inch higher, leaving no more than a moment to react. But Beck *did* react. With as much dexterity as his chains would allow, he gave Joelle a vicious yank to the side. Covering her body with his own, he hit the ground. So did a bullet. It smashed into the rocks and sent up a wild spray of debris.

For a heartbeat, the two of them stayed exactly as they'd landed. Him, on top of her. Her, staring up at him with those drown-in-me green eyes. His bonds created a sharp barrier between them, but it wasn't enough to completely drown out the distracting softness of her body. At least it wasn't until he remembered the gunman undoubtedly had another bullet on the way.

Thinking quickly—and moving in sync with his fast-paced planning—he lifted his wrists and their shackles. He slid the chains smoothly under Joelle's head and down to her shoulders, tugged her hard against his body, and he rolled. Once. Twice. Three times. When they came to rest beside the good-sized boulder he'd noted before, Beck pulled his arms free and sprung to his feet. He got up just in time. Another shot came firing his way. This one didn't penetrate the ground. Instead, it somehow managed to skid along the surface, leaving a stream-like rivulet in its wake. And the armed man was already taking aim again.

"Get behind that goddamn rock!" Beck hollered at Joelle.

He didn't look back to see if she'd listened; he had to assume she was smart enough to take cover. What he *did* do was dive out of the line of fire, catch one of his ankle manacles on a protruding mess of tree roots, and land facedown in the ice-crusted ground. Spitting out dirt, he fought to free himself from the foliage before his attacker could simply peg him off. The roots didn't give easily. Beck kicked harder. He twisted his body, all the while bracing for the inevitable bullet. It didn't come. Still struggling, he looked up in search of an explanation. Or maybe a miracle. The gunman was stalking toward him, a look of grim determination on his face. He didn't stop until he was only two feet away.

"Not taking any chances this time, Mr. Samson," the man said.

"I thought you wanted me alive," Beck replied.

"Alive doesn't have to mean in perfect condition."

He lifted the barrel and pointed the muzzle at Beck's knee. But he'd waited a second too long. It gave Beck just the moment he needed. With a grunt, he shot out his hands and took hold of the other man's ankle. He gave a vicious tug, and his assailant toppled, dropping his weapon.

Despite the fact that he was still stuck, Beck didn't waste any time making his next move. He pulled the man in even closer, wrapped his bound arms around his neck, and squeezed. He ignored the flails and kicks. He paid no attention to the nails digging into his flesh. All of his energy was concentrated on bringing the gunman to heel.

Beck didn't know how long it took. Thirty seconds? A full minute? Enough time that he broke a sweat and was sucking wind. At last, though, the guy ceased his fight and went limp. Beck let him fall to the ground, then turned his attention back to his tangled feet. Without the pressure of being shot at, it was much easier to get free. A few seconds, and he had his chain-encumbered mobility back.

As he tried to catch his breath, he grabbed the dropped gun and flung a look around in search of any other potential threat. He saw none. He did, however, see Joelle. She sat on the ground beside the boulder, her eyes shifting from the unconscious man to Beck. Her raw shock was apparent, and an unusually strong wave of emotion flooded into him. He didn't want her looking at him like that. Like *he* was the bad guy. In fact, he wanted to pull her into a reassuring embrace, and make sure she was all right.

Don't be ridiculous, Samson.

He settled for a question. "You okay?"

"I'm fine." Her eyes went back to the gunman,

"He's not dead," Beck told her, tucking the pilfered weapon

into the rear of his waistband. "You can use your nursing skills to verify it, if you want."

"No, I . . ." She trailed off, swallowed, and tried again. "I don't have to check."

"You sure about that?"

"I believe you."

"Good." He meant the word more than he should've, probably.

"Who is he?" she asked.

"Don't know." It was the truth, at least in the strictest sense. *And the strictest sense is all she needs to hear about,* he told himself firmly.

A frown overtook the shock on Joelle's face. "Hang on. You don't know who was just trying to kill you?"

Beck answered without thinking it through. "Pretty sure he made it clear that he wasn't trying to kill *me*."

The nurse's skin paled again, and her voice was a match to her expression. "Right."

Fighting another urge to offer her some kind of comfort, Beck cleared his throat and reminded himself that he was as eager to change the subject as he was to get the hell away from the crash site.

"Aside from on the plane and just now with the gun, I haven't seen the bastard before in my life," he said. "Doesn't matter anymore anyway. What I need right now is more important."

Joelle blinked again. "What is it that you think you need?"

"An inventory."

"Sorry?"

"Who *is* dead?" he asked. "I saw you looking around."

She swallowed. "The real flight attendant, Wanda. And one of the guards."

"Allan?"

"Was that the guy who was supposed to be sitting with you?"

Beck nodded. "That's the one."

"No, it wasn't him that I saw. It was Marty Strom. The one beside me."

Her attention started to slide away, then quickly came back to him—like she didn't want to see whatever was in that direction. Again, Beck had to battle back his concern over her and her feelings.

"Maybe the guy named Shane Dreery, too?" she added. "I can't . . . there are a few bodies."

"Okay," he said in a clipped tone. "Let's switch this up. Did anyone else make it?"

Joelle didn't answer right away. She looked a little uncertain, and the extra moment gave Beck time to consider what he hoped her answer would be. On the one hand, he didn't wish death on anyone. On the other, though, it'd be a shit ton easier to escape without a hot pursuit.

"Ms. Diedrich," he prodded after another silent second. "I need to know what I'm up against."

She blew out a breath. "Darby O'Toole. He's the only one I'm sure is alive."

"Of course he is," Beck muttered, then sighed and shook his handcuffs in her general direction. "Wanna give me a hand finding the keys for these?"

"You're kidding, right?"

"Not in the slightest. Hard as hell for me to get out of here when I'm in chains."

Her eyes dropped to the bindings in question. "You know I can't do that."

"You can't?" he countered. "Or you won't?"

"I'm a part of a prison transport. I have obligations. It's my job, Mr. Samson." Her voice was stiff.

"We're stranded on a mountain because our plane crashed, and I just fought off some guy who was trying to maim me and kill you. So I'm pretty sure normal rules no longer apply, prison transport or not." He paused and tried to soften his words with a smile. "I'm also pretty sure you're safe to call me by my first name at this point."

"Beck, then. But it doesn't matter what I call you. I still can't free a—" She stopped herself and bit her lip.

"A convicted murderer?" he filled in.

She breathed out. "Yes."

"I'd tell you I'm innocent, Miss Diedrich, but every asshole behind bars says that. Truthfully, I don't have time to do it anyway. Either buddy with the gun will wake up and try again, or one of his friends will turn up and do it."

"Joelle is fine."

"Sorry?"

"You said to call you by your first name," she told him. "I'm saying the same. Call me Joelle."

He echoed the cadence of her moments-earlier reply to his own suggestion. "Joelle, then. But it doesn't matter what I call you. You still can't free a convicted murderer. Not even one like me, who has his *own* obligations."

Her expression was apologetic, and the genuineness of it nearly made Beck laugh. Under the dark amusement, though, he felt an unusual need to convince her that he was deserving of her assistance. Except there really wasn't time. No matter how green her eyes were. No matter how sweetly she pursed her lips and waited for something more. Not even no matter how much she reminded him—for the first time in memory—of the fact that he was a man and not a number. He had to get out of harm's way and off the damn mountain. People were waiting for him. Counting on him. So if Joelle wasn't going to help him, he had to help himself. He held her gaze for another moment, then pressed his lips together and turned away.

"Wait!" she called.

He tossed his reply over his shoulder. "Unless you're going to tell me exactly where the keys are, I *can't* wait."

He kept going, heading back toward the area of concentrated wreckage and the possibility of escape. He stopped beside a patch of scorched ground and scanned for the most likely candidate—Allan. His sweep yielded a roll of his gut before anything else. There were casualties, just as Joelle had stated. Beck was certain that the first sprawled-out man he saw was dead. The unnatural angle of his head gave it away. No doubt there were others who had met the same fate. He let himself dwell on the loss for a moment, then ordered himself to complete his task.

Another look, a few more steps, and he found Allan. The guard was lying on the ground, faceup, splayed out, eyes closed. For a second, Beck assumed the man was dead. When he moved closer, though, he saw the ragged rise and fall of Allan's chest. Unexpected relief hit. It wasn't specifically *Allan* being alive that brought the feeling. If anything, it would be easier if every single person on the plane had perished. But the relief was there all the same.

Beck shook his head at his own bleeding-heart self. He wouldn't celebrate these assholes' deaths, but they didn't deserve a concentrated amount of his sympathy.

Moving with extra caution, he sank down beside the guard. Gently, he took hold of the keys. Even more carefully, he removed them from the belt loop, then repositioned himself a decent distance away before he bent down and got to work on the first lock. As he did, Joelle spoke up from behind him.

"Is he still alive?" she asked.

"Yes," Beck replied, moving the key from his ankles to his wrists. "Don't worry. Allan will get to continue his personal enjoyment of belittling inmates for years to come."

She ignored his facetious comment. "What will happen now?"

"They'll track the crash and send in a rescue team." He assumed it was true, regardless of the intentions of its passengers.

"How long do you think that will take?" Joelle asked.

"Not sure." He finished freeing himself, stretched a very satisfying stretch, and met her eyes. "Why? Are you calculating my odds of getting away? Or maybe just planning on trying to stop me?"

Her cheeks colored. "Neither."

"In that case . . ."

"You're going."

"I am."

She bit her lip then shook her head like she'd changed her mind about whatever she'd been about to say. "Okay."

"Okay," Beck echoed. "Stay safe, Joelle."

"You, too." The pink in her cheeks heightened as she realized what she'd just said.

Touching the gun in his waistband for reassurance, he offered her a tight smile, then headed for the wooded hills, trusting that his survival skills would serve him better than anything he might waste time looking for in the wreckage.

Chapter Five

Beck didn't get far before a mix of guilt and regret made his feet want to slow. He didn't let it happen. Not immediately, anyway. But it didn't stop his mind from churning. From hanging on Joelle and her green eyes.

What was he supposed to do? Ask her to come with him? Suggest that a Medical Escort from inside the prison system become his fellow fugitive? Or better yet, insist that she did it? She sure as shit wasn't likely to come easily.

He kept going, but as the trees started to thicken around him, Joelle's question played back in his head.

What will happen now?

"Not my problem," he said under his breath.

Except he couldn't help imagining that things could play out badly.

The man with the gun would wake up at some point. Likely before any rescue attempt came through. Joelle had seen the guy's face. Seen what he wanted to do.

He was going to kill her before. He won't let her live now.

The thought made Beck stop so abruptly that he nearly tripped. Cursing himself for not seeing the obvious conclusion in the first place, he spun back. He half expected to find out that Joelle had been smart enough to leave the crash site on her own. Maybe even followed him. Of course, she hadn't. There was no sign of her red hair, parting the foliage. No flicker of movement that indicated someone was trying to stay out of sight. With the exception of the smoke, all evidence of the wreck was invisible.

He muttered a curse then strode back, not slowing until he saw that telltale flash of crimson. And knew why she hadn't followed. Joelle was crouched down beside Allan, her fingers pressed to his neck. Beck watched her for a moment as she went through the motions of checking over the guard. She was calm. Gentle. Compassion somehow radiated from her actions in a way that told him she was absolutely in the right profession.

But I still can't leave her here. Especially considering the other thing that occurred to him right then. *If—when—the gunman wakes up and takes her out, he has a readymade scapegoat for her murder. Me.*

Somewhere nearby, someone unseen let out a groan, hammering home the fact that danger could rear up at any moment. Beck had no clue what else his attackers had planned. All he knew was that they'd do anything to achieve their goal of capturing him to get what they wanted.

"Joelle," he called, keeping his voice as low as he could while still drawing her attention.

She tipped her head his way, surprise registering on her face when she saw him. She gave the guard's arm a small squeeze, then stood up and came closer.

"Change your mind?" she asked.

"About sticking around and getting shot in the kneecap then hauled off against my will? Hardly. But I need you to come with me."

"You can't be serious."

"Rarely been more so," he said.

Her arms crossed over her chest. "No."

"It's not really a request."

"What are you going to do? Toss me over your shoulder and carry me off screaming?"

He gave her a speculative look, and she took a small step away.

"I'm not going with you, Beck."

"If you stay, you'll wind up dead." He said it matter-of-factly, and her green gaze sharpened.

"Less than five minutes ago you told me that a rescue team would be sent in," she reminded him. "Was that a lie?"

"I don't mean the elements are going to get you. It's our trigger-happy friend that'll see to it."

"*You* have his gun. And I can take care of myself."

"Maybe, maybe not," said Beck, not bothering to tell her that the man likely wasn't acting alone or that the whole damn crew and her co-workers might've been involved, too. "But I can't risk it."

She frowned. "What do you mean? It's not you who's risking something if I come with you."

"Really? Who do you think will take the blame if you get shot?"

Understanding flickered across her face. "Oh."

"Am I going to have to find a way to force this?" he asked softly.

"I—" She cast a look toward the guard. "If I stay, I might be able to help some of these people."

"You might," he replied. "But you won't be doing anyone any good if you get killed in the process of trying."

She swallowed. "All right. I'll come without a fight. But shouldn't we try to find something to take with us?"

"Like what?"

"I don't know. Food. Water. Gear."

He shook his head. "Waste of time."

"Water is a waste of time?" She sounded incredulous.

"Do you see anything in view?" He swept his hand out wide. Her eyes followed. "No. Nothing. But still."

"Look. I don't have time to justify my choice. Nor do I have time to make a search that might end up fruitless. We'll make do." He paused. "Still coming without a fight?"

"Yes," she said after a small hesitation. "Still coming without a fight."

Beck stared at her. He had a feeling that she'd left out two words at the end of her second acquiescence—*for now.* But if that was all he could get from her, then he'd just accept it. He'd be grateful. And he'd be on his guard for when that unspoken promise of a fight became a reality.

*   *   *

Joelle was uneasy. More than uneasy. She was scared. She didn't like the idea of leaving behind the only known factor. Even if the factor in question happened to be the fallout of a plane crash accompanied by some wacko with a gun. And it kept crossing her mind that she might've fought harder to stay at the crash site. Maybe if she'd just argued a bit more, she wouldn't have to be on alert for some means of real escape. And yes, she was planning on making a break for it as soon as she was given the slightest chance.

The slightest chance that doesn't involve just running for my life and hoping I make it, that is, she silently amended.

She definitely needed more than that. In fact, if she simply wanted to run, she could've done it a dozen times by now. Beck wasn't paying much attention to her at all. His focus was on slicing through the foliage and making his way across the rough terrain. The only time he checked on her was when she fell behind a little, or if he had to pause to hold back some branches so she could pass more easily.

It didn't matter. She'd already decided that her best bet was to figure out what Beck's exit plan entailed, then somehow use it herself. But so far, he hadn't shown any sign that he was going to share it. In addition to half ignoring her, he'd barely spoken. Was he using markers? Or maybe the position of the sun to guide their way? It'd be easier to think so if the sun were actually visible. What was his secret?

Maybe he doesn't have one, said her subconscious. *Maybe he's just as aimless as you would be.*

Joelle refused to accept the suggestion. He *had* to have a plan. Aside from those minimal moments pausing to assist her, he was walking like a man on a mission. It made her ridiculously thankful that she hadn't tried to force herself to wear the too-big flats. She would never have been able to make this journey, let alone keep up with Beck.

She studied the back of his head as they continued along their overgrown path. Maybe her eyes even bored into those dark locks. As though she was hoping to find an explanation for all her questions there in his hair. All she saw was that he had a small scar where his hairline met the back of his neck. Before she could stop herself, she wondered how he got it. Doing something bad, or something good? It seemed like it couldn't possibly be something in the middle. Because there was no denying that Beck Samson was a contradiction. A convicted murderer who helped her navigate the foliage more easily. A man who warned her about a hazardous dip in the ground but knew how to throttle someone unconscious with his bare hands.

Joelle pursed her lips. Why *was* Beck's attitude toward her so at odds with his actions and history?

His actions? You mean defending himself against someone who was trying to shoot him?

Her brow furrowed. She hadn't yet come up with a theory about the man with the gun. And when she thought about it now, she knew there were far more questions than answers. Who was the shooter? How had he managed to get the gun on the plane? Did the crash itself have anything to do with him?

Why was he after Beck, and did Beck really not know him at all? It seemed unrealistic. But she believed him anyway.

Mentally, she shook her head. She could probably drive herself crazy with trying to unknot Beck's motives.

Except now that she was thinking about it—about him— Joelle realized that despite the strength of the fear that crawled through her veins, it wasn't directly linked to Beck. Which was odd. Possibly not very smart, either. But even when she drew her attention to it and asked herself why, it remained true. The man himself had nothing to do with the bounce of her nerves. She felt more trepidation at the thought of being lost in the forest than she did about being alone with Beck.

Great, she thought with a self-directed eye roll. *You're not afraid of a killer. Congrats. But that doesn't mean you should stay with him.*

She needed to go back to concentrating on finding that plausible means of escape rather than thinking about Beck Samson's scars. The problem wasn't just that she had zero idea how to get off the mountain. It was also the fact that she wouldn't survive long on her own. It was already cold. If their trek lasted any amount of time—and by Joelle's estimate, it'd already been at least twenty minutes or so—it would get colder. Already, the sky seemed to be growing grayer. The mountain air had a bite. Fresh snow was inevitable, and she shivered at the thought.

She had another problem, too. One that was more immediate than the impending winter weather. It was the fact that every time her brain stopped gnawing away at a solution, some part of her body reminded her rather pointedly that she hadn't come out of the crash unscathed.

There was a throb in her right calf and a concerning sting in the upper left side of her abdomen. Her head kept trying to renew its ache. Worse than before, if she was being honest. She wasn't exactly dizzy, but now and then the world lost a bit of clarity. She was likely concussed. She *had* been unconscious for an indeterminate number of minutes. Had she been her own patient, she definitely would've been checking her pupils. And on that note, maybe she ought to be mentioning her injuries to Beck. Perhaps even asking him to slow the pace to account for them. Except truthfully, she wasn't sure she wanted him to know. Sure, he was chivalrous now. But he was still a fugitive. And she hadn't yet figured out what that meant for her.

Still mulling it over, she sidestepped a patch of ice. Or she tried to, anyway. Her foot caught the edge of the frozen ground and sent her leg sliding out wider than was comfortable. Right away, her side panged a protest at the extra stretch. And—like he could feel it, too—Beck slowed, then stopped. Joelle followed suit, halting next to him.

"Is something wrong?" she asked, careful to keep the pain out of her tone.

He tipped a look from her head to her toes. "I don't know. You tell me."

"I'm fine," she lied.

"*Fine* fine?"

"Of course *fine* fine. Why wouldn't I be?"

"Pretty sure I could supply a whole list in response to that," he said. "But I won't." He gestured to a fallen log that blocked the path ahead. "Just thought we could stand to take a breather, and nature provided a seat in this very convenient spot."

Joelle considered arguing. As much as she wasn't relishing the hike, she also wasn't particularly keen on the prospect of lengthening it by indulging in a break. But before she could open her mouth, Beck was already sinking down onto the wood. And standing over him felt awkward, so she bent her knees and perched herself beside him, trying to maximize the space afforded by the log.

Beck lifted a dark eyebrow at the small gap in between them. His mouth twitched. But if he'd been about to comment on it, his words were cut away by a strong gust of wind that kicked up some snow and sent a shiver running down Joelle's spine. She tried to adjust her jacket to compensate. The chill had other ideas, easily penetrating the newly torn holes with breezy vigor. Joelle's teeth did their best to chatter. And after another heartbeat, Beck took matters into his own hands, angling himself to block the wind. His new position effectively removed any hope of maintaining some physical distance, but it also made it so that the all-over iciness dissipated, so Joelle could hardly justify voicing a complaint.

"Thank you," she said, meaning it.

"No problem." He gave her a smile, then added, "Nut allergy?"

Caught off guard, Joelle frowned. "What?"

He reached into his pocket, pulled free two small packages, and held one out. "Almonds. Pilfered from the plane before we started our untimely descent."

"No nut allergies," she replied, taking the proffered food. "Thank you. Again."

"A good kidnapper supplies his hostage with her needs."

"Is that what this is now? A kidnapping? I thought you were saving my life and avoiding being blamed for my murder."

A dark, pained look passed over his face, then slid away quickly into a smirk that seemed a bit forced. "Maybe not a *kidnapping* kidnapping. But let's give it a few more hours, then we'll take a vote."

She rolled her eyes, but both his brief expression and the words *a few hours* pinged at her anxiety. Trying to push it aside, she pulled open the package of almonds, then popped one into her mouth. Surprisingly, the savory flavor *did* steer her attention away from the worry. She was hungry. Thirsty, too. But she didn't want to bring up water again, only to be told it was a waste of time. So for a minute or so, she ate in silence, just enjoying the unexpected snack. But as the seconds ticked by, she decided she really ought to pursue some kind of greater understanding about their situation.

"Can I ask you something?" she said.

"You can ask me whatever you want," Beck replied.

She made a face. "Let me guess. That doesn't mean you'll answer it?"

"Precisely."

"Gee, thanks."

He tossed an almond up in the air, tipped his head back, and caught it. "Why don't *I* ask *you* something instead?"

"Go for it. Maybe *I'll* even answer."

"What made you decide to take this job?"

She knew he was talking about the Medical Escort position. But she sensed something else—something she couldn't quite pinpoint—under his words. A misdirect of some kind, maybe. And she also suspected the casualness of the query wasn't quite so casual at all. So she deliberately answered the same way.

"Half of it was timing," she said. "I finished my degree in the same week that the posting came up on the job board at school. And the other half of it was because I didn't enjoy my hospital practicum, and I was looking for something different."

"Prison nurse and Medical Escort definitely fit the 'different' bill."

"Yes, they do."

He sent up another almond and caught that one in his mouth, too. "Makes me wonder why Dr. Karim would walk away from it."

"What makes you think he walked away?" Joelle replied. "They told me he was sick."

Beck shrugged. "Dunno. Guess he doesn't strike me as the get-sick type."

"But he does strike you as the walk-away type?"

"No. Not that either."

His eyes found and held hers, his gaze intent. Joelle's curiosity was even more piqued. What was he really trying to ask her?

"We should get going," he said abruptly.

"Hang on," she replied. "I didn't get to ask my question yet."

He paused with his hands set to push off from the makeshift bench. "So you're saying my warning that I might not answer didn't deter you?"

"Are you saying you really wanted to know why I took this job?" she countered.

"All right. Ask."

Joelle narrowed her eyes at the evasion, but she chose not to comment on it. In fact, when she opened her mouth, the question that popped out wasn't one she'd even realized she was thinking about.

"Did you do it?" she said.

His forehead wrinkled. "Did I do what?"

His confusion seemed genuine. And it gave her a chance to backpedal. But she didn't take the opening.

"Did you kill your business partner?" she asked instead.

Beck went still. So silent and so motionless that every other noise in the immediate vicinity was amplified. The trill of a bird in the distance. A blast of wind whining through the trees and the muffled hush of snow, just starting to fall. Their breaths, drawing in and out in a strangely synchronized pattern.

"Are you sure you don't know the answer to that already, Joelle?" Beck said at last, the words edged.

Joelle didn't know what kind of response he was looking for, but he clearly didn't find it in her face. And her voice seemed to be stuck in her throat anyway, so she was relieved when he shook his head, and his expression cleared.

"Everyone in prison is innocent," he stated. "Didn't we already establish that?"

"Right," she replied with false lightness. "I guess I forgot."

He nodded, then pushed to his feet and held out his hand. Without thinking about it, she pressed her palm to his. Immediately—before she could even stand—the heat from his skin zapped straight into her, startling her. She jerked her face up and met his eyes. There was a new intensity there. A different one. One that reminded Joelle that when she'd first seen Beck in the back of the SUV, she'd been struck by his good looks. Now, with the wintery mountainside as his backdrop, the strength in his grip, and the way his gaze dropped to her lips for just a moment, it hit her again.

He's also a convicted murderer, J.D. You really must be suffering from a head injury. Call off your over-active imagination. But even as she had the thought, she questioned it. *Convicted murderer, yes. But was the conviction deserved?*

He gave her a small tug, and she let herself be pulled up. Except as she stood, the pain in her side screamed a protest so forceful that her teeth clenched together. And as he released her hand, a fresh wave of real dizziness hit. The world around her blurred.

"Beck?" Her voice sounded faraway.

"What's wrong?" he replied, concern lacing the question. "You look like you don't—"

Whatever else he said was lost as Joelle's equilibrium failed her. She toppled over, heading straight for the ground, unable to get her hands in front of herself fast enough to break her fall.

Chapter Six

Beck reacted instinctively. He shot out his arms, scooping Joelle up just before she earned herself a mouthful of dirt. Her head lolled to one side, and worry spiked through him. He shifted her so that she was cradled against his chest, then carried her over to the log they'd just abandoned. Still holding her close, he seated himself and brushed her hair away from her face. Her eyes were open but glassy. Her breathing was even, and that was somewhat reassuring, but not quite enough.

"Hey," he said gently. "You still with me, honey?"

The endearment slipped out before he could stop it. It didn't matter, though. His concern over her well-being overrode all else.

"Joelle?" he prodded.

She muttered something that was either too quiet to hear or just plain incomprehensible, and Beck's worry deepened.

"You've gotta give me something to work with here," he said.

"It hurts," she said.

"What hurts?"

"Me."

Her hand fluttered to the side of her stomach, and when his attention followed, his breath caught. Under her jacket, her blouse was stuck to her abdomen, pulled tight by an easily identifiable crimson liquid.

Oh damn.

"Is it bad?" she asked.

Beck looked up and tried to cover his feelings. He knew he didn't succeed. Joelle's eyes closed.

"It *is* bad," she said. "I can tell from your face."

"Why didn't you tell me you were injured?" he replied.

"So you could nurse the nurse?" she said without opening her eyes.

"So that I could slow down our pace. At the very least."

"Or leave me behind somewhere."

He was glad she couldn't see his startled expression, and he kept his tone even. "Why would I do that?"

She sighed. "Deadweight."

"I didn't keep you away from that son of a bitch with the gun just to leave you behind," he said.

"Because then you couldn't be blamed."

"That's not the only reason."

"Or so you want me to believe." Her eyelids fluttered, and her emerald irises made an appearance.

Beck couldn't quite stop himself from touching her cheek. She leaned into his hand just the tiniest bit, and she closed her eyes again. A surge of unusual emotion surged in.

He spoke softly. "Listen to me. I don't have any idea what you think you know about me, but I promise you that I am *not* the kind of man who abandons a woman on the side of the mountain under any circumstance, okay? So we need to find some shelter. I want to clean up that wound and get you warmed up."

Her eyes opened. "There's something good about being cold."

"What's that?"

"No fever."

"Yeah, not sure I'm buying that story."

"Feel my forehead," she said.

Beck was going to argue and tell her they had more signifi-cant things to focus on, but her hand came to his wrist, and she guided his palm to her head. Her skin *was* relatively cool. Knowing that made Beck more relieved than he would've expected. She was hurt, but she didn't have the first signs of an infection. Not yet.

"No fever," he conceded gruffly. "Assuming your medical expertise accepts a forehead check as a good enough means of assessment. But we still need to find somewhere warm and dry."

She wiggled, and he realized she was trying to free herself from his arms. He tightened his hold.

"Aren't we going?" she asked.

"We are," he said.

"Then why aren't you letting me go?"

"I don't think you're in any shape to walk."

Her still-glassy gaze sharpened just a little, and the flush in her cheeks darkened. "Are you implying that you want to *carry* me to some . . . I don't know. Some *cave* somewhere?"

Despite the situation—the ongoing threat to his life and the reasons for it, her injury and worsening physical state, and the fact that the snow was swirling with increased intensity—a chuckle found its way up out of Beck's chest. "A cave isn't a bad idea, actually. If we can find one. Not entirely sure about your cave*man* insult, though."

"Is it more insulting to call you a caveman, or more insult-ing to imply that I can't stand on my own two feet?"

"I'm not 'implying' a damn thing. I'm stating it outright."

"I can do it," she insisted.

"I don't think you can," he replied. "Or that you should."

"I feel a bit better now that I'm not standing up."

He didn't point out the irony in her statement. He eyed her wound. He winced. Then he decided it was easier—and quicker—to let her try than it was to keep arguing about it.

"Okay," he said. "Letting you go now."

He loosened his arms, shifted so that she could put her feet on the ground, and waited. Joelle pressed one hand to his shoulder. Slowly, she stood up. For a second, she was fine. Or at least as fine as a baby deer was when it was using its legs for the first time. Then she wobbled. She teetered. She toppled. And her fall landed her right back in Beck's lap. Only this time, she was face forward. Her body was between his legs, her soft curves pressed against his chest.

The new position sent a thump of unexpected want through Beck. It caught him off-guard. Not because he wasn't aware of just how attractive he found her. Her striking features had been what prompted him to speak to her in the first place. Her thick red hair. Her creamy skin. Those green eyes that made a man want to lose himself in them. Her beauty was a given. What hit him right then, though, was something else. A below-the-surface feeling. She was stubborn in her efforts. Brave in her interactions with him, even though she knew he was a convicted murderer. Kind to him before the crash, too. Those things made him want to know more about her.

Any other time, Samson, and I'd say you're on your way to liking her. As in like *liking her.*

It was an emotion that had zero place in his life, and even less place in relation to a woman whose loyalties were unknown. He had no room for feeling anything, actually. His goal was to get off the mountain, track down his contact on the other end, and take care of the business that had set this trip in motion in the first place. Nothing else was on the agenda. But as Beck moved to free himself—or to free Joelle, depending on how he looked at it—her arms came up to his shoulders. Quite suddenly, their position was even more intimate. Practically an embrace. Her head lifted, and they were almost nose to nose. So close that Beck felt the heat of her lips.

"Hi," she said.

"Hi," he said back.

"I fell again."

"You did."

"Sorry."

"Don't be," he replied. "Just agree to letting me carry you."

"You can't just warm me up and do triage here?" she said hopefully.

Beck couldn't fight another laugh. "No. I don't think that would be in our best interests on either front. And in case you haven't noticed, the snow is starting to come down pretty hard."

Joelle tipped her face toward the sky. On the way up, her chin brushed Beck's cheek, making him want to tighten his hands on her hips. He forced himself not to.

"All right," he said, unwilling to sit through the torment any longer. "As your resident kidnapper, I'm making the decision."

He didn't wait for further argument. Swiftly, he helped her to her feet, scooped her from the ground, and resumed his trek into the woods.

* * *

The weather went from impending storm to full-out tempest in under two minutes. The wind pushed hard against Beck's back while a mix of snow and freezing rain slapped against every bit of exposed skin. He did his best to shield Joelle from the elements. She was small and light, and she clung to him, shivering. She felt fragile in his arms. It only made him more worried about her injury and her vulnerability. He pushed on.

A few more minutes, and the trees grew sparser, the terrain rougher. Even though Beck was confident that he was still headed in the right direction—east and lowering in elevation—the going grew hillier. His thighs protested as the hike turned into a climb. The weather intensified, too. Gales pushed and pulled and pushed again. Every step required restabilization. The snow and rain became pellet-like, hitting with enough force that Beck wondered if he might find himself covered in welts when it was over. The clothes on his back did nothing to protect him, and despite Joelle's jacket, he suspected she was freezing as well.

He was about to give in and tell her that his plans needed to be altered—likely to creating a makeshift shelter rather than finding a natural one—when he spotted something. A dark shadow in the rocky face ahead. Beck squinted through the continuing onslaught. He couldn't be one hundred percent sure that it was a cave, but it was at least worth checking out.

He bent his head down to let Joelle know that he'd found a potential solution. When he started to speak, though, he saw that her eyes were closed. Not in the tight way that would indicate she was trying to shut out the storm, but rather in something that resembled repose.

"Joelle?" he said, the wind dragging away his voice.

She shifted the tiniest bit in his arms, but she didn't answer. Beck couldn't pretend it didn't set off alarms in his head.

Probably my cue to hurry up, he thought.

Once more, he set off. He picked up his pace as best he could, battling the whole while against the rage of wind and ice. The potential cave was farther away than he'd initially estimated. Twice, he had to stop to catch his breath and adjust his hold on Joelle. Both times, he spent the extra moments studying her face and watching her inhales and exhales for a sign that something was worse. Each visual confirmed that her vitals seemed stable, and his relief was a physical thing.

"Just a bit longer," he murmured as he started the final leg.

At last, he got near enough to the looming hill to see that it was most definitely a hollowed-out space. If it wasn't quite a cave, it was damn close. Being certain made him move even faster. In fewer than two minutes, he reached the mouth, where he paused to search for any indication that the cavern was inhabited by wildlife. When he found none, he ducked his head and carried Joelle inside.

The change was immediate. Near darkness swathed Beck's vision. The roar of the wind slid into background noise, and the wild, hail-like snow couldn't reach them. It was still cold, but the packed dirt and rocky walls created a temperature buffer that made it a few degrees warmer. The space was just the right size. Big enough to accommodate and shelter them while not being cavernous. The best Beck could hope for, he supposed.

Wishing he had a coat or sweater to cover her—or both so he could cover her *and* give her something to lie on—he settled Joelle into a spot on the ground. Then he leaned back and studied her sleeping form. Her skin was pale, but not unhealthy. Her breaths were even. With the wound hidden by her jacket, she really did look like she was just sleeping.

Because technically, she is *sleeping,* Beck said to himself.

He wasn't anywhere near qualified to diagnose something specific, but he'd been living in a prison for two years. Fights were common behind the walls. Minor injuries needed to be dealt with regularly, and the men preferred to keep their cuts and bruises away from the attention of the guards. So he was well-versed in first aid. Joelle had been conscious and lucid just a short bit ago, which meant that if she was suffering from a concussion, it was fine for her to rest. Better than fine. Rest was a necessity. As far as her injury was concerned . . . as she'd pointed out herself, there were no signs of fever. She couldn't possibly have developed an infection that quickly, anyway.

"You're going to be fine," he told her near-still form. "You'll wake up from your nap, we'll get that cut dressed, and then we'll tackle the rest of the mountain."

Despite the reassurance, he didn't move away. Instead, he leaned in and pressed the back of his hand to her forehead. It was still cool.

Too cool, maybe?

He tapped his fingers on his thigh for another moment before realizing the longer he sat around overanalyzing things, the less action was being taken. There was no reason why he couldn't get to work on prepping for when Joelle did wake up. Starting with some heat.

He stood up and turned away from the sleeping woman, letting his eyes roam over the dim space. Building a fire in a cave wasn't a fantastic idea, survival skills-wise. There was smoke to consider. Worse than that, too much heat could cause expansion of the walls and prompt a collapse. So he'd have to be cautious.

A fire that's not a fire is what I need.

Again, Beck's fingers strummed his thigh. He made another visual sweep. This time, a small pile of stones caught his attention, and an idea struck. His hand stilled. He'd need a few more things, but aside from some moss that would make a good starter, none of it was inside the cave. Which meant he had to head back out into the storm. He was loath to leave Joelle unattended, but what other choice did he have?

Gritting his teeth and casting a silent apology her way, Beck braced for another smack of winter and made his way out of the shelter. He was pleasantly surprised. The wind had mostly abated. The freezing rain was gone, replaced by thickly falling snow. Already, the surrounding area was becoming blanketed in white. Soon, the mountains would be a winter wonderland.

Beautiful, he thought, wondering a little absently if Joelle would like it.

The scenery was liberating. Expansive. Despite the snow, he swore he could see for miles. The forest and the hills. The cloud-dotted sky. For the first time since the crash, he paused and let himself think about his freedom. He'd been behind bars for two excruciating years, biding his time and seriously considering if he'd ever get the justice he deserved. Assuming—maybe consciously, maybe not—that it would never happen. Now, looking out over the mountains, it seemed within reach.

He breathed out and closed his eyes. It was almost worse to feel genuine hope. The truth was, he would never be free unless he got off the mountain and did what he was meant to do. He might be physically unencumbered at the moment, but there was so much more to it than that. Even the current moment was indescribably complex.

Had the plane been brought down on purpose? If so, how many innocent people had died, just to get to Beck? The pilot? Other crew members? Had there been anyone else on the plane? What was the likelihood that the crash was unrelated to him at all? Whether it was an unintended consequence or not, the people who were after *him* were the ones responsible. But he knew that now wasn't the time to muse it over.

Shaking off the renewed discontent, he forced his eyes open and focused on the challenge of finding the supplies he needed for this hiccough in his plans. For once, luck went his way. An overhang of rock just outside the cave sheltered the remnants of a fallen tree. In a single swoop, Beck was able to grab three of the things on his mental list—a straight stick, a flat piece of tree trunk, and some kindling. A bit more digging around in the same area, and he found himself a rock that would make a decent tool. He tucked it all under his shirt and slipped back to the cave, where he checked on Joelle. Satisfied that her condition remained stable, he set to work.

He performed the simplest tasks first, starting with rearranging the loose stones into an approximation of a hearth. Next, he broke the kindling into tiny pieces and tucked them between the rocks. Then he balled up the moss from the cave to create a tinder bundle, which he set atop the rocks and kindling. With that done, he moved onto the more strenuous steps. He used the rock to whittle one end of the stick into a point. He used it again to make the needed drill board out of the flat tree trunk by creating a notch in the middle and a notch on the side. His hands ached, but they were accustomed to the manual labor he'd undertaken at the prison. Working with wood felt like second nature, and it was almost soothing to feel the familiar protest of his muscles. But the hardest part was yet to come.

Beck let himself take a fifteen-second break. He stretched his arms and flexed his fingers, then rolled his shoulders and wiped the beading sweat from his forehead. He cast a look at Joelle, who'd continued to slumber through the whole thing. Then he went back to work. He positioned himself on a raised piece of ground so that he could place his feet on the newly crafted drill board to hold it in place. Breathing out, he put the pointed stick into the notch and started twisting the stick between his palms. Faster and faster he twirled, careful to keep downward pressure on at the same time. He had no concept of how much time passed. It was a seemingly mindless task, but it actually required focus. If he slowed or eased up, the effort would be in vain.

Soon, his palms were burning. His eyes watered. His forearms tightened. He kept going anyway. From experience, he knew that losing friction for even a second or two would result in having to start over. In fact, only once in all his weekend wilderness trips had he successfully created a fire like this.

But all that was at stake then was my ego, he reminded himself.

A hint of smoke made an appearance between the stick and the board. He spun faster. Harder. The smoke became a miniature plume. At last, the needed ember formed. Once it was there, Beck didn't waste any time. He spun for a few more seconds, then released the stick, brought the board to the tinder bundle, and tapped the ember into the moss. A spark lit. He dropped to all fours and blew gently on it. The moss crackled. He blew again. The kindling took. Glowing orange spread through the rocks.

"Yes!" The exclamation and the accompanying fist pump were spontaneous and admittedly sort of comical, and right away, they earned a tinkling laugh from behind him.

Beck shifted to face Joelle, a smart comeback on the ready. It fell away, though, when he caught sight of her. His breath stuck in his throat. She had a single eyebrow raised at him, and her lips were parted with residual amusement. Her red hair was an untamed mess, her face flushed. The white blouse was damp from the storm, and under her jacket it clung to her curves in a way that made him have to concentrate on keeping his eyes on her face.

"What?" she said lightly as he continued to stare. "Have I got something between my teeth?"

"Do you know the LaBelle crime family?" The unrelated question burst free before Beck could stop it, but as soon as it was out, he realized he needed to know exactly where she stood.

Chapter Seven

Confusion made Joelle frown, then echo Beck's words back to him. "The LaBelle crime family?"

Of course she'd heard of them. Because who hadn't? But why did he want to know?

Before she could ask for more clarification, he stood up and began to pace the small space, his big form making shadows flicker along the walls of the cave. He stayed silent as he moved. And somehow, that silence ricocheted louder than any sound. Joelle didn't know what to say. His movements were restless, yet tightly wound. One second, she'd been watching with amusement as he celebrated his fire in a pleased, classic little-boy fashion. Now it was far too easy to imagine him behind a barred cell door. Which only sealed her mouth even more.

He stopped abruptly in front of her, his blue eyes a stormy shade as they bored into her. "Do you work for them?"

It took her five long seconds to clue in that this second question was connected to the other one he'd just asked.

"The LaBelle crime family?" she repeated, just to be sure.

"Yes, dammit," said Beck. "Do you work for them?"

It struck her that maybe he had a personal reason for

asking. One that lined up with being an accountant, shooting people, and sending distinct "messages."

"Do *you* work for them?" she asked.

The responding expression on his face was impossible to describe. First, his cheeks seemed to go a bit wan. His mouth worked silently, then closed. His eyes widened. Narrowed. Widened again. He lifted a hand and ran it over his jaw twice. Again, his lips parted. But he snapped them shut without a word. Finally, just when Joelle was about to ask if *he* had suffered a head injury, too, he let out an enormous laugh. He actually doubled over, his hands on his knees as his body shook with mirth. And Joelle was speechless again. She waited for him to finish and offer some kind of explanation. But when the laughter finally died down, all he did was shake his head and sit beside her on the floor.

"Let's have a look at that wound," he said, gesturing for her to take off her jacket.

Joelle didn't move. "I don't understand."

"I want to see what we're dealing with," he replied. "If it's something that probably should've had stitches, we might need to do something about that before we get going again. And by we, I mean you. Because I suspect you've got a hell of a lot more experience in that department."

Her puzzlement grew. But she shrugged out of her jacket anyway, obliging in his request to check out her injury. He wasn't wrong, after all. If it needed attention, it needed attention. She peeled back the edge of her blouse, wincing as it pulled on the cut. Her work didn't allow any room for being squeamish, but looking at her own wounds wasn't high on her enjoyment list, so she focused on Beck's face instead.

"How is it?" she asked.

He leaned in a little closer. "Messy."

"Great."

"I don't suppose you've got any secret stashes of antiseptic hidden somewhere?"

"Like where?"

"I live in a prison, and you work in one," he said as he sat back and grinned up at her. "Use your imagination."

She made a face. "In all seriousness, though, we should definitely wash the area around the wound and make sure there's nothing stuck in it that shouldn't be."

"Is that the medical way to describe it, Nurse Diedrich?"

"Maybe it is."

He lifted his hands in mock defeat. "All right. I won't argue with the expert. Any objections to using some melted snow in place of rubbing alcohol?"

"No," she said. "Not unless *you* have something else hidden somewhere."

"Not this time." He winked, then pushed to his feet and headed for the mouth of the cave.

Joelle watched him disappear, her mind churning. There was no doubt that he was deliberately avoiding the very subject he'd brought up. *The LaBelle crime family.* They had their fingers in an awful lot of illegal pies—racketeering, money laundering, and the like—and the name found its way into the news often. Joelle had heard the family referred to at work as well. But she couldn't recall whether anything had come up recently.

She worried at her lower lip as she thought about it. What kind of involvement did Beck have with them? And why would he ask her if she knew who they were—and ask if she worked for them, of all things—then completely switch topics? She still had zero logical explanation by the time he returned, and she couldn't think of a good way to ask, either.

He positioned himself beside her again and held out a

palm-sized leaf full of already melting snow. "Hold this for one second?"

Joelle took it gently, careful to keep the contents as intact as possible.

"How attached to your jacket are you?" Beck asked.

"What? Why?" said Joelle.

In response, he lifted the jacket from behind her, reached inside, and yanked at the lining. A rip permeated the air, and when Beck pulled out his hand, he was holding a strip of fabric.

"Hey!" Joelle protested.

"Beggars, choosers . . . all that," Beck replied, taking the sopping leaf back and dipping the cloth into it. "Show me the cut again."

She wrinkled her nose, but also grabbed the hem of her shirt and brought it up, holding her breath as he dabbed the skin with the dampened piece of her jacket. He worked in silence, and after a few seconds, she let herself relax. His touch was gentle, his fingers warm. A few *more* seconds, and her eyelids drooped. It was almost enjoyable. So when Beck spoke, his voice was startling.

"How's your head feeling?" he asked.

Joelle's eyes flew open. "What?"

His mouth quirked up. "That thing attached to your neck. How's it feeling?"

"Very funny," she replied. "But now that you've brought it up . . . I actually feel a lot better on that front."

It was true. The residual dizziness had faded, and despite the relative darkness in the cave, her vision was clear.

"Guess your nap did you good." Beck's smile widened even more.

She had an unreasonable urge to stick her tongue out at him. But before she could follow through, something about the way he shifted reminded her that he'd literally carried her to the spot where she sat now. She also remembered that he'd assured her in one of the sincerest voices she'd ever heard that he would never have left her behind. And instead of mustering up any sass, her face warmed.

"Thank you," she said. "I really appreciate that you've looked after me."

"No sense in saving you from getting shot if I'm just going to let you freeze to death." He shrugged, then sat down and draped his arms over his knees. "I'm glad you're all right. Glad you rested, too, because it's not a good idea to stay in one place for any longer than necessary."

"We're in a cave in the middle of the mountains in a snowstorm."

"I'm aware."

"You really believe someone is going to come after us up here?"

"There are some very determined people in this world." His mouth set into a line, his jaw ticking with irritation.

No, not quite irritation, Joelle thought. *More like . . . bitterness.*

"Beck . . ." She said it softly, but he grimaced anyway.

"Don't," he replied.

Despite his protest, she pushed for more. "Determined people . . . like the LaBelle crime family?"

"They might fall under that umbrella."

"And you think they might be after you?"

"I don't *think* it, Joelle."

Her heart did a nervous jump. "So if you know they're after you, why did you ask if I worked for them?"

His hands flexed in the low firelight. "Because anyone can work for them."

"Anyone but you," she countered.

He grimaced again, then let out a sigh and dropped his gaze to the ground. "I'm not on their radar because I'm in the habit of cooperating with them. I'm sure having faith is in short supply right about now, but on that, you can trust me."

Something in his tone made Joelle ache to reassure him, and she reached for his arm without thinking about it. "I trust you."

His eyes came up, and there was a whole world of emotion in their ocean of blue. Sadness and anger. Hurt. Hope. And a warmth that drew Joelle in. She was suddenly more aware of his proximity. She could feel his body heat, smell his understated masculine scent. She could see the stubble dotting his cheeks and a few errant gray hairs mixed in with the dark ones at his temple. His attention flicked down to her lips for a second, and she recalled that he'd done the same thing right before she'd collapsed. He *liked* her mouth, she decided, blushing a little. And she *liked* that he did. So when his hand came up, and his thumb traced the very edge of her lower lip, she didn't pull back the way she should have. The way she normally would have. If anything, she leaned into the touch. And when he dropped his fingers from her face, a rush of disappointment swept in.

"I'm going to check on the storm," he said, his voice rough-edged. "I'll put the fire out when I get back, and we'll keep moving."

Joelle wanted to protest, but Beck got to his feet and slipped away so quickly that she couldn't even call his name before he was gone.

*   *   *

Beck didn't realize he was holding his breath until he had already stepped outside and expelled it. Even then, he really only noticed because the forceful exhale sent with it the last hint of Joelle.

Joelle.

He cast a look back. It was too easy to imagine her sitting there, staring after him with a tiny crease in her brow as she puzzled over his abrupt exit. A stab of guilt made his feet want to retrace their short path back to her. To a woman he didn't know. One to whom he owed nothing.

One you damn well near kissed. Who seemed to want to kiss you, too.

"What the hell am I doing?" he muttered. "This is ridiculous."

He stared at the opening to the cave for another second before he made himself turn away. The itch to return still didn't recede, so he stalked in the other direction, trying to put some space between himself and temptation. He needed to clear his head. It was more difficult than he wanted to own up to. His mind was too full of red hair and pink lips and green eyes. Even the chill in the air couldn't sweep away the heat.

What the hell was it about her that made him feel like letting his guard down? What made him want to believe her when she said she trusted him, and what made him want to reciprocate it?

Not once in all the days he was behind bars had he inadvertently mentioned the LaBelles. Not to either of the two men who'd shared his cell. Not to Gary, the elderly inmate who'd taught him how to use the woodworking tools with skill. The only person he'd spoken to about the crime family was his contact on the other end of this trip, and it'd taken that particular man *months* to drag it out of Beck. Yet somehow, he'd spat out the name to Joelle within a couple of hours of knowing her.

Dammit, Samson. Don't you remember what happened the last time you trusted someone? said his subconscious.

He answered aloud. "As if I could forget."

Rolling his eyes at the understatement, he trudged out farther in the snow—which was creeping up past the soles of his boots now—and let his mind shift to the past. Or to be more accurate, he forced them there. They moved from red hair to blonde. From green eyes to brown. True kindness to manipulation.

Tonya.

He usually kept thoughts of her secured in a mental box. One he'd both welded shut and locked with a combination he tried his damnedest to forget. Making himself focus on those memories now meant unlocking that box and letting other things out, too. Her deceptively girlish giggle slipped in first. With it came the recollection of one of their final conversations. It temporarily blocked out the snow and the mountains.

"They won't give you long to decide, Beck," Tonya said.

"I don't know why you're making it sound like a choice, T."

"Oh. Well, that's a relief."

"Yeah?"

"For sure." She stood on her tiptoes and kissed his cheek. "I'll let them know."

Some of the tension in his shoulders eased. "And that's a relief, too. For me."

She let out one of her giggles. "And why is that?"

"Because I have no desire to give the family bad news."

"Wait. What?"

"Letting them down will come easier from you. They like you." He laughed, but it was tinged with bitterness.

Tonya didn't even smile. She flipped her hair over her shoulder in one of the moves Beck had come to know meant she was annoyed.

"You just told me there was no choice," she said.

Unease made him stuff his hands into the pockets of his dress
pants. "There isn't. I can't do what they want."
"You can."
"I won't, then, if you feel the need to split hairs."
She took a small step away, and somehow her whole self
changed with that one movement. Any softness disappeared.
"You don't want to do this, Beck," she said, and the words
were nothing but a threat. "But I can see from your face that
you're going to."

Beck had let out a breath then—right before Tonya walked
out—and he let one out now, too. The rough terrain came into
view again, but he didn't quite let himself slide back into the
present.

In retrospect, the way he'd been duped was embarrassing.
Maybe he'd been looking to become a savior. A hero, pulling
Tonya from what he'd believed was the wreckage of her life. In
the process, he'd become something else entirely. He couldn't
afford to take the chance it would happen again, no matter how
slim the odds.

Shaking his head, he swung back toward the cave. It was
gone. Or rather, *he* was gone. He'd been so focused on his own
thoughts that he hadn't realized how far away he'd walked while
trying to give himself a bit of space. The snow was coming down
in large flakes, obscuring his view. The rocky hillside was homo-
genous. Gray and white. Tree dotted. For a panicked second,
Beck genuinely believed he might have some trouble making his
way back. Then sense kicked in. He dropped his gaze, found his
tracks in the snow, and started to move. He only took one step,
though, before a cracking noise made him freeze.

Slowly—silently—he swiveled toward the sound.

Don't let it be what I think it is. Let it be a bear. A moose. A ran-
dom elephant, for crying out loud. Just don't let it be a person.

The hope was in vain. The source of the noise was most definitely a person. A man. He stood on an elevated piece of rocky ground; just near enough that Beck could make out the details of his appearance. The guy was vaguely familiar, so Beck assumed he'd been on the plane, too. He wore a black suit, torn at one shoulder. A loosened tie hung from his neck, its silvery hue catching the light as it got picked up by the wind. All of those things were secondary, though, to a couple of other important facts. One, the man's attention was zeroed in on Beck. Two, he held a club-sized tree branch in his hands. Then a third thing came into play, too. The man charged.

"Shit," said Beck.

His mind kicked into high gear. He had to defend himself. He had to protect Joelle. He had to make sure Joelle was safe, even if he wasn't successful in fending off this new attacker. He needed a weapon.

The gun! his subconscious hollered.

He reached to the back of his waistband in search of it. His hand found nothing but fabric and air.

"God*dammit*," he snapped.

He didn't know what had happened to the gun, but there was literally no time left to do anything about it. Nor was their time to search out an alternative weapon. The man was practically on him, club raised. All Beck could do was dive out of the way. So he did. As he hit the ground in a roll then scrambled to recover, something unexpected happened.

From the corner of his eye, he caught sight of a flying object. It sailed through the air, flashing darkly through the falling snow, then smacked straight into the back of his assailant's head. The man's eyes widened, then rolled back. The club fell from his fingers, and he tumbled to the ground.

Startled, relieved, and wary at the same time, Beck lifted his gaze in search of his rescuer. He didn't know what—or who—he was expecting to see, but it wasn't a tangled head of red hair.

Joelle. Thank God.

She stood about ten feet away, staring at the fallen man with a stricken look on her face. Beck said her name softly, and she jerked her attention to him.

"Are you okay?" she asked, exhaling.

"I'm fine," he replied. "Are *you* okay?"

"Yes." Her eyes darted around the surrounding space. "But I think we need to go. Like, now. I came out of the cave because I was worried about how long you'd been gone. Then I heard two voices. *Two*, Beck. So I don't know where this guy's buddy is, but I'm sure that he has one."

Beck's sense of urgency picked up, and he stood quickly, brushing off the snow as he did. Part of him wanted to suggest hiding out in the cave. A bigger part of him knew that doing so put them at risk of becoming trapped.

His mind went to the gun. He wanted it. Needed it, probably.

Not an option to spend time looking for it, he told himself.

"Time to get out of sight," he said, grabbing Joelle's hand and tugging her toward the nearest patch of trees.

They only got partway there, though, before she abruptly pulled herself free.

"Wait one second," she said, then took off toward the man on the ground.

Beck clamped his jaw shut to keep from calling after her. Tapping his fingers impatiently on his thigh and scanning the area for any sign of the second possible attacker, he watched her stop and bend over.

What the hell was she doing?

He got his answer just a moment later. Joelle came sprinting back with the gun in her hand and Beck realized *it* was the object she'd used to knock out the man in the suit. Relief surged up.

She held it out. "Here."

"You're a genius," he said, taking the weapon from her. "I could practically kiss you."

The words came out by themselves, and they brought him right back to the very reason he'd left her alone in the cave in the first place. His eyes found her mouth. He cleared his throat. But he didn't get a chance to make an awkward retraction. An unseen man hollered out just then, and they had no choice but to run.

Chapter Eight

Even though Joelle was feeling significantly better than when they'd first left the crash site, their new trek was more taxing. The pace was just this side of gruelling. The mountain was unforgiving. Though the snow had abated, the wind was howling. The ground remained uneven; the brush never seemed to wane.

Soon, sweat made Joelle's clothes stick to her back and legs, and the only good thing about that was that she didn't get a chance to be cold. Beck held her hand intermittently, sometimes to tug her along even faster, sometimes to guide her through a particularly challenging area. And all the while, she kept asking herself the same question.

Why did I help Beck Samson instead of Shane Dreery?

Because even though she hadn't said it aloud, that was who the man she'd knocked out was. The Onboard Transport Coordinator. Supposedly one of the good guys.

But her brain scoffed at the idea. *How many good guys do you know who go around* clubbing *people to subdue them?*

And in the moment that she'd stepped out and seen what was about to happen, there'd been no doubt. No second guesses. Beck was the one being attacked. Beck was the man who'd carried her through a blizzard and tended her wound. The convicted murderer to whom she'd handed a loaded weapon.

It was tucked into his waistband, just as it likely had been when they'd been walking earlier. But now, she was extra aware of it. She could've held onto the weapon, at least for a while. Or she could've simply left it behind. And if she'd been thinking straighter, maybe she could even have grabbed it without Beck knowing. She'd been able to tell from his expression that he hadn't known that what she'd thrown at his attacker was the gun.

She just wished she had a better idea of why she'd done it. And strangely, she wished she could ask her mother. The thought of doing that made her smile sadly. What *would* her mom say about all of this if she could see it? Nothing good, probably.

Except for those blue eyes of his, said her mom's voice in her head. *Those, I'd definitely approve of.*

"Joelle?"

At the sound of her name, she looked up and realized she'd stopped walking. Beck was a dozen steps ahead of her, his handsome face pinched with concern.

"Everything all right?" he asked, stepping closer.

"Yes." She fought a blush and swiped her hair back from her face.

His gaze dropped to her abdomen. "What is it? Is it your—"

"It's not. I'm fine. We can keep going."

"It's okay if you're hurting. We've put enough space between ourselves and them that we can take a rest," he said.

She shook her head. "I seriously feel okay. And the cut didn't look so bad once it was cleaned up. My professional opinion—given with zero sarcasm—is that it doesn't need anything more serious than a bandage."

"You sure?"

"Yes. I'd tell you if it was a problem."

"Okay."

But the moment they started walking again, a question burst out of Joelle's mouth. "Why are you being so nice to me?"

He stopped and spun back so abruptly that she bumped right into him. His hands came to her shoulders, steadying her.

"See?" she said. "Why would you do that?"

"Why would I make sure you didn't fall over?" he replied.

"Yes. And why do you sound so confused by my confusion? You're a convicted felon. A fugitive. And I'm just following you through the woods like that's normal. It's . . . it's . . ."

"It's what?"

"Confusing!" The word came out loud enough that it made Joelle blush.

Beck, on the other hand, let out a laugh, his deep chuckle somehow sounding at home in the woods.

"I'm sorry."

"Are you?" she countered without much force.

"I am," he said, his expression sobering. "Look. I know none of this is funny. Nothing could be more serious than what's going on, and the reason I'm so nice to you is that I genuinely don't want you to get hurt."

"Why not?"

"Really?"

"Yes. Really."

"Why didn't you just shoot that guy back there?" he asked.

"What does that have to do with anything?" she replied.

"I'm trying to prove a point."

"Well, you're not doing a very good job."

"You could try answering the question," he stated.

She crossed her arms over her chest. "I don't know how to fire a gun."

"I . . ." He trailed off and scratched his chin, his mouth seeming to want to turn up again. "Okay, forget that, then."

"Forget what?"

"It doesn't matter."

"Obviously it does, or you wouldn't have used it to try to make your so-called point."

Another chuckle escaped his lips, and Joelle rolled her eyes.

"You're not going to make this any easier, are you?" he asked.

"Probably not. And we should go," she said. "Before your 'very determined' friends show up again."

She tried to slip past him, but his hand closed firmly on her elbow, and he spoke in a dark tone. "None of these people are— or have ever been close to—being my friends."

He released her arm, then pushed ahead, his pace only slightly slower than it'd been a couple of minutes earlier. Joelle hurried to catch up.

"I didn't mean to insinuate that they were really your friends," she said.

Beck held back a branch for her, his face still broody. "I know. It's just a sore spot for me."

The statement made Joelle even more curious than before. She had to bite her lip to keep from asking more questions. She wasn't sure why it mattered so much to her. It *shouldn't* matter to her. In all likelihood, the less she knew the better off she'd be at the end of it. She let a few silent minutes tick by, and then it was Beck who finally broke them.

"The point I was trying to make before is that there's a lot of gray in the world," he said.

Understanding made Joelle nod. "So you thought I was going to tell you that I didn't shoot him because there was another, less lethal option available?"

"Yes. Since that wasn't the case . . ."

"I didn't think about it, to be honest. I saw the guy getting ready to clobber you, and instinct kicked in."

"You've got instincts that make you *throw* a gun?" he said.

"As a matter of fact, yes. I played softball in high school." She narrowed her eyes, daring him to laugh.

He just lifted an eyebrow and kept walking, albeit a little slower. "Tell me more about that."

"About softball?"

"About your life when you're not escorting felons on planes."

She was going to argue that small talk seemed odd, but then changed her mind. Maybe if she told him some things about herself, he might reciprocate.

"Well," she said, "I don't play softball anymore. And putting aside the fact that you're my very first felon on a plane, mostly what I do is work."

"That sounds like a copout," Beck replied. "You don't like to read? Do yoga? Spend time with family?"

Her heart panged at the mention of family, and she forced a light tone. "No family left. Not quite slick enough for yoga. But yes, I do have an impressive collection of books, and I've got a particularly weird weakness for rock star biographies. What about you?"

"Ditto on the family and yoga," he said. "The celebrity biographies, not so much."

"Not just *any* celebrities. Rock stars only. And I meant what do *you* do when you're not being escorted as a felon on a plane?"

"Well, I like long walks in cement halls. Making shivs. The usual prison-life things."

Joelle blushed. "Right."

"Occasionally, I build stuff out of wood in exchange for credit in the commissary," he added with a grin.

She let it drop. Instead, they chatted about old movies and hockey and the rain. She waited for a better segue into discussing Beck himself—and more specifically, his case, the LaBelles, and why someone was out to kill him—in more detail. But every time she steered the conversation toward his life, he redirected with a question about hers instead. And after what had to be at least an hour more of hiking, she was starting to think it wouldn't come up naturally. She was about to give in and make another direct query when Beck paused and jerked his thumb to the side.

"Hear that?" he asked.

Joelle stopped and listened. Under the sound of the wind was the rush of water.

"A river?" she said.

"Yep." He resumed walking, now leading a route toward the noise. "With any luck, it'll lead us down the mountain."

It was as much of an opening as she'd had so far, so she jumped on it. "And then what?"

"Then I do what I have to do." His tone was clearly intended to cut off the conversation.

"You know this isn't really fair, right?" said Joelle. "Wanting me to tell you everything about my life but not telling me anything about yours."

"It's not my *life* you want to hear about."

"Yes, it is."

He tilted his head and studied her face. "That extra bit of pink in your cheeks tells me you're not being entirely honest."

She resisted an urge to try to scrub away the immediate heat that crept up her skin. "I'm a redhead. If you look at me the wrong way, I go this color."

"Uh huh." His voice was dubious, and he turned away to push yet another bit of foliage out of their path.

Again, Joelle was going to persist. And again, outside forces stopped her. Their next couple of steps brought the river into view. The water was about four feet down, its banks maybe five feet apart, and it ran with medium swiftness over a rocky bed. It was breathtaking. But if Beck noticed, he didn't show it. He swung in a circle, then strode closer to the edge and knelt so that he could peer down.

"Too deep to wade through it," he said after a second. "We'll have to find a way to go over instead."

"You want to go across that?" Joelle eyed the ravine skeptically.

"Yes. It's a good way to put even more space between us and the guys who're after us."

"But . . . can't we just walk down until we find a place narrow enough to walk over it?"

"There's no way to know how long that will take." He was up and moving again. "And nature provided a bridge."

She frowned. "What? Where?"

He didn't answer. Not with words, anyway. He disappeared into the trees for a few seconds, and when he reappeared he was dragging a thick, tall log. As Joelle's mouth worked in silent surprise, Beck pulled the log to the gully. With a grunt, he forced it upright, then sent it sailing across the small gorge.

"There," he said, wiping his hands on his pants. "A bridge."

"You can't be serious," Joelle replied. "That's hardly my idea of a bridge. And I don't think it counts as 'nature' if you put it there."

He chuckled, then stepped onto the log, moved back a foot, and held out his palm. Staying put, Joelle glanced toward the water. It seemed to be rushing faster now.

"I'm not a strong swimmer, Beck," she said.

"Can't swim . . . can't shoot . . . You really need a few lessons in wilderness survival, don't you?" he teased.

"I *can* swim," she replied. "Just not well. And I don't usually *need* survival skills."

"Says the prison nurse."

"That's why there are prison guards."

"I'll reserve my rebuttal on that subject for now," he said. "Come on out here. It's stable."

He bounced his feet. And to be fair, the log barely moved. So despite her wariness, Joelle put her hand in his and inched out after him. But a heartbeat later, she made the mistake of looking down and her breath caught in her throat, freezing her to the spot. It wasn't that the drop was all that far. It was just that being above the river let her see into its swirling churn, and the vertigo was immediate.

"Hey," said Beck. "Look up at me."

Her eyes didn't want to move, and she whispered, "I can't."

"Yes, you can," he replied. "Ask me what you really want to ask me and move while you talk."

She swallowed, and her brain tried to let itself be distracted, but she still couldn't make herself look up as she took his suggestion. "Are you guilty for real?"

"Do *you* think I did it?"

"No."

"No?" he echoed.

"Or maybe I just don't *want* to think so," she amended. "Because the fact that you're avoiding the question makes me kind of nervous."

"Does it matter a lot if I'm guilty?" he asked.

Her gaze finally lifted. "Of course it does."

"Why?" he wanted to know.

"Because."

"Because why?"

She knew her face was flaming, and she couldn't quite manage an answer. At least not out loud. In her head, her subconscious felt a need to pipe up, sounding almost gleeful.

Because if he's a murderer, it said, *then you probably shouldn't like him as much as you're starting to. Or at all, for that matter.*

She flailed for a different explanation. One wouldn't come.

"We're almost there," Beck said gently, misreading her panic.

Joelle glanced over his shoulder. He was right. A few more steps, and they'd be on the other side. But the rushing river caught her eye again, and she swayed.

"I'm guilty," Beck said suddenly.

Joelle jerked her eyes up. "What?"

"I'm guilty," he repeated. "But not *guilty* guilty."

"What does that—"

Joelle didn't get to finish. Because a bird burst out of the trees overhead. It let out a raucous cry, then dived toward them, startling them both so badly that they lost their balance and were suddenly falling off the makeshift bridge.

Trying not to panic, Joelle squeezed her eyes shut and braced for her body to hit the water and go under. She sucked in a breath and held it. And the anticipated plunge *did* happen. Just not how she expected it to.

For a second, the river closed in around her. She could feel the pressure of it. The swell of the current, pushing her along while the undertow sucked her down like a weight. Then she felt something else. Something more solid than water. Warmer, too, in a distinct contrast to the icy torrent. It pushed her up, buoying her to the surface.

Not it, she realized. *Him.*

It was Beck. His body was cushioning hers. Chest to back.

Arm wrapped protectively around her waist. Legs kicking a steady rhythm as he pulled her across the river. Another few moments, and they were in the shallows, safe from the threat of being dragged away. Beck pulled her up a little farther, and then his hold on her loosened, and he collapsed backward against a slope on the riverbank, breathing heavily. Joelle stayed where she was. Her body was half sprawled across Beck, but she didn't care. She needed the human comfort. Her inhales and exhales were as quick as his, though the source was fear and shock rather than exertion. When she did finally shift, it was just to push herself into a more comfortable position. His arms came up and pulled her closer.

"Hey," he said, his voice soft and gruff.

"Hey," she repeated back to him.

"You okay?"

"I don't think I drowned, if that's what you're asking."

He let out a laugh. "Well, that's good news, right?"

"It could be worse," she agreed.

She meant the statement lightly, but somehow it managed to sound like she was referring to the fact that she was currently cradled in his arms. And it was kind of true, anyway. Despite the cold and the wet and the unintentional plunge into the river, Joelle had been in far less comfortable places than pressed against Beck's well-muscled form. The intimacy of the situation only increased when his hand found the back of her head and ran down her wet hair.

"You know . . ." he said. "If you wanted to prove you were right about the log not being a bridge, you didn't have to go quite that far."

His tone was serious. A contradiction to the obvious joke in his words. And Joelle answered in the same way—kidding, but in some way masking something less than humorous.

"Is that your way of apologizing?" she replied.

"I *am* sorry. In retrospect, it was probably a reckless choice." His fingers began gently detangling a knot. "In my defense, though, it's been a long time since I was responsible for someone else's well-being."

"Hmm."

"What?"

"I feel a bit torn. Part of me wants to tell you that I can take care of myself, and part of me wants to tell you that you're doing a pretty good job of taking care of me, even if you're rusty."

He finished with the knot, then settled his palm under her jaw, his thumb sliding across her cheek. "Both things can be true, can't they?"

Joelle's heart was racing again, but now it was in an entirely different way. For the first time since hearing the two strange men's voices outside the cave, she remembered that right before Beck had gone to check on the weather, they'd been in an equally close pose. On the precipice of a kiss. In fact, she'd been certain that was what had driven him to walk away—the need for some space. And in the moment, she'd appreciated it. A kiss was a complication they didn't need. A very bad idea on all fronts for a dozen different reasons. She'd gone over those reasons multiple times after he'd left. She'd even half planned on mentioning them to him, just to be sure they didn't almost slip up again.

But now?

Now she couldn't recall a single one of those reasons. The two of them were alone in this battle against the wilderness and the men following them. What if they died out here? It was a real possibility. What if they perished, and the very last thing she stood her ground on was a series of excuses for not kissing

Beck Samson? Wasn't it better to at least steal this one small bit of pleasure?

"Joelle." Her name was a throaty whisper.

She tipped up her face, meeting his blue stare. It was heated. A cloudless summer day, searing her skin in the most pleasant way possible.

His hand still cupped her cheek, and it gave her the lightest pull toward him. The nudge was all she needed. Her eyes sank shut. She leaned in. And his mouth met hers, sending an explosion of tingles through her whole body. His touch was soft. An exploration. Or maybe a question. One Joelle felt compelled to answer.

She twisted so that she was properly facing him. Her left hand clung to the back of his neck while the right one clutched at his soaked shirt, and she deepened the kiss. She let her tongue dance along the edge of his lips. He groaned. The sound played a seductive rumble across Joelle's mouth, and she couldn't stifle a gasp.

Both of his hands dropped to her hips, tightening in a possessive way that made her want to melt into him. Maybe she *did* melt into him. Because her body was suddenly flush with his, every hard line of him matched up against her softer, more yielding parts. And he was a perfect fit. A perfect feel. Joelle wanted more.

As if Beck could read her thoughts, he gripped her a little harder, then sat up so that she was straddling him. Her thighs were locked around his hips, and his palms slid under her shirt. His touch skirted around the site of her recent wound, and the extra care—whether it was consciously done or not—made her heart swell to the point of aching. She eased back, slowing the kiss so that she could look into his eyes again. She saw her own desire reflected back at her. The same need. The same heady, heavy-lidded want.

His name found its way to her lips. But it didn't quite make it all the way out, because a wood-cracking crash echoed all around them, dashing away the passionate moment. They both froze. They both whipped a wild look down-river toward the thick trees in the not-too-distant bend. And the crash sounded again.

Chapter Nine

For a too-long second, fierce irritation stopped Beck from reacting. No way in hell did he want this moment to be over. He wasn't even close to being done with kissing Joelle. Then sense kicked in. Kisses didn't have much value to dead people. Joelle seemed to be one step ahead of him on that front anyway. She was already disentangling herself from their embrace, her eyes scanning the surrounding area, likely in search of cover. Beck followed suit, his gaze joining hers.

They spotted it at the same time. A lone evergreen. It was growing horizontally out of the gully wall, its trunk jutting at a near perfect perpendicular angle while its branches formed a reasonably thick umbrella a couple of feet off the ground.

"There," Beck whispered just as Joelle lifted her finger and pointed silently.

By unspoken agreement, they pushed up to a crouch. Then, still keeping low, they hurried toward the prospective hiding place. Beck kept himself positioned slightly behind Joelle. If the need called for it, he'd become a human shield. Whatever it took to give her a better chance at getting away. Thankfully, though, the sacrifice wasn't needed. They reached the tree, ducked beneath it, and huddled together in silence.

In his head, Beck was already formulating a rough plan. First, he'd need to try to figure out if the person at the other end of the ravine knew they were there, or if the intruder hadn't yet seen them. If he *hadn't* seen them, they might be able to wait it out. If he *had* seen them, Beck would take action. Bait him. Draw attention away from Joelle and their hiding place.

All I need is to—

"Don't," said Joelle, the whispered order stopping him mid-thought.

He swung a look her way and replied in an equally low voice, "Don't what?"

"Whatever it is you're thinking about doing."

"I'm not thinking of doing anything."

"You are."

"We should be being as quiet as possible," he said.

"I'm not being quiet until you agree not to do it," she replied.

He scrubbed a hand over his chin. "I can't *not* do something that you tell me not to do if I don't know what that is."

She narrowed her eyes. "I'm not going to bother unpacking that. But I think your plan has something to do with you running out there like a crazy person while I wait here. And you can't do that."

"Joelle . . ."

"I'm serious, Beck. You promised me that you weren't the kind of man who'd leave a woman alone on the side of a mountain."

"If all I can do is give you a fighting chance, then that's what I'll do," he told her.

"If you die, but *they*—whoever they are, because you still won't tell me that—live, I'll die, too." She lifted a hand, silencing him before he could start to argue. "I'm not being dramatic. I can't fire a gun. Especially not with any accuracy. My self-defence skills would be best described as mediocre. And even if you manage to single-handedly kill every person who's after us but also die in the process, I'm not going to make it. I have no idea how to build a fire like you did. I wouldn't even know what direction I'm supposed to go so I can get off the damn mountain."

"Okay. Maybe you have a point about some of—"

Yet another noise—a thumping sound, heading their way on the riverbank, he thought—interrupted him.

"Dammit," he swore under his breath.

Joelle's hand found his elbow, her fingers holding it tightly. Beck didn't blame her for her fear. Their cover was visual only. The foliage wouldn't protect them from a rain of bullets.

I won't let it get that far, he told himself.

Silently, he shifted enough to free the gun from its spot in his waistband. He tried belatedly to recall how many bullets were left, but he hadn't even stopped to check what size the weapon was. Or what type. He could see now that it was a sub-compact handgun. That probably meant six rounds altogether.

In the current moment, the initial attack back at the crash site seemed like something that happened a long time ago, and he couldn't quite remember how many times his attacker had fired. Three, maybe? He decided to settle on the idea that there were at least two bullets in the chamber. A third was likely. Any more would be a bonus.

Two or three well-aimed shots. I can do that. Even if there's more than one of them. I can manage.

He gently shook off Joelle's hold, gave her a look he hoped passed as reassuring, and eased forward. Holding his breath, he dared a look between the evergreen's needles. *Nothing.* There was no sign of whoever had made the noise. Not even a flash. Where were they?

Beck would've preferred not to attempt a closer look. He just didn't feel like he had any other choice. The thumps had stopped, but if the person who was making them got much nearer, the hiding place would undoubtedly be spotted. He needed some kind of advantage. To know the intruder's size. To see if he appeared to be armed. To find out if it was a lone attacker, or if there were multiple people out there.

Exhaling now, he leaned out a little more. At last, he saw something. A dark shadow, moving down near the water. Splashing *in* the water, actually.

It wasn't a person at all. It was a bear. A big black one. With a fish between its ample paws.

Beck's body sagged. From behind him, he heard a muffled laugh. He twisted and found Joelle so close to his back that she was almost touching him. Her hand was over her mouth, her green eyes brimming with poorly hidden amusement.

"What are you doing?" he said.

"Well, I *was* planning on jumping on your back to stop you from running out there, but I'm guessing that I don't have to now?" Another laugh followed her response.

"You won't think it's very funny when we get eaten by that bear," he replied.

"Bears don't eat people, they maul them," she said. "I feel like you should know that, Survival Man."

"That's *Mister* Survival Man to you, and FYI, about one in a million black bears will eat a person. We have no way of knowing if he's the one. Even if he's not, I don't relish the idea of being mauled."

"Better than being shot."

As soon as she'd said it, the last of the mirth in her eyes

faded away. A pensive silence followed the change in her expression, and Beck's own heart tightened. He itched to reach out and pull her close. To kiss her again.

Something you shouldn't have done in the first place, he thought. *And something you should* tell *her you shouldn't have done.*

But he couldn't make himself say it, and he cleared his throat instead. "While we're on the topic of shooting, I think it'd be prudent if I showed you how."

"In case you have to abandon me in the woods?" she said, the lightness in her tone audibly false.

"In case something beyond my control happens."

"Fine. I'll let you show me. But only on that condition. Deal?"

"Deal," he replied.

He knew full well that he'd break the promise if it meant saving her life, and he had a feeling she knew it, too. Neither of them said anything about it, though. After another few seconds, Beck checked to make sure the bear had moved on, then held out his hand and guided Joelle from their hiding place back into the open air.

"Okay," he said. "The first thing you want to do is learn how the moving parts work. And check if it's loaded."

He slid out the magazine and counted the bullets in the clip. He was relieved to find it fuller than he'd expected. Four of six rounds were left.

"Pretty sure we already knew it was loaded," Joelle said dryly.

"It was safe to assume the guy hadn't emptied it," Beck agreed. "And it's actually best to treat every firearm like it's loaded until you know otherwise, but it's still good to find out for sure." He paused and adjusted the gun so he could point. "These are the obvious parts. Barrel. Handle. Trigger."

"Got it, got it, got it."

"Great. Next are the sights. The front sight post and the rear sight notch. See them?"

"Yes."

"Okay. Final thing is this lever here. That's the safety."

"Got that, too."

"All right." He held out the gun. "Take it, and make sure to keep your finger straight and away from the trigger."

Gingerly, she did as he asked, gripping the gun with inexperienced awkwardness.

"Flick the safety off," he said.

She bit her lip and did that, too.

"Now flick it back on," he added.

She looked up at him. "What?"

"We only want it disengaged if we're actually going to shoot, and I think a loud bang might draw some unwanted attention." He smiled, but she didn't look any more relaxed, so he gave her free hand a squeeze. "You've got this."

"Are you sure about that?"

"Definitely. Except for the part where you're holding the gun like it's a dirty sock."

"It *feels* like a dirty sock."

Beck laughed. "Let that thought go and adjust your hold. You're right-handed?"

"Yes," she said.

"All right. Rest the gun in your right palm, wrap the bottom three fingers around the handle, and leave your trigger finger extended. Then bring up your left hand to cover the exposed part of the grip." He watched her position her hands. "That's perfect. But make sure you're holding the gun just a little tighter than you think you should. It's small, but it will still have kick."

She exhaled. "Okay. Tightened up."

"Good. Now let's talk about stance. Feet shoulder-width apart, knees slightly bent. Comfortable, but braced so that you don't injure yourself."

Automatically, he shifted his position to match his description. Joelle studied him, then nodded and matched his pose.

"Good," he said again. "Next, extend your arms. Bend your elbows slightly but don't lock them. Find your target and square your shoulders toward it."

Her eyes fixed on something in the distance. "Ready."

"You're going to want to lean forward a bit so you can use your weight to counteract that kick I mentioned."

She did. And for a second, Beck was distracted by the way she looked. Soaking wet. Holding the weapon like she knew how to use it. A determined set to her delicate jaw. Powerful and sexy. There was no part of him that didn't want to drag her into his arms and kiss her breathless.

"Beck?" she said, pulling him back to what he was supposed to be focused on. "Am I doing it wrong?"

He cleared his throat. "No. You've got it exactly right. It's time to align the sights. The rear and front sights should be level so you know where the bullet will go."

She squinted.

"That's it," said Beck. "Now you're ready to fire."

"So I just squeeze the trigger?"

"Yep. But slowly. It's more sensitive than most people think. And don't forget to breathe."

She released a tiny exhale, then let her arms drop. "Am I really expected to remember all of this?"

"Probably not, but it's better to have some idea of what to do than none."

"I guess so."

Her lips pursed, and her eyes probed his. Tensing, he waited for another of her direct queries. In all honesty, he was finding it harder and harder to be evasive with her, and he was almost certain that whatever she asked right now, he wouldn't be able to stop himself from answering. Except she didn't voice the concern in her gaze. Instead, she just held out the gun.

"Here," she said. "We should probably keep moving, right?"

Beck opened his mouth, then closed it.

What are you going to do? he wondered. *Demand that she asks something, then do your damnedest not to answer her?*

Of course he wasn't. But as he nodded and took the weapon from Joelle, he was surprised to find himself feeling disappointment rather than relief.

Chapter Ten

Joelle wasn't sure exactly how much time had passed since they started following the river. She just knew that the minutes seemed to keep coming slower, and with each one she became more aware of her discomfort. Her clothes showed no sign of drying. If anything, they'd somehow gotten damper. At some point, one of Joelle's socks had slipped down and exposed her heel to the inside of her shoe. She hadn't noticed then, and she'd since pulled it back up. But now, the skin was raw and sore.

Her body hurt. Everywhere. There wasn't a muscle that didn't remind her that the months she'd spent grieving her mother's death hadn't also been months at the gym.

The ache in her abdomen wasn't exactly back—not with the sharpness of before—but she did feel it again, and that was bad enough. The only good thing about the pain was that it kept hunger at bay. A few almonds wouldn't have sustained her for that long, otherwise. Thirst was a whole other thing. Her mouth kept getting dry. Her throat remained parched. Beck had allowed them to pause once at a spot on the river where he felt the water was clean enough, and they'd each taken several scooped gulps. But that was it.

To add to all of that, the air had dropped a few degrees. Before too long, the sun would start to set. It would get even colder, and darkness would encroach, too.

And then what?

She didn't know. And she shivered at the uncertainty as much as she shivered at the increasing chill.

Ahead of her on the path, Beck was relatively silent. He still hadn't offered her an explanation for what he meant by not *guilty* guilty, and he hadn't commented on their brief but intense moment of passion. Not that Joelle particularly wanted to discuss it either. The color crept up her cheeks just thinking about it. But there was a part of her that couldn't help but wonder if she was deliberately avoiding it for more than just general awkwardness and embarrassment at being swept away.

She shook her head. She didn't need another reason. Nevertheless, her mother's voice filled her head.

You need to fall in love, J.D.

Joelle almost tripped. It was a real thing her mom had said to her. An oft repeated suggestion, actually. One that had zero relevance in the current situation. They were also the very last words her mother had ever spoken to her. Or to anyone.

And what did you say back? her conscience asked.

She tried to steer her thoughts away from the bad memory, but exhaustion made it impossible to control the turn of her mind.

I told her that my love life was none of her business. That my life was none of her business.

The memory and the accompanying guilt pressed down on her shoulders. Her throat burned with it. Somehow, time managed to slow even more. And now her brain was holding onto old emotional pain as well as the new physical ones. So when Beck suggested that they make camp for the night before it got too dark, she'd never been more relieved. She didn't even argue when he told her to take a load off while he did what needed to be done. Survival techniques were his area of expertise anyway, and she was sure she would've just slowed down the process if she'd tried to assist him.

With tired eyes and a heavy heart, she watched as he collected branches—both stripped of leaves and heavy with coniferous foliage—and created a lean-to that would make the most skilled boy scout envious. The only real downside to not helping was that by the time he was done, Joelle was shivering uncontrollably. Her teeth chattered as Beck helped her crawl into the shelter.

"Don't worry," he said as he settled her into the small space. "I can't light a fire in here, but human beings generate as much heat as a hundred-watt bulb. We'll be surprisingly toasty in no time."

Joelle had her doubts. Even when he tucked her under his arm and pulled her close. But after a few minutes, he turned out to be right. The small space *did* warm up. The all-over ache eased, her skin stopped prickling, and she was able to take a look around. It was small inside. Just barely big enough for the two of them to fit. In fact, even sitting down, Beck's head brushed the ceiling. They were completely enclosed—the entrance had been covered by a large branch—and the only source of air and waning light came from a one-inch gap in the far top corner. There was a pile of leaves and moss beneath them, and Beck had kicked out a small hollow near their feet. Even without any kind of survival training, Joelle could surmise that it was meant to draw in and hold the colder air while they stayed above it.

"Remind me to never get lost in the mountains without you," she said after a few more quiet minutes.

Beck chuckled. "Remind *me* to never get lost in the mountains again at all. It's not quite as enjoyable as my fellow weekend warriors led me to believe."

"You make it look easy, if that helps at all."

"It does stroke my ego a bit."

"Glad to be of service."

His forefinger traced a circle on the back of her hand. "Tell me something?"

"Sure," she replied.

"What were you thinking about back there?"

She knew without any explanation exactly which moment he meant. Another jolt of sadness made her breath do a little hitch, but she surprised herself with an honest response.

"My mom," she said. "And how much I miss her."

"I'll get you back to her," Beck replied. "I promise."

A laugh managed to bubble up under her sorrow. "Please don't promise that."

"What?"

"I'm not quite ready to become acquainted with the afterlife."

"With the—oh. Damn. I'm sorry, Joelle. I didn't mean to come across as insensitive."

She smiled, then dropped her gaze to her fingers. "You didn't. And you couldn't have known."

"I'm still sorry," he said. "You were close?"

Joelle nodded, and she surprised herself again by offering more information than she normally would have. "She was my best friend. My dad died when I was too young to remember, so it was just the two of us. My mom was a travelling photographer, and she homeschooled me until eighth grade. I know it sounds lame, but we had a bond. Losing her was the hardest thing I've ever gone through."

"It's not lame. I get it. My parents are both gone, too. A few years for my mom, and a decade for my dad." He paused then, his expression growing heavy. "I shouldn't have kissed you before."

The seemingly unrelated statement caught Joelle just off guard enough that she didn't blush, and she blinked at him instead. "What?"

"There are lots of other obvious reasons why I shouldn't have," he said, "but if I'd realized what you were going through . . ."

Joelle's heart did a funny dance—expanding and contracting in quick, syncopated succession—and she felt a smile try to creep up. "Are you worried that you took advantage of my emotional vulnerability?"

"I know what it's like to be in that state. It makes it easier for people to take advantage."

His statement sparked her curiosity about *his* emotional vulnerability, but Joelle brushed it off in favor of reassuring him that her grief wasn't his fault.

"It's been three months," she said. "It's not a completely fresh wound."

He studied her for a moment. "Fresh enough."

A lump formed in her throat, and she couldn't quite clear it away.

"It hasn't been easy for me," she admitted. "That's actually part of the reason I took this job. I thought it might distract me."

"Got a bit more than you bargained for, I guess."

"You might say."

"Has it helped?" he asked.

A laugh escaped. "You'd think, right? But no. I've been thinking about her more than ever."

His fingers slid between her knuckles, then curled around to her palm. "Sorry about that, too, if it's my fault."

Joelle bit her lip. It *was* his fault. But not in the way he meant. And not in a way that she even wanted to start to try to explain.

"I guess we should probably get some rest," she said.

"Is that what was going through your head just now?" he replied.

"No."

"All right. I guess I'll allow the obvious change of subject."

"I wasn't giving you a choice," she told him with a smile. "And I'll take first watch."

"Oh, you will, will you?" he said.

"Yes. I had a very satisfying nap earlier, and someone recently taught me how to fire a gun."

"Yeah, well, the guy who taught you *might* be a convicted felon," Beck replied.

"True," said Joelle, tipping her face to look his way. "But he's not *guilty* guilty."

He met her gaze in the dark, and for a second, she thought he might actually divulge something more about his case. But he just lifted his hands up, put them behind his head, and closed his eyes.

"Night, Joelle," he said.

She frowned, wanting in an unreasonable way to ask him to open up. But all she said was, "Sleep tight, Beck."

* * *

Beck didn't actually believe that he'd fall asleep. It wasn't as though he slept well under normal circumstances. Or abnormal, as the case had been for the last two years. He really only closed his eyes because he felt some pretty damn irrational irritation at the way Joelle had changed the subject away from her mother's passing. He had no right to be privy to her personal life. He had no ownership of her grief. He sure as hell wasn't even the right man for the job of shoulder-to-cry-on. Lord knew he was familiar enough with the problems created by giving too much trust to a person too soon. He was aware more than most how easily betrayal could come. How a world could shift from average to nightmare in the span of a day. It was what had gotten him into the mess to begin with.

So why did he resent the fact that Joelle didn't want to confide anything more? Why did he want to pull her into his arms and tell her that she could trust him with that hurt he could see in her eyes? Why did the revelation about her mother's death twinge every bit of curiosity and protectiveness in him?

And why does it feel so natural to be stretched out beside her like this? he wondered.

Alongside that question, his annoyance slid to the wayside. It *did* feel natural. Oddly so. He'd met Joelle just hours ago. There was no logical reason to be experiencing a sensation like this. The opposite, really. Yet here he was, genuinely thinking about how well she fit against him. Not only that, but also how much he liked it. Which was stupid. But still true. As he considered what it might mean, real drowsiness crept in, then took hold. His thoughts became slippery, wakefulness elusive. And the next thing he knew, he was being shaken awake, and Joelle's voice was whispering in his ear.

"Beck," she said. "I think there's someone out there."

He was immediately on alert. Head tipped, breathing under careful control, ears open. For a moment, he heard nothing. Then the silence was broken by the sound of muffled voices, carrying through the walls of the shelter. Beck couldn't make out what they were saying, but there was no doubt in his mind that whoever was out there was searching for him and Joelle.

No one else would be hanging around on the mountainside under the cover of night.

He let his eyes close again for a second, imagining what the shelter looked like from the outside in the moonlight or the glow of a flashlight. He'd been conscious of the need for discretion when building it. He'd made sure it was nestled against a very large stump, fully disguising it on one side. Moss covered the branches, acting as both insulation and as camouflage. In his opinion, the people tracking them would have to literally stumble into the lean-to in order to find it. The fact that they were this close was a miracle.

And if they somehow manage to get even closer . . .

They would have him and Joelle in a very bad position.

He opened his eyes. "We need to get out of here."

"What?" Her shock was evident despite her quiet voice.

"If we're moving, they're less likely to find us by accident."

"And stumbling around in the dark is a better idea?"

"At least if we're out in the open, we can run."

He didn't wait for her to respond. Expediency mattered. He gave her hand a little squeeze, then shifted his body and crawled to the cover he'd put over the entryway. He paused to listen for any indication that their pursuers were getting nearer. Finding none, he carefully pushed the extra foliage aside. Then he waited again. The voices were slightly louder, but no less clear. It strengthened Beck's belief that they still had a good window to escape. Slowly, he moved forward. He poked his head out, cast a glance side to side, then made his way more fully into the open.

Sometime in the night, the sky had cleared. The air was cold but not icy. Overhead, the moon was bright, and when the wind rustled the treetops, shadows danced over the forest floor. There was no visual on the people who'd tracked them there, but after a moment of stillness, Beck heard them again.

Southeast, he thought, mentally cursing the fact that it was the same direction he and Joelle needed to travel.

They'd have to find a way to skirt around while not losing their own path.

Silently, he pushed to his feet, then turned back to wait for Joelle. When she'd finished exiting, he extended his palm and helped her stand. As soon as she was up, he started to pull his hand back, but she held fast.

"Wait," she said, her voice low but urgent.

"Wait for what?" he whispered.

"I shouldn't have kissed you back there, either."

"You want to tell me this now?"

Her head moved in a quick shake. "No."

"Then why are we stopping?" he replied.

"Because kissing you now is a bad idea, too."

"Kissing me—"

She cut him off by standing on her tiptoes and pressing her lips to his. For a moment, he was too startled to react. A belated second later, his body and his brain caught up to what was happening. His hands lifted to the small of her back, pulling her closer. His mouth eagerly returned her kiss, and desire flooded in. But as surprisingly as it started, it also ended.

Joelle pulled back, sank down to her heels, and spoke softly. "There. Now we can remember this properly. Just in case we don't get another chance to make a bad decision."

Beck felt his lips quirk up, and his heart tugged with an unusual prickle of emotion. "It's probably wrong to admit this, but I'm going to try pretty damn hard to make sure we get to make at *least* one more bad decision."

He touched her cheek then slid his hand to hers and pulled her away from the shelter. Silently, he guided them deeper into the forest. He didn't want to take them too far off course, and he fully intended to make his way back to the river as soon as they'd steered clear of the people on their trail. So his plan was to walk wide of the voices, take himself and Joelle to a certain point out, then cut back in again. Yet he found himself doing something else instead.

Maybe it was because the voices remained constant, and he unknowingly suspected what they'd find before they got there. Or maybe it was something even more subconscious than that. Like a need to see who was after them. Either way, he still went wide, but not out. He circled them far nearer to their stalkers than he'd been planning—near enough that he could smell smoke in the air and see an orange flicker through the trees. He might have gotten even closer if Joelle hadn't stopped walking and given his hand a hard yank.

He turned a look her way. Her expression was understandably concerned, and she shook her head and jerked her thumb over her shoulder. Beck shook his head, too, and put his finger to his lips. Her mouth opened. Before she could whisper a protest, though, the voices spoke up again. They were loud enough now that Beck not only understood their conversation but also recognized one of the speakers. It belonged to the man who'd been dressed as a flight attendant. The one who'd tried to capture him and kill Joelle when they'd first crashed.

"So . . . what next?" said the guy in question, his words and tone far too clear for comfort. "We haven't seen any sign of our runaway and his new friend."

"Could have something to do with the fact that it's too damned dark to see *anything* at the moment," replied his buddy.

"Aren't you supposed to be some kind of genius?"

"A high I.Q. doesn't equate with being able to see in the dark."

"You know that isn't what I meant," said the phony flight attendant. "And this job was supposed to be easy."

"Easy?" the other man scoffed. "Why the hell would you think that?"

"Boss told me it was straightforward, Corbain. One perfectly talented pilot and one perfectly orchestrated plane crash. One perfectly good explanation to make everyone believe a snitch was perfectly dead."

"See, that's your problem right there, Kit. Things are never perfect in this business."

Confirmation that the crash had been on purpose should've been the thing that struck Beck. Instead, it was hearing the men's names. *Kit and Corbain.* The former actually meant nothing to him, but the latter made his mouth want to go dry. The only Corbain that Beck had ever heard of was a contract killer. A mean one. A smart one. One who was sent to do the dirty work when someone wanted it completed cleanly and with no conscience. There was zero chance this wasn't the same man. His presence was a very bad sign. What the hell was he doing there? Had he been on the plane somewhere, too? He had to have been. It seemed far too unlikely that he'd been deployed to the crash site somehow. Just how deep did this thing go?

Doesn't matter, said a dark voice in his head. *You just have to do something about it.*

He tried to imagine following through on the idea. Could he sneak up on the two men without attracting their attention? If he managed that, could he follow through? Was it worth the risk that he might fail? Self-defense was one thing. This would be something else.

His gut churned, and it took Beck a moment to refocus on the conversation.

"Still," Kit was saying. "Regardless as to whether our so-called trick pilot fucked up the crash, Samson should never have walked away from it. It was the whole damn point. The guy's obviously smarter than our boss gave him credit for."

"Doubtful," the other man replied. "He's just managed to hit a lucky streak. It's going to run out sooner or later."

"Hopefully sooner." Kit paused. "You really believe in luck?"

Corbain sighed so loudly that it echoed off the surrounding trees. "Sure, Kit. Why?"

"Because I think it's that redheaded bitch's fault."

Beck went cold. He felt Joelle stiffen beside him, too.

"How so?" Corbain asked.

"She's the unknown factor. The only one. We had all the guys inside the prison crew. The co-pilot. The dude on the ground. It was all *perfect*. No matter what you say. Then *she* turned up."

"Well, she's not the one who fucked up the custom crash landing, is she?"

"Not directly," said Kit. "But if she's Samson's lucky fucking charm . . ."

"I doubt Samson considers any of this shit storm lucky," Corbain replied.

"He's gotta be close, doesn't he?"

"We'll wait for the fire to go out, then we'll take a final look before we go to sleep. If we don't get him tonight, we'll get him tomorrow for sure."

"And her," Kit added, his voice darkly hungry.

That, Beck took as their cue to go. He couldn't risk Joelle's life. He wouldn't. So he took hold of her hand again, and this time, he didn't mess around with their exit.

Chapter Eleven

The path away from the two men at the fire was treacherous. Shrouded in darkness. Uneven under their feet. Littered with natural debris and dotted with unpredictable hazards. It required serious concentration to stay on track.

One ear on the river, the other on alert for any incoming threat.

One eye on the position of the stars, one on what lay ahead.

But Beck was glad. He needed something to focus on so that his mind wouldn't do its best to gnaw away at the recent revelations. Eventually, he'd have to deal with all of that. Just not right now. If he started to think about the intentions behind the crash and collateral damage, he wouldn't be able to stop. He'd been down that road before. He didn't want to do it again. Not with so much on the line. Not with *Joelle* on the line.

And speaking of Joelle . . .

She was the one thing that managed to override the concentration needed to steer through the forest. More specifically, the obvious fact that she was in even more danger than Beck had assumed. It was only going to get worse, too, the longer this went on. The more time she spent with him. It would compound. As far as his joke about wanting to make more bad decisions went . . . he could forget about it.

No, he thought. *Not just forget about it. Stuff it into a box and forget it ever crossed your mind.*

His jaw tightened. He moved faster. Or he tried to, anyway. As his pace quickened, Joelle made a little noise beside him, and he realized he was pushing more than he needed to. Enough minutes had passed that going at a full clip was no longer necessary.

Beck slowed. Another moment or two of silence ticked by, and then Joelle spoke up quietly.

"You knew one of those guys back there, didn't you?" she asked.

He offered a tight nod without looking at her. "I know *of* him. That's more than enough. His name is Corbain, and he's bad news all around."

"They're not going to give up looking for you, are they?"

"No."

"What happened, Beck? Why are these guys so desperate to catch you? They caused a plane crash to do it."

He let out a breath. Then he paused in his walk and met her gaze. The sky was the tiniest bit lighter now, and he could see her eyes perfectly. There was nothing but concern there, and all of it was on his behalf. It suddenly occurred to him then that she probably hadn't shared her grief over her mother's death lightly or easily.

So maybe you owe her a bit of emotional quid pro quo, he thought.

"Can you promise not to judge me?" He meant it to sound like a joke, but it came out in a serious tone.

Her eyebrows knit together in puzzlement. "Sure?"

He resumed walking, and Joelle kept pace.

"The last woman I kissed before you . . ." he said. "She was mixed up in some bad things. I knew it when I met her, and I didn't go into the relationship blind. Not on that front. But Tonya fooled me in other ways. I thought I was saving her. In reality, she was trying to sucker me into joining them."

"Joining who?" Joelle asked.

He didn't answer. A moment passed. Then another. And then Joelle filled in the gap.

"Tonya is part of the LaBelle crime family," she stated softly.

"She wanted to be," Beck replied. "And that's even worse."

"But you said you *didn't* work for the LaBelles." There was a hint of poorly disguised hurt in the statement, and Beck felt a need to assuage it.

"I didn't," he told her. "I wasn't a criminal, and I had no interest in becoming one. Which was a problem. When Tonya realized that I wouldn't come to her side of the fence, she cut me loose and went elsewhere for her needs."

"Was she the one that had the affair with your business partner?" Joelle asked.

Beck blinked, his feet stalling again. He hadn't planned on adding in that particular piece of information. Not because he was embarrassed that he'd been duped. Yes, at the time, it'd been humiliating. Two years to mull it over had given him enough perspective to realize he wasn't naïve; he just hadn't had any experience dealing with murderous liars until then.

"I'm sorry," said Joelle, clearly reading his face. "I shouldn't have mentioned it."

Beck cleared his throat. "It's fine. I just didn't think that my personal life was general knowledge."

"The guard who was sitting beside me on the plane told me about it," she replied. "He said that your girlfriend cheated on you with your partner, and that was the reason you killed him."

"Right," said Beck. "I guess I should've realized that factored into the official story."

"Does that mean there's an *un*official story?" she said.

"No. There's just the official story, and there's the truth."

"A truth you won't tell me."

"A truth that could make you more of a target, too."

"You don't think I've become one already?" she countered. "You didn't hear the same thing that I did, back there?"

"Right now, you have a bit of plausible deniability." Before he could think to stop himself, he slid his hand over hers and clasped her palm. "It's not safe for you to know the rest."

"I don't see what difference it makes at this point," she replied. "They know I'm with you. They have no way of knowing what you've told me and what you haven't. I don't think they'll stop and ask, and even if they did, they'd just assume I was lying."

Her words hit him straight in the gut. She was right. A minute earlier, he'd been thinking the same thing—that her life was in danger just from being near him. Her words only drove it home. Guilt coursed through him, making his chest ache. He needed to find a way to get her out of harm's way.

But how?

"Beck?" she prodded.

He had to think. He pulled his hand away and tried to smile, but his reply came out sounding strained.

"Guess I'll just have to make sure they never get a chance to interrogate you," he said.

She didn't answer him, but he could feel the frustration emanating from her. He was sure she was trying to work out some way to get the information she wanted. After all, he was focused on the opposite—trying to find something to say that would convince her she didn't need to know anything more. He'd given away too much already.

So why did *you tell her those things, then?* he asked himself. *Why do you keep digging yourself farther into this too-much-information hole?*

He needed to find a way to stop himself from doing that almost as much as he needed to keep her safe. Maybe it would help if he tried to think of her as a work colleague. Or a client at his old accounting firm.

Or a fellow inmate, suggested his subconscious.

He stifled a snort. He'd certainly never had a problem maintaining distance there. But his peers in the prison hadn't been beautiful redheaded women with kind eyes, soft skin, and caring hearts. Joelle was all of those things. More, too. So the only solution was to resort to using an extraordinary amount of self-restraint. To give himself a mental kick every time he strayed to wanting to touch her or reveal anything else. Possibly with an accompanying pinch of the physical variety.

Then, as if to prove just how hard it was going to be to follow through on that, Joelle's hand found his arm. Where her fingers met his skin, heat radiated inward. A shockwave of desire rammed straight through him. Likely, the overly visceral response came from the fact that he was ordering himself *not* to have one, but knowing that didn't change anything. It was so distracting that he nearly missed the actual reason she'd stopped him.

"Look," she said, pointing.

Beck turned his head and did as she requested. Just ahead of them, the trees thinned, revealing a steep slope. The river wound around it, flowing dangerously wide and thick. It was wild. Breathtaking on its own. The sunrise, though, made it sublime.

Mottled purple sky. Orange bursting through the bruised clouds on the horizon. The colors dancing down in a cascade of blues and grays.

"It really is amazing, isn't it?" said Joelle.

"Prettiest one I've seen," he replied gruffly.

She leaned into him and let out the smallest sigh. Automatically, he slid an arm around her and pulled her against his side. She turned just a bit—just enough—and tipped up her face. She exhaled, the small puff of air tickling his lips. It was all Beck could take. His very recent resolve to maintain a professional distance—or a prison distance—or any kind of distance at all crumbled.

He cupped her cheek, dropped his mouth to hers, and devoured her with a kiss. She met his amorous onslaught with a matching fervor. Her hands came to his neck. Her body pressed to his, her curves making him groan. It wasn't enough. He wanted more. Needed more.

He put his hands on her hips. Slid a knee between her thighs. Started to lift her from the ground. And then things went wrong. The heel of his boot caught in a divot, knocking him off his balance. His loss of equilibrium shifted to Joelle. She wobbled in his arms. He tried his damnedest to steady her, but his efforts only succeeded in making himself less stable, which in turn made her shakier. In the end, he lost the fight to stay upright.

Together, they hit the ground. In a tangle of arms and legs, they rolled down the embankment. Rocks jabbed, and roots and twigs scraped until at last the two of them came to a stop at the bottom of the hill. There, they lay breathless, Joelle's petite frame on top of Beck's large one. Several seconds passed, and then a chuckle built up in his chest.

"Was that as good for you as it was for me?" he teased.

She groaned. "Really? That's the line you're going with?"

He lifted an eyebrow. "What makes you think I'm joking?"

She made a face, but her green eyes turned serious. "You know you can trust me, right, Beck?"

He was going to tell her that he *did* trust her. He was also going to let her know just how much that surprised him, given his history. What came out instead was something completely different. Something unexpected. Something very honest.

"I can't be responsible for another death, Joelle. Especially not yours."

* * *

There was a slight catch in Beck's voice—one so small that were it not for their close proximity, Joelle was doubtful she would have heard it at all. And it made her heart ache. It also made her sure of what Beck had meant when he'd said before that he wasn't *guilty* guilty. She could feel it rolling off him. And she could relate to the deep sense of accountability.

"The LaBelle family killed him, didn't they?" she asked softly as she eased off him and came to a seated position on the ground. "Your partner, I mean."

He stayed where he was, his eyes on the dawning sky, his reply laced with poorly hidden emotion. "It should've been me."

"That's not true." Joelle said it fervently.

"If I'd agreed to help Tonya, she wouldn't have gone to Ward instead of me. And if she hadn't solicited his help instead of mine, they wouldn't have had a reason to murder him."

She put one of her hands over one of his. "There's no way you could've known what would happen to your business partner."

"But if I'd just—"

"Compromised your principles, broken who knows how many laws, and become a lifelong criminal, then maybe your partner would be alive?"

"Yes," he said. "All of that."

"Or not," she replied.

"What?"

"Maybe he—Ward—would've done something else that ended the same way."

Beck grunted, then sighed. "You think there's some other situation that would've ended in his execution?"

"I know you're being sarcastic," she said, "but whatever he did to get killed, Beck, he did himself. And I don't mean that he deserved it, or anything close to that, but you didn't make him choose to get involved with your ex. Or with the LaBelles. I assume that he was presented with the same option as you, but chose to go in the other direction? You can't hold yourself responsible for that."

"I wish it was that easy."

"I understand how it feels."

"Do you?" He sounded deflated and disbelieving at the same time.

"Yes, as a matter of fact, I do." As soon as she'd said it, she knew she'd spoken with too much fervor.

She bit her lip and hoped that Beck hadn't noticed. The hope was a vain one. Letting her hand go, he sat up and studied her face.

"You've got a lot of experience feeling responsible for murders?" He said it lightly, but Joelle could hear the genuine curiosity under the question.

She didn't want to explain. She didn't want to say it aloud and relive the bad memories. Except when she looked into Beck's eyes, her own words echoed through her head.

You know you can trust me, right?

There was something in his blue gaze that made her sure she could have faith in him. It felt good—and just plain right—to be sitting there beside him having this conversation. So as much as her chest compressed with sadness and despite the quaver that she knew would creep into her voice with whatever she said, she spoke anyway.

"I'm responsible for the car accident that killed my mother," she told him. "So like I said . . . I *do* know how it feels."

Beck sat up straighter, and both his hands came out to close around hers. "Do you want to talk about it?"

"Not at all, usually," she admitted, looking down at their clasped fingers. "But maybe a bit right now."

"You don't have to."

"I know. But I want to."

He brought her hand to his lips and kissed her knuckles. "Tell me as much or as little as you want. I'll listen."

She brought her gaze back up, seeking solace in his eyes before she spoke again. "I told you before that she was my best friend, and it's true. We had *so* much in common. Same taste in books. Same taste in movies. Same sarcastic sense of humor."

"Sounds like a mother–daughter match made in heaven," Beck said.

Joelle nodded. "I really think it was. We got along perfectly about ninety-nine percent of the time. But that day, we had a fight." Her throat tightened and her eyes stung, and she had to pause to gulp a breath before she went on. "No, that's not quite the truth. We were *having* a fight when the accident happened. Literally. We were on the phone. I lived it like I was right beside her. But I was helpless to do anything about it."

She stopped again because the tears were really coming now, and it was too hard to speak through them. In her head, she could hear the screech of tires, followed by her mother's yelp. A horrible, deafening crash. Then silence. So much terrible silence. It paralyzed her then. It paralyzed her now. But Beck came to action. He put his arms around her, pulled her right into his lap, and cradled her against his shoulder as she cried. When her tears finally tapered off, he spoke into her hair.

"It's not your fault, Joelle," he said. "An accident is just that—an accident."

"I distracted her. If I hadn't been talking to her . . . If I hadn't been *arguing* with her . . ."

"Let me ask you something," he replied. "You said you got along almost all the time. But was that the first time you'd *ever* argued with your mom?"

"No, of course not."

"Did any of your other fights lead to an accident?"

"No."

"And if *this* accident hadn't happened, would you have argued with her again?"

"I—"

"Be honest," he interjected before she could finish. "Don't take what you know now into consideration. If you'd carried on with life as normal, would you have never disagreed?"

Joelle swallowed. "No. We would've disagreed about something at some point."

"So it's fair to say that while fighting wasn't an everyday occurrence between the two of you, it's *not* ridiculous to say that it happened occasionally."

"Yes." It was a whisper.

"Because that's *normal*," Beck stated. "Disagreements with the people you're close to are pretty damn common. The fact that your mom got into an accident during a fight is just really, really terrible luck. The worst kind of horrible coincidence. It's not your fault."

She didn't say anything. She didn't tell him about how her mom had held on at the hospital until they got to say their silent goodbye. And she didn't mention her mom's final words—*You need to fall in* love, *J.D.*—even though they slid through her mind. It was almost ironic. Here she was, sitting in a man's arms in a way that would've made her mother positively gleeful while confessing the truth about what had happened.

You'd probably be laughing your butt off about that, wouldn't you, Mom? Joelle thought.

A small smile broke through her tears. But she didn't pull away from Beck. Not quite yet. She just continued to lean against him, absorbing both heat and comfort from his wide frame. It was the first time since her mother's death that she'd thought of her without a deadening ache. Oh, the pain was still there. Things like that didn't just disappear. It felt good, though, to think about her mom's laugh and not be overwhelmed with thick guilt.

"How are you doing down there?" Beck murmured after another few moments.

"I'm okay," Joelle replied.

"You don't have to be. And you don't have to say you are just because you think it's what I want to hear."

Her smile actually got a little wider, and she leaned back so she could look up at him. "You're a nice man, aren't you?"

He chuckled. "I've been accused of that a time or two. Pre-prison, of course."

A new question surfaced. "How did you wind up in there, anyway? I mean, I know what you were sentenced for obviously, but what made the police decide you were a suspect in the first place? Just because of Ward's relationship with your ex?"

Beck's expression darkened, then closed off completely. And when he answered her, it was an evasion.

"Not the kind of thing you want to discuss on an empty stomach," he said.

He shifted her out of his lap, stood up, and held out his hand. She was going to argue. She felt like she'd just bared her soul, and now he was shutting her out. But her stomach rumbled loudly just then, and she knew that whatever protest she might have, she wasn't going to win it while her body was siding loudly with Beck.

Chapter Twelve

Once again, Beck was glad to have a task to occupy both his mind and his body. He might've let his resolve about keeping his hands to himself slip, but that didn't mean he had to do the same thing with his words. He guided Joelle right down to the river and sought out a shallower, slower-moving portion of the water.

"Wait here," he said, gesturing to a piece of driftwood.

"I can't keep sitting around all the time while you do the work," she protested.

"Oh, I'll put you to work," he promised. "It'll just take me a minute to get what I need."

"A *minute* minute?"

"Or less."

"Fine. But I'll be counting," she said.

"By all means," he replied.

She narrowed her eyes. "One."

Suppressing a laugh, he hurried away to scavenge for the required supplies. First, he sought out a long branch, thicker at one end than the other. Next came an edged rock and a half-inch stick. Finally, he grabbed a length of bramble, which he began stripping of its leaves as he made his way back to Joelle.

"Fifty-eight," she said as he reached her side. "You got lucky."

"No luck required," he told her, trying not to think of the two men who'd said Beck's luck was about to run out. "It's all about mad crazy skill." He extended the long branch in her direction. "Take this and hold it steady for me."

Brow wrinkling, she did as he'd requested. He moved to the narrow end of the stick, where he used the rock to split a gap near the tip. With that done, he took the stripped offshoot of bramble, slid it through the newly created hole, and wound it around, lashing it in place.

"Are you making a fishing rod?" Joelle asked.

"No," he replied. "*We're* making a fishing rod."

"I don't think you can call my contribution a part of the craftsmanship. I'm basically a glorified vice-grip."

He gave the creation a tug to make sure it was secure, then finished the final step—attaching the short twig to the loose end of the bramble.

"A vice-grip is still a necessary tool." He looked up as he said it, and her eye roll made him laugh. "We all have to start somewhere in the hierarchy of survival skills. Wanna help me next by finding some worms?"

"I think I'll pass," she said dryly.

"I thought you didn't want to sit around."

"I'll amend that to have the caveat of not sitting around unless the alternative involves things that are slimy."

"Suit yourself."

He took the fishing rod from her and set it on the ground, then got to work searching out some bait.

"Where did you learn all of this?" Joelle asked after a few seconds of watching him dig around in the dirt.

"My dad, at first," Beck told her. "He had a real bug up his ass about being prepared for anything. Drove me nuts when

I was a kid. I *had* to know how to change a tire. I *had* to know how to collect rainwater. I got more into it by the time I was a teenager. We camped every weekend, and after a while, I was the one challenging him to do things."

"And yet you became an *accountant*?"

"That might've been my mom's doing. She taught high school math. I'm damn sure my dad is out there in the afterlife somewhere, teasing her mercilessly about it right this very second. He was always telling her that *his* skills would come in handier in the long run."

"Well, I can't say I disagree with him at the moment," Joelle replied. "I'm personally pretty thankful for the bug up his butt."

Beck laughed again and kept lifting rocks until he at last found what he was looking for. "Aha! Want to see him?"

"I think I'm good."

"Okay. Avert your eyes for a second, then meet me down at the river."

He hopped up, apologized silently to the worm for needing its cycle-of-life services, then baited the wooden hook and strode toward the water with the rod in his hands. A few moments later, he heard the light tap of Joelle's feet as she joined him.

"Ready to see a master cast?" he asked.

"I'm absolutely giddy with excitement."

"You mock me now, but when we're eating a feast of trout and dandelions, you'll be sorry."

She snorted, but as he sent the makeshift line out into the river, she went silent and inched closer to him. It was peaceful. Relaxed. For the first time since the plane had crashed, Beck felt a sense of freedom. They were nowhere near out of the woods yet—metaphorically or physically—but he felt like he could breathe. Like he *wanted* to breathe. It made him almost regretful when his line worked just the way it ought to in far less time than he would've expected. He was half tempted to toss the fish back in and claim that it was an accident. He might even have done it if not for the fact that the moment Joelle saw the trout lift from the water, she let out a sigh of relief and told him she really was hungry.

"Did you doubt my fishing prowess?" he teased.

"Maybe. But only for a second, I swear," she said.

"I'm deeply offended. Does this mean you also have doubts about my cooking abilities?"

"Should I?"

He shook his head. "Definitely not. But now I feel a need to prove myself."

"Well . . ." she replied. "I guess you'd better get to proving, then."

He tried his hardest to make an unimpressed face. He knew he failed, though, because a laugh burst from Joelle's lips. And Beck couldn't remember the last time he'd felt quite so good.

* * *

Preparing a meal in the woods with Beck was almost surreal. It struck Joelle that the forest was like a strange version of his own personal kitchen. He knew just where to find things. Just how to move through the space with easy familiarity. He cleaned and prepped the fish, and he got the fire going. He instructed her on how to find several kinds of fragrant, edible plants. Together, they tore the greenery into pieces so they could stuff the trout and set it to cook over the flames, and before long, they were dividing up the meal to eat off some river-washed stones. And as they sat side by side on a log that he'd procured from somewhere nearby, Joelle felt like the only thing missing was a glass of wine. When she told that to Beck, he laughed.

"I genuinely can't remember the last time I tasted wine," he said. "Or any alcohol, for that matter."

"Not a prison hooch guy?" Joelle asked.

"A pretty by-the-book guy, to be honest."

"Except when you're out in the woods, acting like some kind of mountain man, you mean?"

"Nah." He gave the fire a poke with a stick. "Still pretty by-the-book out here, too. Does that bother you?"

She frowned. "Why would it bother me?"

He shrugged and quirked a smile her way. "I dunno. Maybe you like a bad boy."

She couldn't help but laugh. "I get just about all the badness I can handle at work, trust me. I don't need any more rebels in my life."

"Guess that's good news for me and my boy-scout ways." His smile slipped for the briefest second after he said it, and Joelle was sure she knew why.

It doesn't matter what I like in a man, she thought. *Not where Beck is concerned.*

For all the stolen kisses and moments of heated attraction and flirting, ultimately they meant nothing. They *couldn't* mean anything. Not now, not a day from now, and not at any time in the future. The fact weighed on Joelle more than she would've expected. Twenty-four hours ago, she didn't have a clue who Beck Samson was, but at that moment, her world seemed very full of him. And she couldn't help but wonder if that meant it would seem empty when this was over.

You want this to keep going? her subconscious asked. *You want to keep getting chased by evil men who are hell-bent on killing you and—at the very least—capturing him?*

Of course she didn't. But there was an odd lump in her

throat, and she was almost positive she wouldn't be able to clear it away.

"Tell me about your wine," Beck said then, interrupting the pensive turn of her mind. "What would it taste like, if you had it?"

"I'm not exactly a connoisseur," she replied, "but maybe a cheap sauvignon blanc?"

"A sauvi-what-now?"

"It's a white wine. It's usually dry and pairs well with—" She stopped and narrowed her eyes at him as she caught the teasing glint in his gaze. "You know exactly what it is, don't you? You probably own a vineyard or something."

He lifted an eyebrow in what Joelle now knew was a signature expression of amused doubt. "Do you picture me as the type of man who owns a vineyard?"

"No. I picture you as the type of man who drinks dark whiskey on a bearskin rug in front of a log fire."

Her comment earned her a rumbling laugh. "I own a one-bedroom condo in South Surrey. The fire lights with a switch, and the only rug is the one under my coffee table."

She sent him one of her own eyebrow raises. "I don't believe you."

"You think I'm lying about my *home*?"

"Yes."

His deep laugh sounded again. "Why?"

"Where do you keep your camping gear?" she replied.

"Storage locker."

"Where do you keep your giant truck?"

He swiped a hand over his mouth like he was trying to cover a smile. "I drive a hybrid. Two-door hatchback, to be specific."

"You expect me to believe that, too?" said Joelle.

"Why would I lie?"

"Because I told you that I like good men."

She blushed after she made the joke, but she didn't avert her gaze. And Beck's expression softened to something that looked an awful lot like tenderness.

"I have something for you," he said. "A bit of a gift."

"A *gift* gift?" she replied, feeling a bit of giddiness but also wondering what he could possibly have procured for her there in the wilderness without her noticing.

"Close your eyes."

"Seriously?"

"Please?"

"I can't say no to that, can I?" She closed her eyes as she said it, and the giddiness grew.

"You don't have any *non*-nut allergies, do you?" Beck asked.

Her eyes opened. "What? No. Why?"

"No peeking," he replied, and Joelle let her lids drop again. "I asked you about nuts before. Now I'm just covering the rest of my bases. That way, I don't kill you or get sued."

"How reassuring."

"Open your mouth."

"Is it going to be wine that you made from tree bark and the tears of a mountain lion?" she asked before letting her lips drop open.

Beck's laugh was low and somehow extra personal—like it was just for her. "Sadly, no. No sauvignon blanc or Riesling, either. No wine at all. Just *this*."

An explosion of sweetness danced over Joelle's tongue, and she opened her eyes again. Beck had angled himself to face her. He had a self-satisfied smile on his face and a pile of berries wrapped in a leaf in his palm.

"Dessert," he said.

"How the heck did you sneak these past me?"

"I'll never tell. But don't worry. It's not the same way people sneak things past the prison guards."

She made a face. "Ew."

He winked and popped a berry into his mouth. "You're welcome."

She helped herself to a couple more pieces of fruit and chewed in silence as Beck's attention went to the waning fire. The quiet moment gave Joelle a minute to study his now-familiar profile. The last twenty-four hours had been the strangest and scariest of her life. The previous morning seemed far away. Like a strangely distant memory. One that started with her never having heard of Beck Samson, moved to one where she'd been told that he was a murderer, and culminated with her knowing that he was a victim rather than a criminal. And now he was the bright spot in all of it. Which made it seem almost funny to consider that she'd ever had any doubts about what kind of person he was. She couldn't quite help but wonder what her mother would've thought of him. But it took only a second to decide that there was no question at all. Her mom *would* have liked him. And that realization brought a stab of emotion. Regret and sadness and guilt mingled together, dulling the sweetness of the berries. Fresh tears tried to well up, and Beck's hand found hers.

"Hey," he said. "Are you thinking about your mom again?"

Under any other circumstances—and with anyone else—Joelle likely would've deflected the question, but right then, she just nodded wordlessly.

"What can I do to help?" Beck asked.

She felt her mouth twist. "Maybe stop being so likeable?"

He brought her palm to his lips and dropped a kiss in the center of it. "You'd feel better if I called you names and kept the berries to myself?"

"Yes."

He snatched the last piece of fruit. "You smell funny."

A tear-laced laugh slid up her chest. "Is that the best you can do?"

"Not normally. But with you . . ." He lifted his fingers and dragged them along her cheek. "An insult would be a lie."

"So it wouldn't be an insult *insult*."

"Definitely not."

He leaned a little closer. Joelle could already feel the heat of his mouth. The thought of its warm touch filled her with heady anticipation. Her lids grew heavy, her lashes fluttering until they settled. And his lips did find hers. Lightly. Sweetly. *Briefly*. Then he pulled back and murmured against her cheek.

"All right," he said. "You're a hideous beast."

Her eyes flew open. "What?"

"A hideous beast. Now give me my food back." He grabbed the last piece of red fruit from its spot on the leaf, popped it into his mouth, and grinned. "Feel better?"

Joelle laughed; she couldn't help it. "I probably shouldn't, but I do anyway."

Beck's teeth flashed, but his expression quickly sobered. "Joelle . . ."

"No," she replied quickly, shaking her head. "You're about to say something all serious and meaningful, and I'm not sure my heart can take it."

"I think you need to hear it anyway."

"And if I don't want to?"

"Then I guess you'd better plug your ears."

She was tempted, for a second, to literally do as he suggested. To press her hands to her ears and maybe add a childish, *Nyah, nyah . . . can't hear you*, to the mix, too. But she didn't.

Instead, she closed her eyes and leaned her head against his shoulder.

"I'm listening," she said softly.

"Actually . . ." he replied. "I changed my mind. *I'm* listening."

"I'm not saying anything."

"You were about to tell me what makes you so sure you're responsible for your mom's accident," he said. "Because I know there's something more to it than the argument."

For a second, Joelle didn't answer. She'd held the words in for so long that it felt like they didn't *want* to be released. But when her eyes landed on Beck's hands—river-clean, strong, and work-damaged—she felt indescribably safe. She opened her mouth. And it was a flood.

"My mom wanted me to date," she said. "And that sounds really silly, but it was a thing we butted heads about. She loved my father beyond all reason, so she thought that's what it was like for everyone else, too. She was a true romantic. Soulmates. Two halves of a whole. Everything impractical and not all that modern, you know?"

She went on, explaining her own poor attempts at meeting someone. Her short-lived relationships. How she preferred to focus on her career and wasn't shy about sharing that fact with her mother.

"That's what we were fighting about when she got into the accident," Joelle said, her voice shaking in anticipation of what was coming next. "She told me that if she died before I gave her any grandchildren, she was going to be *so* disappointed in me. And that's how she died. Disappointed."

"Joelle."

"Beck."

"You know that's not true."

"You're right. I do know. I swear I do. Or at least I know that it's not *true* true. She was just doing her best to give me a hard time. A bona fide guilt trip. But it doesn't stop me from thinking about it. It doesn't stop me from wondering if I really did let her down at least a little in that regard."

"Everyone who's ever lost someone wonders what they could've done differently," Beck said. "The key is trying to let that go. The past can't be changed."

"Is it that straightforward for you?" she countered. "Does me, promising you that it's not your fault, make you feel like you're not responsible for Ward's murder? If I tell you that your decisions didn't cause his death, will you just smile and nod?"

A low chuckle vibrated from his chest. "No."

"So there you have it. We're an unreasonably guilty pair."

"Unreasonable, maybe. But not guilty. You didn't cause your mom's death."

"And you didn't cause Ward's."

"I just have to convince myself it's true, right?" he said.

"I'll help," Joelle offered. "I'll just keep repeating myself until you're so sick of hearing it that you agree."

He laughed again, then used his thumb and forefinger to tip her face toward him. This time, his kiss was longer and slower. So deep that she could feel it with every inch of her body, starting with her curling toes and working its way up to the tingle of her scalp. The world slipped pleasantly away. But Joelle no sooner let herself fully sink into it than a man's rough-edged voice yanked her out once more.

"Isn't this sweet?"

It only took her a second to recognize who was speaking. *Darby O'Toole.* A second more to turn toward him. And a third for him to sweep in, dig his fingers into her hair, and pull her to her feet.

Chapter Thirteen

Beck leapt up. His first instinct was to draw back a fist and drive it right into O'Toole's face. He was close enough to deliver the blow, and it was the simplest solution to sending the man onto his ass and away from Joelle. It was also something that'd crossed Beck's mind each and every time he'd encountered O'Toole in the past. So that was a bonus. But something in the other man's eyes stopped him. There was a challenge there. A dare. Another moment passed, and he found out why. An unmistakable metallic glint flashed from between the nearby trees, and a second man stepped into view.

"Mr. Samson," said O'Toole, "meet my good friend, Mr. Redburn. He's got a finger on the trigger, and I'm sure all this chasing you down has made him a tad . . . itchy. You want to come at me and see whether or not he slips?"

"We both know you're not going to kill me," Beck replied.

"No?"

"I have something you want."

"True." O'Toole's mouth curved into a cold smile. "But it's not yourself you need to be worried about, is it? It's pretty little Miss Diedrich here. It's her that my friend might hit inadvertently."

Beck ordered himself not to react as the other man gave Joelle's hair a sharp pull. "What makes you think I care?"

"Gee. I dunno. Maybe something about the way your lips were locked when I walked up, that's what."

"I've been behind bars for two years. My last piece of action was a bearded man who wouldn't take no for an answer."

O'Toole let out a dark laugh. "As much as I appreciate the visual, I think you're full of shit. You like this girl. So if you don't want to see her die, then you're going to put both hands behind your back so I can put you back in the chains where you belong."

"I'm sure you heard the irony in that last bit."

"I might've. Doesn't change my order a bit, though. Do what I told you to do, Samson, before I lose my patience."

Beck positioned his hands as instructed and met the other man's eyes. "If you hurt her, I won't tell you what you want to know."

"Ah, so you *do* care." O'Toole smiled again, then turned to Redburn. "Have you got the cuffs?"

"Sure do, boss."

"Good. Throw them my way. But keep that gun pointed on the girl. Wouldn't want anyone to get any ideas."

"On it."

With his gaze narrowed, Beck watched as the second man shifted to grab the handcuffs while continuing to maintain his aim. He did it expertly. Like a man who'd performed the task—or one like it—numerous times before. A fact that Beck didn't think boded well for their escape. And they *had* to escape. Soon.

Very soon, he thought. *Because if we don't . . .*

Their other two pursuers—Kit and Corbain—would catch up, too. He and Joelle would be outnumbered as well as out-armed.

The handcuffs clattered down at Joelle's feet, and despite the lightness of the noise, it was undeniably ominous.

"Pick them up," said O'Toole.

For a second, Beck thought the man in question was giving *him* the order. Then he clued in. O'Toole wanted Joelle to do it. He released her and gave her a little shove, and after a bit of a stumble, she bent down and grabbed the cuffs. She held them like they were poisonous. O'Toole was indifferent to her obvious discomfort.

"Now walk over to your boyfriend and put them on his wrists, nice and tight," he said. "When they're all done up, I want you to pull on them hard enough that I can *see* the way it stings."

Joelle blew out a small breath. Her eyes closed for a fraction of a second. Then she stepped toward Beck.

"I'm sorry," she whispered.

"Don't be," he murmured back. "This isn't you."

As he moved so that she could have easier access to his arms, it struck him that the three-sentence interaction bore a strange resemblance to their much longer one about guilt. Her mother's accident wasn't Joelle. Ward's murder wasn't Beck. Yet it was so easy for the two of them to feel a need to hold onto that responsibility.

Beck suppressed a wince as the cuffs circled his wrists. They were icy against his skin. Uncomfortable—by design—as always as they clicked into place.

"You're going to have to do them tighter than that," he said when she started to pull away.

"Are you sure?" she asked.

"I'd rather it be you than him."

"Right. Okay." Her fingers came back to the bonds, and she squeezed them so that they clicked again. "Good?"

"One more," he replied. "They need to be at the point of *not* good."

A second later, the metal was digging into his flesh and O'Toole was commanding attention once more.

"Much appreciation for the extra effort in your compliance," said the other man. "Now if the two of you would be so kind as to start walking, I'd be even more delighted."

"Any particular direction?" Beck asked dryly.

"Let's stick with the path you were already on," O'Toole replied. "You two can walk ahead. We'll follow behind, and my friend Mr. Redburn will be sure to keep an extra eye on Ms. Diedrich."

"How thoughtful," said Beck.

He sent a look in Joelle's direction, hoping to offer her a bit of silent reassurance. And he could see from the expression on her face that she *did* believe in him. Only knowing it offered him no relief. Instead, as he started off along the natural path beside the river, a new sense of responsibility set in. She didn't just believe in him—she was counting on him. He'd obligated himself to her safety. If something happened to her, it would be his fault.

I should never have forced her to come, he said to himself.

Beck knew, though, that he'd had no other option. Leaving her at the crash site would only have brought her harm more quickly.

Sure. But she never would have been on this trip if not for your "need" for a medical escort. He started to shake off the thought, but he stopped mid dismissal as a question surfaced.

"What happened to Dr. Karim?" he asked.

"Dead," said O'Toole, with chilling nonchalance.

Cold guilt and white-hot anger melded along Beck's spine. "You're a real bastard, aren't you?"

"I'm a man with priorities and obligations, just like you. We all make our beds. When the good doctor climbed into yours, he knew what the consequences might be."

Beck ground his teeth together. The statements weren't untrue. That didn't make the situation less aggravating or the doctor's murder any less consequential.

"Funny," he said through his clenched jaw. "I manage to associate with any number of people, and I never find myself having to kill any of them."

"Except your buddy at your accounting firm," Redburn piped up from behind. "What was his name? Willie? The whole world knows you killed him."

Beck didn't bother offering a correction on the name, and he kept his tone even—almost blasé—as he answered. "Why would I kill a man who'd eased a burden I didn't want to take on?"

"Maybe you should ask your crazy-ass self that question," replied the man with the gun.

"You know," said Beck, "I truly can't tell if you really think I killed him, or if you're fucking with me right now. I want to think it's the latter. But the former would make me happy, too, because it would underscore your stupidity so thoroughly."

"That's enough," O'Toole interjected. "The more you talk, the longer this trip will feel."

Beck bit back an urge to ask where, exactly, their self-appointed commander thought they were headed. He somehow doubted that O'Toole's goals matched up with his own. In fact, he was damned sure they didn't.

Doesn't matter anyway, he thought. *We're going to get the hell away from them before we get even close to figuring out what their destination is supposed to be.*

He divided his attention between listening to Joelle's footsteps behind him, navigating their journey, and keeping an eye out for any opportunity to get free that might present itself. But no chances came. The land continued on in its unforgiving way. The river rushed beside them. The trees thickened then thinned. The continually uneven terrain had the unfortunate side effect of forcing Beck to have to give an undue amount of attention to his actual steps. With his hands immobilized as they were, a fall would be more unwelcome than usual.

His agitation compounded by the minute. He quickly realized that he had no idea what kind of break he was looking for. The only certainty was that whatever it was, he didn't spy it.

Before long, the sky overhead started to darken with the promise of yet another encroaching storm. Beck wondered if it would create any opportunities. He somehow doubted it.

No one spoke, but their labored breathing and the slap of their feet were enough to fill the air, at least for a while.

More time passed. Seconds. Minutes. Maybe an hour. Sweat built up on his forehead. It dripped down his face and into his eyes, where he was unable to wipe it away. Infrequent droplets of rain joined the salty slather, and soon Beck's vision was blurred enough that he knew he was going to have to ask for a break if he was going to continue to lead the way. It was Joelle, though, who interrupted their trek first.

"Darby?" she said, sounding uncomfortable.

"What can I do for you, Ms. Diedrich?" O'Toole replied, his voice laden with false kindness.

"I have a problem."

"And what 'problem' might that be?"

She mumbled an incomprehensible response.

"Don't waste my time," O'Toole snapped, his polite tone gone. "Speak up."

"I need the little girl's room," Joelle said.

"Jesus. Now?"

"It's not like I have a choice in the timing."

"Fine," said O'Toole. "Everyone can stop walking. You can go behind those bushes up there. We'll wait right here. You have exactly two minutes, and I expect to have you in view the whole time."

Joelle nodded, then scurried off toward the brush. Beck watched her move around in the greenery. She was clearly trying to find a place that would give her enough cover for privacy while still complying with O'Toole's instructions to stay in sight.

Behind his back, Beck's hands flexed in irritation. He understood why the other man wanted to keep an eye on her. Hell. It'd be stupid to let her walk away. That didn't mean Beck didn't feel embarrassed on her behalf. The new situation only made him want to deliver a punch all the more. He settled for fixing a glare at O'Toole instead, and he counted off the seconds in his head.

He reached the two-minute mark. Then the three-minute mark. Joelle showed no sign of leaving the bushes. The black fabric of her jacket stayed visible, peeking out between the foliage.

Beck's heart skipped a nervous beat. Was something wrong?

Redburn cleared his throat. "It's gotta be more than two minutes now, boss."

"No shit," O'Toole replied, then raised his voice and called out, "Ms. Diedrich! You've got to the count of ten to get your ass out here, or I promise you, the consequences won't be pretty."

There was no response. No verbal reply. No movement. Nothing.

As he stood there, worrying, waiting, and thinking, Beck clued in. Joelle had given them the slip.

Yes. Hell, yes.

A smile crept across his face as he waited for O'Toole to figure out that they'd been duped.

*   *   *

From her spot in the tree—eight feet up but only three feet away from the would-be wilderness toilet—Joelle watched as the three men approached. Beck had clearly already realized what she'd done. It was evident in his obvious amusement. His lips kept curving, and the visible stiffness in his shoulders had eased despite the fact that he had a gun pressed between them.

Don't get too excited, Joelle told him silently. *We haven't gotten away with it yet.*

Her eyes shifted to their captors. They'd reached the spot where she'd carefully stowed her jacket at just the right height in just the right way to give the illusion that it was her body that wore it rather than a shrub.

"Fuck," said Redburn right away. "Where did she—"

"Shut up," O'Toole growled. "Shut up and listen."

"Listen to—"

"Shut. Up."

Redburn snapped his jaw shut. He didn't move, either, as his counterpart turned in a slow circle. Joelle held her breath. She knew exactly what O'Toole was trying to do. He was listening for *her*. For an indication of what direction she'd headed. Because fewer than five minutes wouldn't have allowed her to get far. Certainly not out of hearing distance. Not if she'd taken off for real. But the only sound was the rain, pattering onto the leaves around them.

"Anything, boss?" Redburn asked after another few seconds.

O'Toole's reply was a sneer. "Do *you* hear anything, Win?"

"No."

"So do you think *I* hear anything?"

"I don't know, boss," Redburn replied. "I just thought—"

"Well, stop," said O'Toole. "Stop thinking."

Beck spoke up then, his voice full of the same amusement Joelle had spied on his face. "No thinking? I mean . . . it explains a lot. But still. Seems like a bit of a faulty plan."

"How long do you think your new girlfriend will last out here?" O'Toole asked coldly. "No proper coat. Storm building. A few more hours, and it'll get dark again. Freezing temps, too. Then what?"

"She'll be fine." Beck's statement was gruff, and Joelle had to admit that it sounded more like he *hoped* she'd be fine than that he actually believed it.

"If you say so," O'Toole replied. "I just thought you'd like the chance to consider wiping that smug look off your face and also consider giving me a hint on what you think she might do. Which direction you think she might head. That way, we can save her."

"Drop the act, Darby. You don't care if she lives or dies."

"Not quite accurate, Samson. I couldn't possibly give fewer shits what happens to her on a personal level. But professionally, I'd like to make sure she doesn't get off this mountain. And it's always easier to explain these things when we have a body. Isn't it, Win?"

"Yes, sir," said Redburn.

In her hiding space, Joelle closed her eyes and bit her lip. She wasn't afraid of men like Darby and Win during her daily life. But hearing them talk so casually about her murder made her stomach flip then twist.

"Why the hell did you let her on the plane in the first place?" asked Beck.

"I didn't let her do anything," O'Toole stated. "The bureaucrats just picked this *one* moment to cut through their own red tape. That, or they just really value your safety. Either way, it's purely bad luck for Ms. Diedrich, I'm afraid."

"She outsmarted you once," Beck reminded the other two men. "She can do it again."

"We'll see." O'Toole still sounded indifferent. "Maybe we'll catch up with her. Or maybe we'll just find her corpse somewhere along the way."

There was a wordless snarl—presumably from Beck—and then the sounds of a scuffle, followed by a barked laugh.

"You are *so* fucking lucky that we need to get you to a place where we have cell service," said O'Toole. "If that weren't the case, I'd let Win shoot you right here and now for just thinking about hitting me."

Beck spat. "Right. I know how much respect you have for thinking."

"I've heard enough," O'Toole replied. "Let's get moving. Little Miss Joelle is going to be freezing, incapable of surviving on her own, and defenseless. She'll probably come running back before we get more than a mile." He paused. "And Win? Use the girl's jacket to muzzle Samson before we go. I'm tired of his voice."

"Try it," said Beck. "I might wind up dead, but you, Win, will wind up a eunuch."

"Boss?" Redburn sounded uncertain.

"You really think he's gonna take your balls, Win?" O'Toole replied. "What's he gonna use? His fucking teeth?"

But ultimately, Beck won the small battle of wills. O'Toole conceded out of sheer impatience, and Redburn grabbed her jacket without gagging Beck. The three men resumed their journey, while Joelle didn't move. She stayed still, weighing her options. Weighing Darby's analysis of her situation. He was right about two of the three things. She had no real survival skills. And she was definitely already feeling the chill. But on that third supposition, he was wrong. Joelle was far from defenseless. In fact, she had a weapon. The very same gun that Beck had shown her how to use.

By some miracle—maybe nothing more than an assumption that they wouldn't have access to any kind of artillery—O'Toole and Redburn hadn't bothered to search them. And it was just luck that when Darby shoved Joelle to the ground, she'd landed with her face over the spot where Beck had set down the gun while they ate. But no way had she squandered the moment by giving away its presence. She'd grabbed it. Tucked it away. And kept it a secret.

If Beck hadn't been cuffed, she would've found a way to give the gun to him. And if she'd thought there was any chance of overpowering their captors in the course of their trek, she would've used the weapon to do it. But even now, she couldn't take the risk. She might miss. She probably *would* miss, actually. So she had to wait until one of two things happened—either the moment was perfect, or there was no other choice.

Preferably the former.

She took a breath, hopped out of the tree, and refocused her attention on the three men's exit. Their movements weren't subtle. The noise they made carried through the air, and it only took a second to track them. Unsurprisingly, their original trajectory had resumed. They were following the flow of the river. It would make it easy enough to keep up with them. Of course, they'd be more vigilant now. Listening for her the way she was listening for them. But the key—her advantage—was that they'd be expecting to find her in front of them.

Allowing herself a glimmer of a smile at her stroke of cleverness, she waited for another two minutes, then cautiously started her pursuit.

Chapter Fourteen

Joelle had to track them far longer than she would've liked. Maybe it was an hour, maybe more. Or maybe it was less time than that, and it just felt as though it was passing in an exceedingly slow way. But it was definitely enough of a juncture that she worked up a sweat. The rain soaked through, too, and the combined wetness brought her to the point of uncomfortable.

She stayed as far behind the three men as she dared. Sometimes she actually had a view of them. Mostly, she could just hear their unsubtle movement. At regular intervals, she checked her own volume, making sure that it remained well below detection level. She was thankful that they remained in the forest. The denser the foliage, the easier it was for her to remain hidden. Still, her stalking was cautious. One wrong move—one startled reaction to something unexpected—and her work would be for naught.

Several times, O'Toole halted their little party. Once, it happened so abruptly that Joelle actually kept going for too long, putting herself in a position that was too close for comfort. She watched as he held up his hand. She saw how everyone stayed still. O'Toole stood motionless for several seconds, just listening. Then he turned in a circle and swept the surrounding area with his cold gaze. And even though Joelle wasn't quite near enough to really see his expression, she could still feel it shoot through her when it passed by her hiding place. She tucked herself tight against the closest set of bushes, held her breath, and waited for him to call out an order to move on. She didn't let the near miss happen again.

And at last, a chance came. The men stopped yet again. This time, though, it wasn't because O'Toole was looking for her. It was because they had to. They'd reached a clearing in the woods that revealed an impassable point on the mountain—a cliff-like spot that was too drastic of a drop to descend on foot. They needed to navigate a way around and down.

Joelle couldn't hear exactly what instructions and plans were laid out, but it wasn't all that important. The result was what mattered.

O'Toole guided Beck to a small tree. There, he pressed Beck to the ground, unfastened the cuffs, then refastened them with Beck's arms around the trunk. After triple-checking the security of the new arrangement, he pulled Win Redburn aside. They talked in a whisper. And a few minutes later, the other man left the area, probably in search of a new path. And his departure was what offered hope. Because when he left, he took his weapon with him.

For a minute or so after he was gone, Joelle considered whether O'Toole was also armed. She even dared to move a bit closer to see if she could spy any hint of a gun. But she quickly decided that he must not have one. She'd seen no evidence of it when he'd held her captive. His threats to shoot them had been second-hand. And surely, if he *had* been in possession of a weapon, he wouldn't have felt a need to secure Beck so thoroughly right now. He wouldn't be nervously strumming his fingers on his thigh. His eyes wouldn't be so restless. He wouldn't be muttering under his breath, then pacing and cracking his knuckles before he leaned against a tree beside the one where Beck was tied up. None of those things screamed of someone being well-armed.

A voice in Joelle's head asked if she was sure. It wondered why the man in charge of the operation would be the one without personal protections. She didn't have an explanation. Maybe it was simply that he felt being armed was beneath him. Perhaps he was just that arrogant. But whatever the reason was, she shoved off the concern.

No gun, she told herself firmly.

With one ear on the distance, just in case Redburn made a sudden reappearance, she crept along the forested edge near the cliff, her pace slower than a crawl. Her gaze stayed fixed on O'Toole. She wanted to look toward Beck, but she didn't dare risk getting distracted. She paused twice when she thought Darby might be turning her way. Both times, it was a false alarm.

Finally, she reached the last line of trees before the clearing. She inched along, half expecting O'Toole to feel the way her eyes bored into his back. She was almost dizzy with anticipation of a pounce. But it didn't come.

Fresh sweat—a different kind of sweat now—dribbled down her face. It made her hands slippery as she freed the gun from its spot at her waistband. Inner calm was a foreign concept. Her heart hammered, her lips were numb, and her legs did their best to quake. But she forced herself to ignore it all. Almost on tiptoe, she closed the final gap between herself and O'Toole. There was less than a foot separating them now. A tiny amount of space, all things considered.

Still not looking at Beck—though he must have noted her presence by now—she raised the weapon and spoke in a voice that was far more even-keeled than her mind. "Make a move to hurt me or a sound that alerts your friend, and I'll shoot."

To O'Toole's credit, he didn't even flinch. He simply continued to lean against the tree, awaiting her instructions.

Joelle exhaled. "Good. Now put your hands on your head and turn toward me. Slowly."

He did as she'd asked, but when he met her eyes, there was no fear there. If anything, his expression was one of his characteristic disinterest.

"Do you know how to use that gun, Ms. Diedrich?" he asked.

She offered a small shrug without letting the weapon waver. "I know how to fire it. But not very well. So if I *had* to shoot you, I couldn't promise not to accidentally kill you."

"In that case, what makes you think you could hit me at all?"

"I'm far too close to miss."

Nothing about his face changed. "What is it you want me to do? Let you go?"

"More or less," Joelle replied.

"Then what? You just take off into the woods and expect us not to chase you?"

"No. I *expect* you to do everything I say, starting with unlocking Beck."

"And if I don't? What will you do?"

"Shoot you," she said. "But I'd prefer not to let it get to that point. So if you could just free him, I'd appreciate it. And when you've done that, I'd like you to take his place there by the tree. And yes. If you don't, I'll shoot you. Then we'll all wait here for Win to get back. Once he *is* back, he'll hand over his gun. He'll join you down there on the ground. I'll cuff you together. And guess what? If you don't, I'll shoot you both."

For the first time since Joelle had entered the clearing, Beck spoke up.

"I sense a running theme here, O'Toole," he said. "You might want to listen to her."

Darby swiveled a look his way. "Not that you have any bias in the matter."

"None in the slightest," said Beck, grinning.

Joelle breathed out. She didn't want the advantage to devolve into a pissing contest between the two men. And they'd already wasted too much time with the back and forth.

She gestured with the barrel of the gun. "Unlock him now."

O'Toole's eyes narrowed. And he took a good second to act. But if he had anything left to add, he kept it to himself. Joelle followed his movements with the weapon, careful not to take her attention off him for even a heartbeat. She tracked him as he bent down behind Beck. When he shifted to the left, she took a small step to keep the weapon aligned. She lowered her arm just the slightest bit, too, so that he'd know she wasn't relaxing. Even once the handcuffs were unlocked and Beck was pushing to his feet, she didn't let herself breathe easy.

"Sit." She said it like she was giving a dog a command, but her subconscious shook its head at her.

That's an insult to dogs, it said.

And she didn't disagree. She'd never met a dog she didn't like. The same couldn't be said of the man standing in front of her.

"Sit," she repeated more firmly.

This time, O'Toole obeyed. He moved into position, pushed his back to the tree, and slid to the ground. His cold eyes stayed on her as Beck came around and stood beside her, but she didn't avert her gaze.

"I'd really like the chance to clock the asshole," said Beck.

"And reduce yourself to his level?" Joelle replied.

"I said I'd *like* to. Not that I'm *going* to."

"Fair enough. I wouldn't mind hitting him myself."

"You could."

"But I won't."

Beck's hand found the small of her back, tightening there in reassurance. For a second, it was like coming home. Though she still kept both eyes on O'Toole, Joelle also let herself lean into the touch. Tears tried to fight their way up, and she couldn't have said if they signified relieved joy that Beck was both alive and free or if it was just sheer exhaustion. And she didn't get a chance to figure it out. Because in that moment, all hell broke loose.

Win Redburn burst from the trees. His mouth opened. And before Joelle could tell him what she wanted him to do, he yanked out his weapon and fired off a shot.

* * *

Without stopping to think, Beck jumped toward Joelle, closed his arms around her waist, and pushed her hard to the ground. From underneath him, she let out a cry. A prick of guilt at hurting her slid in. But as quickly as it came, he also forgot it. There were more important things to worry about. Like the way that Redburn was readying to fire again. And the fact that O'Toole had already managed to abandon the spot where he'd been commanded to wait.

In one fluid motion, Beck sprung to his feet, grabbed Joelle, and yanked her out of harm's way. At least temporarily.

As the next bullet hit the ground, he experienced a moment of déjà vu. The events closely resembled those that had occurred when the man in the flight attendant uniform had attacked them. This time, though, there were a couple of not-so-small,

not-so-subtle differences. The first was the fact that he had
access to a weapon himself. But it was the second that hit Beck
straight in the gut as he took the gun from Joelle's hands and
stared into her green eyes for a moment.

I don't want to lose her. I can't *lose her. Not like this.*

With that heart-dropping thought in his mind, a furious
growl built up in his chest. He tore his gaze away from Joelle
and brought it back to Redburn.

"I'm done with this, you son of a bitch," he snapped, lifting
the gun.

He tried to take aim, but before he could, O'Toole came flying out from wherever he'd been hiding and slammed his
shoulder into Beck's side. The impact sent Beck to the ground.
The air expelled from his lungs, and the sudden breathlessness
made his chest burn. He did, however, manage to maintain his
hold on the gun. A fact that didn't go unnoted by O'Toole. The
other man, who was already back on his feet, zeroed in on the
weapon and dived again.

Beck had just enough time to roll over, taking the gun out of
reach.

Driven by his own momentum, O'Toole smashed to the
mud, chin first. Watching him spit out dirt and blood and pine
needles might've been satisfying under other circumstances,
but there were no spare moments for gratification. Beck needed
to act. O'Toole was on the ground. His buddy wasn't.

Beck worked to reorient himself. He wasn't quite quick
enough. He got a visual on Redburn just as the man let off yet
another shot. It was nothing but luck that saved him. The bullet
went *just* wide, finding purchase in a puddle a few inches away.
Mud and water sprayed up, hitting everything within a four-
foot radius. In addition to that mess, the rain—which had
abated somewhat in recent minutes—picked up again, coming

down in a torrent. It created just the right amount of chaos. O'Toole was left spluttering and cursing and sliding around.

Beck exploited the moment. He pushed to his knees. He lifted the gun, pointed it at Redburn, and squeezed the trigger. The other man anticipated the attack. As the bullet zipped through the air, he dropped to the ground and avoided the hit. Except it was the wrong move. Joelle was right there to take advantage of Redburn's new position. Her foot came down on his back, slamming him flat despite her petite frame. The gun fell from his fingers. He grunted and tried to reach for it, but Joelle delivered another stomp.

"Bitch," Redburn spat.

"From you, I take that as a compliment," Joelle replied.

Smiling at the contrast between her overly sweet tone and the power she was exuding, Beck adjusted his aim to O'Toole, then stepped over to grab the other weapon from the spot where it'd landed. But his triumph came too soon. He didn't even bend down before Redburn fought back yet again. The man bucked under the foot between his shoulder blades, and his weight and the element of surprise threw Joelle off balance. She staggered, then fell backwards. As her ass smacked into the mud, Beck was left in a lurch. His gun was still pointed at O'Toole, but Redburn was making a new move to grab his dropped weapon. If Beck shifted his aim, the former would attack. If he didn't, the latter would succeed in acquiring the gun.

Just shoot! hollered a voice in his head.

The obvious solution came just a moment too late. Beck squeezed, but Darby O'Toole had already started his charge through the mud and rain. The bullet came nowhere near its target. Even as Beck tried to take another shot, the other man closed in on him. A shoulder found his gut. When he stumbled, a fist grazed his jaw. Another set of knuckles jabbed into his ribs. Pain shot through him, but it was nothing more than a backdrop to two feelings—his anger at being bested and his worry over Joelle. A second later, though, he heard Redburn let out a holler, and he knew that Joelle had at least a temporary upper hand. Beck seized on that fact, focused on his fury, and used it to fuel his counterattack.

With a growl, he swung his own fist. It met with the fleshiest part of O'Toole's stomach, and the other man expelled a wounded gasp. Beck drew back again. He feinted a second punch to the abdomen, then switched out for a jab to the eye. He met his mark, and O'Toole howled in pain. Beck couldn't afford pity. Or triumph. He ducked low and lunged for the knees. His plan might've been successful if not for the intervention of Mother Nature.

Overhead, a flash of lightning startled him just before his body made contact with O'Toole. He jerked an automatic look up. The movement caused a momentary loss of control over his feet, and the grip on his boots did nothing to stop him from sliding along the soggy ground. He still hit the other man, but not with near as much force as he'd intended. Instead of knocking O'Toole to the ground, Beck found himself gripping onto him to keep from succumbing to a fall. That didn't work out either. They both toppled. The ground under them squelched as they wrestled for supremacy.

O'Toole was victorious first. He landed on top, earning him a hold on Beck's throat. His fingers tightened, cutting off the flow of oxygen. Beck choked. His hands came up to claw at the other man's grip. Stars exploded behind his eyes, brighter than the lightning above, and blackness encroached on the edges of his vision. He was sinking.

When Joelle let out a scream, though, Beck dug deep and

fought harder. He lifted a knee and drove it straight between O'Toole's legs. Immediately, the pressure on his neck eased, and the air flowed. Beck drove his knee up again. And again. On the third strike, O'Toole at last fell back and off. He stayed there on the ground, clutching his groin and groaning.

Good, thought Beck.

Assured that the threat was at least temporarily neutralized, he pushed to his feet, swung a look around in search of Joelle, and gasped. His toes were inches from the cliff that had halted their journey in the first place. Another bit of forward motion, and he would've gone over.

"Shit," he said, staggering a few steps back from the drop.

Heart hammering at the near miss, he blinked into the rain. The weather was blinding. The clouds darkened the area to near night-level darkness, and the downpour did the rest.

"Joelle!" His holler bit at the damaged skin inside his throat and drew up a cough that stopped him from calling out a second time.

Where the hell was she? A blur of movement caught his eye. For a moment, hope surged that it was her. Except as quickly as it came, it was dashed. There was no mistaking the tall, wide frame for Joelle. It was Win Redburn. It had to be. Beck tensed. Then he relaxed marginally again as he realized that the man wasn't heading for him. He was just traveling in a slowly widening, oh-so purposeful circle. Searching. Undoubtedly for Joelle.

She got away.

He didn't let himself consider any other option. He also didn't consider letting the man find her. He cast another glance toward O'Toole to make certain that he still lay where he'd landed, then straightened his shoulders and prepared to draw Redburn's attention. His mouth only got as far as opening, though, before the words stalled. Stopped by a touch. A hand. It slid up out of nowhere and meshed with his own, the fingers interlocking with his like they belonged there. The sensation was pleasant. So far from aggressive that not one of Beck's defensive instincts rose up. As a result, he simply looked down to find the source.

When he spotted Joelle crouched beside him in the mud, it relieved him as much as it surprised and confused him. He wanted to scoop her into the safety of his arms. Carry her way the hell away from the spot where he stood. Then bury his face in her mess of red hair and tell her everything was going to be okay. The quick shake of her head told him not to do anything close.

Holding still aside from the turn of his head, he brought his eyes back to Redburn. The man had stopped circling. He was now standing in one spot, scratching his chin with his gun in a casually careless gesture that got Beck's back up.

Give up, Beck willed. *Or disappear into the woods and look for her there.*

The wish was made in vain. The sky chose that moment to illuminate with another battery of lightning. Redburn's attention immediately landed on Beck, then slithered to Joelle. Thunder cracked. The lightning sizzled. Both seemed to be in perfect sync with the man's menacing smile. He pulled the weapon away from his face. Grinning, he held it out. He lifted it, visibly relishing the moment.

"Run," Beck said to Joelle, his voice too hoarse to rise above a whisper.

She didn't comply. Instead, she dropped his hand and gave him a sharp shove. The push was unexpected. He was admittedly still feeling somewhat unsteady. Those two things worked against him, and he stumbled sideways. Still, he might've maintained his footing if not for the mud. His boot treads offered no traction. One heel kicked up. His arms flailed. For a second—the same amount of time it took him to realize he was going to hit the ground—he was embarrassed. But the feeling only lasted as long as it took for the next sequence of events to pass.

Following through in the dark promise behind his smile, Redburn fired his gun. The bullet zinged into the space that Beck had just vacated with his fall. And while the shot missed its target, it also found a different one. An unintended one. *O'Toole.* The man had managed to get to his feet. Judging from his position, he'd been readying an attack from behind. Now, though, he stood still. Arms out. Mouth open. A crimson hole in his forehead. He hung in suspended animation for a moment more. Then he crumbled.

There was barely time to process what had happened before Redburn let out a holler. Sliding in the mud, Beck twisted to shield Joelle and face the gunman. He was charging toward them, his weapon seemingly forgotten.

Beck flung out an arm and pulled Joelle close. It was an unnecessary maneuver. Redburn reached them, and he kept going. It would've been logical to assume that he was headed for his boss. Maybe that *was* his plan. They didn't get to find out. As he reached their position, he lost control of his trajectory. Just as Beck had done moments earlier, he windmilled an arm. Then another. His feet came flying out from under him, and he smacked to the ground with a wet thump. And his body kept going. It skidded across the mud to the edge of the cliff, then over it, his plunge to sure death punctuated by a roll of thunder.

Chapter Fifteen

For a long second, Joelle stayed on the ground, frozen by shock.
She could feel Beck's solid form beside her. He was warm despite the storm, and there was a small amount of comfort in that.
But not quite enough to smooth over what had just happened.

Darby O'Toole's body lay in the mud, a few feet from them.
The rain beat down on his unmoving form, washing away the
blood from the wound on his head. His eyes were open. And
seeing the thick drops hit them was one of the most disconcerting things Joelle had ever encountered. Logically, she knew he
was dead. There was no way for him to wipe away the wetness.
No reason to, either. But it was off-putting anyway. It provoked
an unreasonable desire to crawl over to him and force his lids
closed. She stowed the urge and pulled her attention away from
O'Toole and brought it to the spot where Win Redburn had
gone over.

Is he dead, too? she wondered.

She didn't realize she'd spoken the question aloud until
Beck answered.

"He has to be," he said. "The chances of someone surviving
that . . ."

"Slim to none," Joelle whispered.

"I should probably check." He turned her way. "Will you be all right here for a second?"

She nodded. "I'll be fine."

"*Fine* fine? Or just saying it so I can go?"

"Maybe not *fine* fine. But fine enough. Just be careful."

"I will. You saved my life, and I'm sure as hell not going to waste it." He brushed a strand of her sopping hair away from her face, gave her a quick kiss on the forehead, then stood up and walked very slowly to the edge of the cliff.

Joelle was too scared to watch. She knew he'd be cautious. But she'd also just seen a man plummet over the side after accidentally shooting his boss, so she wasn't entirely sure what the universe had in store for her next.

Nausea rose up, and she closed her eyes and tried to focus on the sound of the rain. But it wasn't as soothing as hearing it patter away on the roof of her apartment. This rain tapped her skin in a way that was almost painful. It hit the ground and trees with a force she'd never experienced before. And even though the thunder and lightning seemed to be moving into the distance now, the downpour showed no sign of easing up yet. It was almost like being punished. *Almost.* Because she wasn't the one who'd done anything wrong.

"Joelle?" Beck's voice and the feel of his hand on her shoulder made her drag her eyes open again.

She could see from his expression that their assumption was correct. Win Redburn was dead, too.

"What now?" she asked tremulously.

"We leave them where they are, and we move on," he replied, holding out his hand. "As undignified as it is, there's no other choice. We still have to get off this mountain. I still have to do what I set out to do."

"The thing you still haven't explained to me."

"Yes. That."

She waited. But he offered no further explanation. And after a second, she dropped the hope that he'd share more, stretched out her fingers, and let him help her up. She ran her eyes over O'Toole's body once more.

"I know they don't deserve my sympathy," she said, "but I still feel bad that they're dead. And I feel even worse about just leaving them here."

"That's because you're a good person."

"Am I? I feel like I just caused two more deaths."

He put both hands on her shoulders and turned her to face him. Then he put his fingers on her chin and lifted her face so that she had little choice but to look him in the eye. At first, she wanted to look away. But there was something in his blue gaze that stopped her. It was a warmth that she couldn't quite place, but that made her want to blush.

"What?" she said. "Why are you looking at me like that?"

He shrugged. "I admire you."

"For feeling guilty about two really bad men being dead?"

"Yes. They did it to themselves. Literally. And despite that, you feel bad. Despite what your job exposes you to every day, and despite the heartache you've been through, and despite this whole situation, too . . . You still see them as people. That's very admirable, actually."

She swallowed against the sudden lump in her throat. "I'd say thank you, but it just doesn't seem like the best choice of words at the moment."

"No thanks necessary at this moment or at any other," he told her, tipping his mouth to her forehead once again. "Let's see if we can't figure out a way to dry off a bit, okay? Then we need to get on the move again. We'll both feel better when there's some distance between us and them."

She started to nod her agreement—she really *did* want to be as far away from the two dead men as possible—but then stopped and looked toward O'Toole as a thought occurred to her. "He said something about getting to where there's cell service. He probably has a phone. And if he's got touch ID . . ."

Beck's mouth twisted. "I can unlock it with his thumb and change his passcode so we can use it."

Joelle was indescribably glad that he'd said "I" rather than "we." She wasn't sure if she'd be able to handle searching for the phone, let alone touching O'Toole's hands. And her face must've given away her feelings because Beck gave her shoulder a reassuring squeeze.

"Don't worry," he said. "I've got this."

It was kind of self-centered, she knew, but she bit her lip and looked away as he stepped over and performed the task that she'd suggested. It was a thankfully quick process. In under two minutes, Beck was heading back to her, tucking the phone into his pocket as he moved.

"All done. No service yet, but we'll keep trying." His tone was unusually flat, and Joelle frowned.

"What's wrong?" she asked.

"Nothing. We can go."

"Let me see the phone."

"I just told you there was no service yet." His mouth was pressed into an even line.

"I heard you, Beck," she said. "Now let me see the phone."

He made no move to do as she'd requested, so she stepped toward him instead. When he didn't attempt to escape her obvious intention, she followed through by reaching into his pocket and yanking out the phone. Her heart thrummed with more than a little bit of nerves as Beck's eyes sank shut. What had he seen? For the briefest second, she actually considered changing her mind and giving the phone back. But she couldn't do it. Not knowing what was on the device would drive her anxiety through the roof.

"What's the new passcode?" she said softly.

He didn't open his eyes as he responded. "One. Two. Three. Four."

With dread pooling in every part of her body, Joelle punched in the numbers. And she didn't even have to scroll to see what it was that had made Beck behave so strangely. Right at the top of the screen was a new text message. An ominous one.

Affirmative, it read. *Joelle Yvette Diedrich must be eliminated.*

Her breath cut away, and the phone nearly slipped from her fingers.

"I tried to warn you not to look," Beck said gently as he plucked the device from her hands.

"They're going to kill me," she replied, fully aware that her voice was climbing. "They've put me on some kind of hit list, haven't they? So even when we get off the mountain, I won't be safe."

"I won't let that happen."

"How are you going to stop it? You're going to do whatever you have to do, and I'm going to go back to what I'm *supposed* to do, and they're going to come after me."

He snagged her hand. "I promise you, Joelle. I will *not* let them hurt you."

"I don't even know who *they* really are," she said. "Because you still won't tell me, will you?"

"No."

"Beck!"

"You can see why, can't you?" His tone was almost as desperate as hers. "The more you know, the harder it's going to be for you to get away from it. I just have to—"

She waited for him to add more. Or at the very least to retract his partial sentence and come up with some alternative. But he didn't. He gave his head a vehement shake, stuffed the phone back into his pocket, and looked at her expectantly.

"You really think I'm just going to leave here without more of an explanation?" she said.

"There's no alternative." His voice was cool in a way that made her eyes sting.

"Fine." She cast an arm out in the general direction they'd been travelling before and spoke through clenched teeth. "Lead the way."

"Joelle."

"I said, lead the way."

He stared at her for another second, the hurt and frustration battling on his face. But he didn't relent. He just spun on his heel and started off into the rain.

*　*　*

Beck was thankful for the continuing inclement weather. It gave him a good excuse not to talk. The unfortunate thing about the silence, though, was that it gave him too much time to think. As he took a wide path away from the deadly cliff, his mind insisted on being as active as his body.

Two men were dead. Two more—at least—were still after them. A dark part of his brain half-hoped they would catch up and be dealt with before the day even ended. But the problem was that those four men on the mountain weren't the only ones after them. Others would be waiting for them at the other end.

God knew how many. The sender of the anonymous text on O'Toole's phone was likely just the tip.

That goddamn text.

When he'd read it, something inside him had shifted. A tight ball of fury at the threat on Joelle's life had made its way into his gut. He couldn't let them kill Joelle. He wouldn't. Not just because murder was unacceptable, and not because he didn't want to be responsible for her death in some second-hand way. Not even just because he valued life in general. No. This was something more. Something that had no place in his mind or his heart. *Christ.* His heart shouldn't even be reacting. Yet there it was. This fierce protectiveness. Unexpected. A little unwelcome. But undeniable. He *cared* about Joelle, even though he barely knew her and even though caring wasn't a luxury he could afford.

He had to find a way to get her out of reach. More than that. He wanted her to be untouchable. He just had no idea how to make that happen. At the very least, it would require getting her to *un*-know everything she'd already learned about him, the LaBelles, and the corruption in the prison system where she worked. Which, of course, was an impossibility. Even if he could convince her to fake it—a feat he doubted would be easy—there was still the issue of the people on the other end of that stupid text message. They wouldn't buy some amnesia story. Hell, even if it was a *true* amnesia story, they wouldn't simply walk away.

"Bastards," Beck muttered low enough that he knew his voice wouldn't carry over the sound of the storm.

He scrubbed a hand over his chin, uselessly wiping away water that would just be back in a few seconds. What options did he have? Did he have *any*?

An unusual sense of futility crept in, and he didn't like it at all. He'd felt something similar when he'd recognized the inevitability of Ward's murder, and that'd been over a man he'd barely liked *before* all the nefarious shit went down. With Joelle, it was a whole other level of concern.

He stole a glance at her. She had her head down and her bare arms wrapped around her body. *Her jacket.* Why hadn't he thought to grab it from wherever O'Toole had dropped it? It was a pretty bad oversight. One that embarrassed him and drove home the fact that he wasn't capable of being the person who protected her. If he couldn't even keep her safe in the middle of nowhere, then how could he possibly consider being the one to keep her safe after the fact?

So far, they'd been shot at twice. Caught up to three times. It was actually kind of ridiculous under the circumstances. He was an avid outdoorsman. Experienced enough to survive for days in the wilderness. Entirely capable of keeping their tracks covered. Yet somehow, a bunch of two-bit criminals kept managing to outsmart them. It was so unlikely that—

He stopped abruptly and spun to face Joelle, who nearly crashed into him and let out an understandable, "Hey!"

"I think we've got a problem," he replied.

Worry and exhaustion flitted across her face, and she cast a look around. "What? More of O'Toole's guys already?"

"No," he said. "Not yet anyway. But I think that the only way we'll be able to stay ahead of them is if we do a full body search."

She blinked like she must've misheard him. "A what?"

"I'm guessing they bugged us somehow."

"So you think we should do what? Take our *clothes* off? Because I don't particularly want to get close to naked out here."

Now Beck blinked. "I said body search, not strip search. I

don't want to take all our clothes off. I just think we should examine every inch of them."

Her face was visibly pink, even in the storm-enhanced darkness. "Oh. What makes you so sure they bugged us?"

"Think about it for a second. There's no other way they could possibly keep finding us out here like this. It's utterly unrealistic to believe that all of those men just happened to be expert trackers. Even if they knew exactly how to get off the mountain and chose a similar path to the one that I chose, what are the chances that they'd just keep wandering into us?"

Joelle's expression became resigned, and she shifted from foot to foot. "Can we at least try to find somewhere with more cover first?"

He nodded. Now that the idea about the bug was in his head, he was eager to do what had to be done. If he was being honest, a big part of him would've liked to just search there and then, but Joelle was right. It made more sense to do it somewhere away from easy view. Moving quickly, he led her out of the sparsely treed area that made travelling easier and into the denser woods. He didn't stop until they were well within the greenery.

"Good enough?" he asked.

Joelle spun a look around. The sound of the rain was slightly muted, and there was enough coverage that someone would have to look pretty damn hard to see them.

"Okay," she said after a second. "How are we going to do this? What exactly are we looking for?"

"Something like what you've seen in the movies, probably," he replied. "Small enough not to be noticed, tucked away so that we wouldn't see it, and not all that easily dislodged."

"So . . . we don't *actually* need to strip, right? They wouldn't have been able to get it into our underwear or an orifice."

The tension he'd been feeling since they left the cliff eased somewhat, and he fought a laugh. "I really hope not. If they're that stealthy, we may have other issues. A pat down will probably be enough. And I promise not to employ the techniques the prison guards use."

The smallest smile graced her lips, and she held out her arms. "Okay, then. I'll volunteer to go first just to get it over with. Although I have to admit that I wasn't aware that there was a lot of demand for GPS trackers inside the federal penitentiaries."

"Of course there is. Right underneath the need for bootleg copies of *Scooby-Doo*."

"Hilarious."

"I thought so. Now turn around, please."

She did as requested, and he stepped closer and put his hands on her shoulders. Except for one small shiver when his fingers brushed her arms, she stayed completely still while he began his search.

Gently, he ran his palms down the sleeves of her blouse, then around the cuffs. He moved as quickly as he could while still being thorough. It took only a few seconds to be satisfied that there was nothing on her sleeves, so he patted inward, sliding his palms along her back. Right away, his touch found a bump under the wet fabric.

"There's something here," he said, probing a little more.

Joelle cleared her throat. "Uh, yeah. That's not a tracker."

"How do you—" He cut himself off as he clued in; it was her bra. "Shit. Sorry."

She cleared her throat again, and this time it was an obvious attempt to cover a laugh. "Don't be sorry. Just try to refrain from undoing it."

"I didn't even recognize what it was. I somehow doubt I'm

adept enough to get it undone without giving you enough time to turn around and smack me."

"No bras in the prison alongside the GPS trackers and *Scooby-Doo* videos?"

He chuckled. "Hardly."

"Then I guess I'll forgive your mistake," she said. "Carry on."

Smiling, he went back to work. He patted down the rest of her shirt, rolling his eyes as he encountered her bra again a couple more times before finishing.

"Moving to your legs now, okay?" he said.

"Okay," she agreed.

As he crouched down and allowed his fingers to traverse the length of her pants, it took some effort to stay focused on looking for the possible bug. Her legs were a perfect blend of softness and tautness, and Beck couldn't quite stop himself from imagining what they looked like under the fabric. Undoubtedly the same creamy shade as the exposed parts of her skin. Maybe with just a hint of the pinkness that often graced her cheeks.

"Anything?" she said then, alerting him to the fact that he'd paused in his perusal.

It was his turn to clear his throat. "No. Nothing down here. Can you turn around again?"

"Sure."

Beck took a small breath, trying to settle the race of his pulse as her spin brought her legs even closer to his face. Trying not to hurry, he ran his hands up along the inseam of her pants, then slid them over her hips. He hoped that standing up would be somewhat of a reprieve. It wasn't. Her rain-soaked scent filled his nose, and he was suddenly very aware of just how snug the downpour had made her clothes.

He swallowed, then took a step away under the pretense of getting better access for his continued search.

"Ready?" The unnecessary question came out in a husky voice.

Her response had a slight catch, too. "Can someone ever really be ready for the continuation of a full body search?"

"No. And I suspect that's usually the point."

He pulled the soaked fabric away from her skin, trying to cut down on the intimacy of the act. It did nothing to help. For every section he lifted, another sucked back against her body. At last, though, he was completely done.

"You're clean," he said.

"That's a relief, right?"

He nodded. It *was* a relief. Except it also meant that *she* was now going to search *him*. And Beck wasn't entirely sure he was prepared to have her delicate hands all over his body.

Chapter Sixteen

Nerves flitted through Joelle's stomach, and she wished she could blame it on concern over being bugged. But it would've been an outright lie. In reality, the quick pace of her heart and the light sweat on her palms had nothing to do with the men chasing them and everything to do with the man standing in front of her with an expectant look on his face. It'd been hard enough to maintain control of her fluttering stomach while he examined her. Every brush of his fingers and palms had made her want to press herself against him, tip her mouth in his direction, and steal another kiss. Her frustration at the secrets he was keeping from her had most definitely taken a backseat. Even now, it was impossible to feel angry.

"All right," she said. "Here goes nothing."

"Well. Let's hope for nothing anyway," Beck replied.

Joelle had no choice but to move closer to start her search. He was half a foot taller than she was, and her arms weren't even close to long enough to both reach his shoulders and maintain the space between them at the same time. And she was thankful that he closed his eyes as her palms met the collar of his shirt. Not being watched took a little of the pressure off.

It was easier to feel confident when the heat in her cheeks wasn't being scrutinized.

"I'm sorry about before," he said as she patted her way down his sleeves.

"It's okay," she replied. "I get it."

"Do you?"

"Yes. I know you're just trying to protect me, but that doesn't mean I like it. And it doesn't feel very fair that you hold all the cards."

"Not all of them," he corrected. "You've got a pretty important one in your hand, too."

"Oh, really? What one is that? Because I'm having a hard time seeing it."

He opened his eyes and tipped a look down at her. "I care about what happens to you."

A renewed blush ran up her neck and fanned out across her cheeks, and she paused with her hands near his elbows. "How is that a card in my favor?"

"It's not just any card. It's an ace." His eyes closed again. "It gives you the power."

She resumed her search, ordering herself not to pay attention to the way his biceps felt under her palms. "Well, that's all well and good to *say*, but I care about what happens to me, too. And I think knowledge is power. So if you refuse to share it with me, then what do I have?"

"Joelle . . . it scares me to think that telling you everything will put you in even more danger."

"How do you think it is from my side? I don't even know what I'm supposed to be scared of. The LaBelles? Getting involved with you?"

"Being scared of both those things is a good start."

She sucked her lower lip in between her teeth. His arms

were done; there was no bug there. And that meant his stomach and chest were next.

You can do this, she said to herself. *You're not incapable of self-control. And he's a person, not a sex object.*

But that did nothing to ease the heady zap of attraction that hit her as her fingers landed on his pecs. They were as defined as she would have expected. So were his abs. It was groan-worthy—in a good way—and she had to work to keep from moving either too fast or too slow. She wasn't exactly *thankful* when it was close to being done. There was nothing even remotely unpleasant about exploring Beck's body. But it also made it hard to breathe. Hard to talk, too, although at least that was a distraction.

She exhaled and hoped her words didn't come out as quivery as she felt. "You don't get to decide what I should be scared of."

"Let me put it a different way," he replied. "I already told you that I feel responsible for Ward's murder because I'm the one who put him in the LaBelles' path."

"Right. And I told you it's not your fault. He made his own choices."

"Exactly."

A frown creased her forehead, and her arms fell to her sides. "What?"

"He made his choices. If I tell you everything, I'm taking away *your* choice." He opened his eyes, lifted a hand, and ran a thumb over her jaw. "I'm sorry that I'm so terrible at this."

Joelle couldn't help but lean into the touch. "All you're doing is confusing me. What are you terrible at?"

He shrugged. "Caring about someone."

"You're not bad at caring."

"Well, out of practice, then. And you know what they say about practice and perfection."

Her heart pulsed with a poignant ache. "I'm not looking for perfection."

"Well, that's a relief. Because I'm a hell of a ways away from perfect."

"This is a mess, isn't it?"

"A big one," he agreed softly. "One that could get both of us killed, if we don't exercise every precaution."

"Is that a hint to hurry up and finish my search?"

"Maybe just a tiny one."

"Turn around, then," she said. "I'll finish your top before I start your bottom."

A cheeky half-smile quirked up his lips at her words, but he did as she'd asked.

"I should warn you that *I'm* not wearing a bra today," he stated. "So if you feel something back there, it's definitely a tracker of some kind."

She rolled her eyes even though he couldn't see it. "Thanks for the heads up."

"No problem."

If she'd thought touching his back would somehow be easier than touching his front, she was grossly mistaken. The muscles on his chest were a given. After all, she *had* been cradled against them a few times already. But the palpable strength in his back was something else altogether. As she carefully felt along the ridges there, heat raced from her palms to her wrists and up her arms. It skated into her chest and down to her stomach. She wanted to gasp, and she pushed her lips together to make sure she didn't inadvertently suck in a too-noisy breath.

"All right." She dropped her hands and squeezed them into fists. "Done with the top."

"You didn't find anything?" Beck replied, turning around.

Nothing that I'm going to admit to, she thought.

"Nope. Nothing yet," she said aloud. "Should I check your pants?"

"Yeah. Just a sec, though." He slipped off his long-sleeved top and handed it to her. "Put that on."

She averted her eyes from his undershirt-clad chest. "You'll be cold."

He shrugged. "You've been cold for a while already. I can take a turn."

"I can't take your shirt, Beck."

"You can't *not* take my shirt, Joelle. If you try to give it back, I'll just cross my arms and drop it on the ground."

"That's ridiculous."

"I know."

"It's wet," she pointed out.

"It's warm from my body heat," he replied. "For now. Put it on."

She narrowed her eyes. "Fine. I'll put it on for as long as it takes me to finish searching for the tracker. Then you have to take it back."

"Take it for that long, plus thirty minutes of walking, and I'll consider it."

"How is this a negotiation? I thought we were in a hurry."

"We are. Put on the shirt."

Sighing, she tugged it over her head, then made a face. "There. Now spread 'em."

He chuckled, widened his stance, and raised an expectant eyebrow. Joelle pretended not to notice that the prickle of warmth that coursed through her stemmed from Beck himself rather than his shirt, and she bent down to examine his jeans. But very quickly, the awkward heat slipped to the wayside anyway. Because the moment her fingers landed on the cuff of his jeans, she felt an anomaly. She leaned closer. There it was.

Something small, hard, and made of plastic in a blue shade that was damn close to that of the denim.

Breath catching, Joelle gave it a nudge with her forefinger. It didn't move. A little pull didn't dislodge it either.

"Beck?" she said, tilting her head up. "I'm pretty sure I found it. Do you want me to try to take it off?"

His jaw tightened. "Yes. Please."

She closed her fingers on the foreign object and pulled. It took a second, but it did come loose. Clasping it tightly in her palm, she stood up, then released her fingers and held it out to Beck. But he didn't take it right away. Together, they studied the innocuous-looking item. It was oval in shape, and far smaller than Joelle would've imagined. When Beck finally lifted it from her hand, a tiny red light blinked on the bottom.

"I do like to be right," he said, his grim tone not matching with his statement at all. "And now I feel a bit better about my wilderness escape skills."

"Are we going to destroy it?" she asked. "Because someone's using it, right?"

"No. If we do that, they'll know we found it. We need to think of something else."

"We could leave it here?"

He frowned. "Maybe. It might make them think it fell off, though."

"That's a bad thing?"

"It just doesn't seem purposeful enough."

An idea struck Joelle. "What if we could keep it moving?"

"How do you mean?" he replied.

"We could stick it to a piece of buoyant wood and drop it in the river."

"That's genius." Beck grinned. "In fact, it almost makes me hope they're relying on it completely. Wanna stick around and see?"

Joelle made a face. "No. Not in the slightest bit. *I* hope it sends them so far away that they never catch up to us at all."

Beck's smile faded. His eyes flicked away from hers for just a second. And for no good reason, Joelle had a feeling that it was a tell. One that indicated that there wasn't much chance that disposing of the GPS brought any closure to their surveillance.

*   *   *

Beck carried the prepared piece of driftwood to the edge of the water, but he didn't release it quite yet. He checked again that the GPS tracker was snug in the space he'd hollowed out, then decided to cover it with a rock as an added bit of security.

"Should we christen the boat with a name?" he asked.

"I've heard it's bad luck not to," said Joelle.

"Got any suggestions?"

"How about *Hope*? Or is that too cheesy?"

"That sounds pretty damn perfect, actually."

He crouched down, set the wood into a gentle part of the flow, and let it go. For a second, it bobbed where it was, and he thought it might need an extra push. Then the current swelled up, tugging the wood in farther.

Beck stood up and watched it go. The rain had lightened to a drizzle while they'd performed their mutual full-body search, and the sky was clear enough to give a good view of the driftwood and its tiny cargo as it started its journey. He kept his eye on it until he was sure it wasn't simply going to tip over. Even when it was gone, he wasn't quite ready to move. It occurred to him belatedly that if someone *was* watching the device's progress—and he had to assume that they were—then they might wonder why he'd suddenly decided to take a trip down the river.

"They might think you're dead," Joelle offered, answering his unspoken thoughts, her tone light.

He raised an eyebrow in her direction. "You could try to sound less delighted at the prospect."

"Well, I wouldn't be delighted if you were *dead* dead, obviously," she said. "But it might not be a bad thing for *them* to think you keeled over and became a corpse in the river."

"I suppose not."

He slid his hand to hers without thinking about it. Like it was an old habit. Except as their palms stayed clasped, it hit Beck hard that however natural it might feel in that moment, their time together was finite.

"I have nothing to offer you, Joelle," he said, wishing the words sounded firmer and less forlorn.

"I'm not asking you for anything," she replied.

He lifted their joined hands. "This . . . it makes it seem like something more is coming, and it's not. When we get to a place where I can use that phone, I'm going to do it. I'm going to follow through on my obligations. I have to. There's no choice. Every extra minute that we're up here, I'm worried that it's a minute too long. And once we're down there, and I've done what needs to be done, that's it. I'm going to become someone else and disappear."

"I know that, Beck."

"So why the hell are you letting me hold your hand instead of shoving me straight into the river along with that tracker?"

She sidled closer, pulled his arm around her body, and settled the hand in question onto her hip. "We just met. We know almost nothing about each other, and it's not as though anything about this situation falls under the business-as-usual category. I don't have any expectations."

"I wish I could tell you all the things I would do if this *were* business as usual."

"What's stopping you?"

"It feels . . . dishonest."

She laughed and leaned her head against his chest. "I'm pretty sure that if you admit up front that it's a fantasy, it's automatically disqualified from being dishonest."

"I meant it when I said I cared about what happens to you," he told her. "And I mostly hope you feel that way about me, too."

"Mostly?"

"I'd be lying if I didn't admit that there's a tiny bit of me that thinks it'd be easier if you hated me."

"Easy way out?" she asked.

"Easy for you," he amended. "And that's what matters."

"Well. Sadly . . . I'm afraid I don't hate you at all."

"You could try. It's not like you don't have good reasons for it. Without me, you wouldn't have been on that plane. You wouldn't have crashed in the mountains. And you sure as shit wouldn't be running for your life like this."

"All true," she said. "And yet . . ."

"What?" he replied. "That's not enough to send you running for the hills?"

"Pun intended?" she teased.

He fought a smile. "Just a bad choice of words."

"You want the truth?"

"Lay it on me."

"This is the first time I've felt anything real for as long as I can remember." She paused and shook her head. "No, that's not quite accurate. I know that exact moment when I went numb."

He squeezed her hip. "I'm guessing that's right around the time when your mom died?"

"Yes. Right then. The world's been . . . gray. Until now. So I guess I'll take the plane and the crash and the running for my life in exchange for having something bright on the side of it all, even if it's only for a short while."

"Do I get to tell you that's insane?"

"You can. But it's not going to change my mind. I care about you, too. You couldn't make me hate you if you tried. And if I can only have whatever this is between us for another day or another few hours, then I'll take it. So tell me, Beck, even if it's just a fantasy. What would you do if things were business as usual? I'd like to hear it."

He eased away just enough that he could look her in the eyes as he answered her. Somewhere along the line—possibly while trudging, handcuffed, through the woods—he'd unconsciously mapped it out in his head. The perfect first date. A quiet dinner at his favorite restaurant. A walk in the park that was tucked around the corner from his old apartment. Wining. Dining. Romance-movie charm. Things that he hadn't considered even once since his incarceration.

He opened his mouth to make the confession, but as she met his gaze, he was overcome by a different need. A desire to show her instead of telling her.

He brought his palm to her cheek, cupped it gently, and tipped his mouth to hers. Joelle's response was immediate. She pushed to her toes and wrapped her arms over his shoulders. Her hands pressed into his bare skin, and her tongue darted sweetly between his lips, eliciting a groan from deep within his chest. Desire, fast and hard, ripped through Beck. Thought was elusive. Primal instinct was far more powerful.

Both his hands dropped to her hips, and he lifted her from the ground. Her legs tightened around him, and he groaned again. He kissed her harder. More thoroughly. Her lips were soft and warm and begged for more.

The same more that you can't give, whispered a voice in his head.

With a regret that was a physical ache, he eased away. He pressed his forehead to hers and waited for her eyes to open.

"I'm sorry," he said.

"For kissing me?" she replied breathlessly. "Or for stopping?"

"For not being able to give you anything more than that."

"I told you—"

"You'll take what you can get. I heard you before. But I know that's not what you deserve."

She tilted her head. "Do I need to tell you again that you don't get to decide things for me?"

"I'm deciding this for me." He let himself graze his lips over hers for one more tiny kiss. "I don't want to be that guy, Joelle."

"Hmm."

"What?"

"If that's the case, you should probably put me down."

"Right."

It took him a second, though, to actually release her. He wished like hell he didn't have to.

"We'll keep going for just a little while longer," he said as he set her down. "Then we'll light another fire and try to get dry."

"And you'll tell me more about the people who want us dead?" she asked, sounding so falsely innocent that Beck laughed instead of getting annoyed.

"Nice try," he told her.

"Do you want your shirt back now?"

"No. And your fake sweetness will get you nowhere."

Her mouth turned up. "Maybe not. But you can't stop me from trying."

He smiled back, but another stab of wistful remorse sliced through him, and he had to look away as they started down alongside the river once again.

Chapter Seventeen

The thought—the explanation—hit Joelle just a few minutes after they'd resumed their journey. It was replaying Beck's words about becoming someone else and disappearing that did it. There were a lot of reasons why people reinvented themselves. But there were only so many ways that a person in prison could actually do it. In fact, only one came to mind. And it fit with everything else, too.

It fit with the things that were *supposed* to be happening. Beck's transfer from one prison to another. His very specific requirements for the person acting as his Medical Escort. And the terribly important meet-up with a contact on the other end as well. And it fit with the things that *weren't* supposed to be happening, too.

Joelle kept her conclusion to herself for a long time after she'd reached it. She didn't want to blurt it out. She was worried that if she did, the lighter mood would be spoiled by an argument. And while she knew the current levity wouldn't last for any great length of time, she wanted to hang onto it at least for a bit longer. But she clearly didn't do all that good a job of hiding her swirling thoughts, because finally, Beck sighed. He stopped walking, faced her, and crossed his arms over his chest.

"Okay," he said. "I've been ignoring the fact that your brain is trying to bore into mine for enough time. Whatever it is you're thinking, you might as well just say it."

"What makes you assume that what I'm thinking has anything to do with you?" she countered. "Maybe my brain has actually been trying to *avoid* boring into yours."

"Then why have I got a sharp pain right here?" He tapped his temple.

"Probably just your alien implant activating," Joelle replied.

"Only if your opinion on something to do with me is what activates it."

She had an urge to stick out her tongue, but her good humor slid away as she confessed her conclusion. "It's witness protection, isn't it?"

She saw the way his eyes tightened, and she heard the strain in his too-casual reply as well.

"That's a strange leap," he said.

"Except it's not." She shook her head. "It explains everything, doesn't it? Why your transfer was so sudden and so secretive. And what you said about being involved with the LaBelles but not working for them. You've got some kind of incriminating evidence against them, and you're going to turn it over to the police. That's why they want to kill you, too, isn't it?" Her brain kept going, and so did her mouth. "But either they aren't sure what you've got, or they don't know where it is, so they can't just shoot you. They have to interrogate you first."

"Joelle." His voice was dark. "You should stop."

But she couldn't. "Your business partner . . . he's the one who *got* that evidence, right? He worked for them. Then tried to blackmail them. So they killed *him*, but . . . what? For some reason, they believed he shared the info with you. And if they didn't know what kind of leverage you had, that meant they couldn't outright kill you then. So that's why they framed you."

Beck was practically rigid as he answered. "There's a hole in your theory. If any of that were true, then why wouldn't I have just ratted them out? Why the hell would I hold onto evidence that could keep me out of prison? Why wouldn't I send them there if I could do it?"

Joelle stared at him. She worried at her top lip with her teeth. She was missing something; that much was obvious. But she wasn't quite wrong. Beck was being far too defensive for her to be that off in her assessment.

But what is it?

"I don't know," she said, answering both his question and her own silent one.

His jaw was so tight that it had to be aching. "You don't want this kind of information in your head. It can be used against you."

"It's a little too late for that."

"Let's say you're circling the truth. Let's say that one day, I'm finishing up some paperwork in my office, when I hear a noise. Let's say I turn around because of that noise. I'm not fast enough. Something hits me. Some*one*. Just the right force, just the right placement. It's the last thing I remember before waking up with a gun in my hands and Ward at my feet. Blood everywhere. Floor. Walls. Soaking the carpet. Soaking *me*. In my goddamn eyes. The horror of it is nauseating. But I know I didn't kill him. It should be easy to prove. I shouldn't even have to try. Except I do. Every fucking shred of evidence comes at me. Anything that doesn't . . . it disappears." He paused, his eyes sharper than a polished sword. "What kind of power and influence is needed to make sure an innocent man is locked away? Imagine what else they could do. And then ask yourself . . . do you want to be on their bad side? More than that, do you want to be on their bad side with no leverage?"

Joelle didn't respond. Her mind was full of a vivid picture of Beck, standing over the shockingly violent scene he'd described. Her heart was focused on how that might feel. She couldn't begin to imagine it. And he was right. No one wanted to be on the bad side of someone who would kill and happily lay the blame on someone else. It was no wonder he didn't want her involved. She wished *he* wasn't involved. So strongly that she had to lift a hand and press it to her chest to soothe the ache.

Beck followed the gesture, and when he spoke again, his tone was gentler. "If our roles were reversed, would you be jumping at the chance to share every detail with me?"

"No." It was a whisper.

"Ward told them I was his failsafe. They just forgot to ask me if that was true before they set me up for his murder."

His words distracted her from the picture in her head. "Wait. Are you saying that you *don't* have the evidence?"

"I'm saying I *didn't*," he replied. "Not then."

"But you do now?"

"In the ongoing hypothetical discussion . . . it might take someone two years and a whole lot of trouble to acquire the assumed evidence. In the meantime—still hypothetically—there would be no one to tell. No one to convince. The legit cops wouldn't believe a convicted murderer. And the convicted murderer couldn't very well make much noise about it, either."

"Because then they'd have figured out you—the convicted murderer, I mean—didn't have the leverage at all."

"Hypothetically."

"But not *hypothetically* hypothetically." Joelle's breath hitched, and she drew in a lungful of air to keep from crying. "I'm so sorry, Beck."

His hands squeezed into fists, then flexed out. "Yeah. So am I."

A desperate need to protect him—one that was far more forceful than was reasonable considering how short a time she'd known him—surged up. She wanted to help him. To somehow take him away from everything he'd been through over the last two years and smooth over the wounds she could see in the sad blue of his eyes.

"What can I do?" she asked.

"You know what I'm going to say." He took her hands. "For a long time, I've had this one thing keeping me from getting a bullet in the head. I want to be rid of it. I sure as hell don't need it to become the one thing from putting one in yours, too."

She didn't want to argue with him, but she couldn't stop herself from pointing out the obvious. "I don't have that one thing, though, do I? They can just kill me because they want to. Because I know too much to be allowed to live but not enough to be kept alive."

"You don't want this."

"You're right. I don't."

"I'm not going to let them hurt you," he said. "I'm going to make sure that they understand that you don't know anything."

"And then what?" Joelle replied. "You'll trust them to take your word for it, after all this?"

He kissed each of her palms, then released her hands again. "It'll just be about talking to the right person. You won't have to trust them. You'll just have to trust me, okay?"

She met his eyes. She did trust him. That much, she'd already established, even if it was strange to place so much faith in a person she barely knew. The problem was, she also trusted herself. And her gut was telling her that whatever he had planned, it wasn't as cut and dry as he was making it out to be. She studied him for another few seconds, and then she made herself stow the doubt. If what Beck really, truly needed was for her to let her questions go, then that's what she would have to do.

* * *

Once they were back on the path again, Beck was acutely aware of their new conversation. Not because it steered too close to all the things he'd been trying not to say, but because it so clearly didn't. It was as though a long-standing fight had at last come to a close.

And you won, he told himself.

Except he really didn't feel that way. Joelle might've dropped the subject in favor of telling him about her lemon meringue pie recipe—a topic they'd managed to get to logically somehow—but it didn't provide any relief at all. As he lifted a branch out of her way and smiled at her, he wondered why the hell he wanted her to start pestering him about it all over again. He had no desire to disclose anything else. He'd spent hours— two days, really—avoiding oversharing.

In between kissing her, you mean?

He acknowledged the thought with an internal nod. It was accurate. Trying not to confess everything to her while also being more attracted to her than he'd been to anyone in . . . ever, probably. It was almost funny. Two years behind bars. Two years hustling his ass off to maintain his sanity, prove his innocence, and do it so quietly that no one noticed. His focus had been on his one purpose—to get the hell out of jail. So he hadn't been thinking about women. Not specifically. Not abstractly. Considering that, in relation to how he felt about

Joelle, made it seem a little unrealistic. A little crazy. Just glancing over at her now made him want to grab her and do things that had been weirdly foreign just days earlier.

Days . . .

The timeline hardly seemed possible for the way he felt at the moment, and a need to mention it superseded his other thoughts.

He gave yet another tree branch a whack out of the way as he spoke. "Hey, Joelle? You said something before about us barely knowing each other, and I don't quite agree."

She stopped walking and gave him a funny look, and it took him a moment to clue in as to why. He'd cut her off, mid-sentence. She'd been saying something about a dog. Sam? Simon?

Beck shrugged and gave up trying to pretend he'd remember. "Apparently, I wasn't listening."

"Apparently not," she said dryly.

"Tell me again."

"I have a feeling that what you were about to say is more interesting than my neighbor's cat, Peggy."

"Peggy the cat?" Beck repeated. "Not Simon the dog?"

"What? Where did you get *Simon the dog*?"

"You didn't say anything about a Simon at all?"

She shook her head. "No. Not even close."

He rubbed an embarrassed hand over the back of his neck. "Whoops. Sorry."

"I'll forgive you if you tell me what you were about to say a minute ago."

"Right."

He paused. Now that the words were no longer so spontaneous, he second-guessed them. Joelle was looking at him expectantly, though, so he pushed past a desire to change the subject once more.

"You were right," he said as he started walking again. "We *don't* know each other. Not in the traditional sense of the word. We haven't spent weeks or months or years filling in the blanks like people do. But I've said more to you over the last forty-eight hours than I've said to anyone since they read me my rights. Literally. But also in the bigger sense."

"I know what you mean," Joelle replied right away. "I've never talked to anyone about my mom's death. I've actually never really been the kind of person who likes to share a lot of personal stuff with anyone *except* my mom. But I told you."

"Is there a special word for that kind of knowing each other?" he asked.

"I don't think so."

"No? Nothing that describes a short, intense connection like ours?"

"Um. A one-night stand?"

A protracted silence followed the suggestion. Then a laugh burst from Beck's mouth.

"Shut up," Joelle grumbled. "That is *not* what I meant. At all."

"And yet . . ." He cast a raised eyebrow her way.

"Didn't I just say shut up?"

Another chuckle escaped his lips. "You're not wrong, though."

"I'm pretty sure I am, actually."

"No. That's what it's like, isn't it? All the adrenaline, and the chemistry, and the rush to get in the best night ever because in the morning it will be gone. Possibly before toast and eggs."

Now Joelle laughed. "I can't decide if that's incredibly over-confident, cheesy, or poetic."

"Maybe it's just accurate," he said.

"Yeah. No."

"How would you describe it, then?"

Her feet slowed, then halted. "I know this is going to come across as ironic considering what I just told you about not having a whole lot of people who I confide in . . . but I'm more of a relationship type than a one-night-stand type. Not that there's anything wrong with a one-night stand, if that's what someone is into, or what they're after. It's just not me, that's all."

Beck stared at her, his chest tightening at her sincere-sounding confession. She stared back. He opened his mouth to answer—to deny the irony, maybe—but before he could speak, Joelle got moving again, twice as fast as they'd been going a minute earlier.

"Hey!" he called.

"Are you coming?" She flung a look over her shoulder, but she didn't reduce her speed.

Beck scratched his chin. "Hold up a sec!"

When she still didn't answer, he took off after her and gently grabbed her elbow to slow her down.

"What just happened?" he asked.

"Nothing," she replied. "We're still supposed to be hurrying, right?"

"I call bullshit."

"On hurrying?"

"Joelle . . ."

"Yes?"

He closed his mouth and kept it that way for a long moment before sighing. "Nothing."

She started off again, just a little slower now. Beck had to fight a second sigh as he followed her. Really, he had no right to demand to know what was in Joelle's head. He definitely had no right to wonder if what she'd just said about herself and relationships had anything to do with him. Most of all, though, he had no right to wish it did. Despite the self-awareness, he was still glad when the terrain took an abruptly tough, downhill turn. It forced them to physically steady each other multiple times as they moved along, and the contact was reassuring.

Reassuring enough that it should be a warning, he thought.

Except it wasn't. When they reached the bottom of the slope, and she stumbled over a rock then reached for him, he held onto her for an extra moment. She felt warmer now, under his touch, and he was glad.

"Just in case you were worried—at all—it's fine by me that you aren't the one-night-stand type," he said, then shook his head. "Shit. That sounded a lot less self-centered in my head."

"It didn't sound that way out loud, either, Beck," she replied. "And honestly, I'm not worried about what you think. Not the way you mean. But not being the one-night-stand type is the problem."

"I don't get it."

"If that *was* the kind of thing I was after, I wouldn't feel so bad about knowing that by this time tomorrow, this is going to be over."

Again, Beck was left momentarily speechless. It was exactly what he wanted to hear, but actually listening to her say it just drove home the fact that there was no hope of it mattering.

"More irony, I know," Joelle added. "Stranded, chased, almost killed . . . but like I said before . . . it's the best I've felt in months."

He forced a smile. "New hobby?"

"I think I'll pass, thanks," she replied.

Their eyes met, and Beck sensed a heaviness behind their jokes. As good as she might feel—and as much as he liked thinking he had something to do with that—the other part was also true. He was the source of all that danger, and he didn't want to be.

"It doesn't change anything," he said, "but for what it's worth, I'm not a one-night-stand guy, either. Even when I'm not locked up and unable to hand out my phone number to a bunch of random women."

"You always make sure your random women stay for their eggs in the morning?" she joked.

"I rarely date at all," he admitted. "After everything that happened with Tonya, I never felt much of an urge to invest a whole hell of a lot of myself into anyone else. And that was before the shit went down with Ward. And since I'm not interested in anything superficial . . ."

"Why bother with a series of lost causes," Joelle filled in. "I was always saying that to my mom. Trying to explain to her that I didn't want to go on forty first dates a year. I'd tell her that for a woman who claimed to believe in fate, she had an awfully bad habit of meddling in my love life."

"I bet she told you that you have to make your own fate, didn't she?"

"Every time. How'd you know?"

"It's something I believe, too."

She smiled at him, but it was a sad one. "She'd love you for that."

Guilt stabbed at Beck. *And she'd hate me for leaving you at the end of this, I'd bet.*

He cleared his throat. "We need to get going. I think the weather's going to turn again. But I should probably mention that we have to circle back a bit."

Joelle frowned. "What? Why?"

"Because we've been headed in the wrong direction for about ten minutes now."

"Oh. You're sure?"

"Entirely."

She blushed. "Sorry. That was a silly question. Maybe I should've asked *how* you know. Or how you've known which way to go the whole time, for that matter. Because it mostly looks the same to me."

"Nothing more than basic orienteering," he told her.

"Because everyone has a total understanding of exactly how that works." The statement was accompanied by an eye roll.

"Okay, point taken," he said, smiling for real this time. "First off, I've been using the sun to give us the correct direction. The slope of the mountain helps, too, because we want to keep moving down. And the flow of the river is a pretty good guide as well. And you know those flight trackers on the backs of the seats on the plane?"

"Yes."

"I took a look at mine about a minute before we crashed, so I had at least a little idea of how far we were from where we needed to be."

"So which way is the right way?" she asked.

He lifted a finger and pointed to the hills in the distance. "That way. East."

She turned in that direction, took one step, and stopped. "Beck. There's something over there."

He tensed, immediately on alert. But as he squinted into the distance and saw what she'd spied, his muscles relaxed. He knew exactly what he was looking at—another plane crash, this one three decades old.

Chapter Eighteen

Joelle's first reaction to the metallic glint was fear. She assumed that somehow, their pursuers had outsmarted them. Tracked them despite their ruse with the driftwood in the river. But as she watched Beck's face morph from grim into something that bordered on little-boy excitement, the fear slid away.

"What is it?" she said.

"Come on," he replied. "I'd rather show you."

He grabbed her hand and tugged her into a run. Beck's palpable enthusiasm was contagious, and by the time they crested the hill where Joelle had seen the flash, she was laughing along with him. She stopped short, though, when she realized what they'd found. Her mouth went dry. The memory of the smell of burning plastic filled her mind. But Beck didn't seem the least bit bothered by it. In fact, he seemed overly pleased by the discovery.

He swept a hand wide and struck a gameshow-host pose. "Joelle, welcome to the *Marauder*."

She surveyed what was left of the plane. The wreckage was much smaller than the one they'd come from, but there was no doubt that it'd crashed there. The aircraft had hit the hill at a wild angle. Its nose was buried in the dirt, and the front of the haul had a crumpled look. One wing was missing. The other jutted straight up, and it seemed likely that it was the piece she'd spotted from afar.

She turned a frown Beck's way. "Is this supposed to mean something to me?"

"Only if you're a survival buff," he replied.

"Which we both know I'm not."

He grinned. "Okay, listen. Thirty-three years ago, this plane and its two passengers—the pilot and her husband—disappeared in the mountains. They sent out a search party, but a freak snowstorm hit, and they had no choice but to call it off. It was a blizzard that lasted four days. Little chance of survival, the experts said. The snow eased up on that last day, and they assumed they'd be doing a body retrieval. But when they got out here, the couple was missing."

Joelle flicked another look at the plane. "Is this going to end in a ghost story? Because I *really* don't think I need another reason to be scared right now."

"No," Beck said with a laugh. "Not quite a ghost story. The search party kept looking for two more days, and they still didn't find the pilot and her husband. They called it off. It'd already been a week."

"I'm not seeing the entertainment factor."

"That's because I haven't finished. Ten days later, the two of them turned up on the other side of the mountain. They'd set off before the storm started, got pretty far, but were way off course for making their way down. When the snow came, they holed up. They were both into wilderness stuff. But get this. The reason they took so long to get off the mountain was that the husband had a head injury. He was delirious, and the wife couldn't convince him that they didn't actually live on the mountain."

Joelle groaned. "You're making this up. It's like your stupid seagull story, isn't it?"

"It's completely not," he replied. "And my seagull story was hilarious."

"Riiiiight."

"I'm dead serious about the *Marauder*, though. No word of a lie. You can look it up."

She made a face. "Oh, trust me. I will."

"Come on," he replied with a grin. "Let's go see if there's anything useful."

She followed him to the remaining bits of the plane, noting the evidence of years passing. Greenery had pushed its way over and through parts of the metal. The lettering on the fuselage had faded from some unknown color into a monotone gray, and rust bled out around most of the exposed bolts. The window of the pilot's side was cracked. But remarkably, it wasn't shattered. Through it, Joelle could see evidence of the people who'd left it behind. A beaded seat cover. A tattered book. Something that may have been a photograph at one time.

"How come they didn't come back for it?" she asked.

"Cost, I guess," said Beck. "Or maybe they just deemed it unfeasible." He gave the door a hard yank, and it creaked open. "Don't worry. I'm sure they wouldn't begrudge us a little breaking and entering." He gestured forward. "Ladies first?"

Joelle fixed him with a look. "I think I'll let you go in and clear out the rodents, bugs, and potential death hazards before I even think about getting in there, thanks."

"Suit yourself."

She watched him slide his wide frame into the plane, then listened as he rummaged around. For at least two minutes, there was silence. Worry actually crept up. Joelle started to call out his name, but just a heartbeat before she did, he let out a noisy curse. There was a bang. Then a thump. Another curse. And she finally stepped closer and leaned in.

"Are you fighting with a rabid squirrel in there?" she asked, her voice raised. "Because if you are, let me know so I can run the other way."

"I'm disappointed to hear that you wouldn't fight by my side," he replied. "But at the moment, I'm just eating a cookie."

"Yeah, right."

But a moment later, he popped his head out, and he really *was* chewing on something. "Want one?"

"A thirty-three-year-old cookie?" She wrinkled her nose, but the scrunch was immediately undercut by the way her stomach growled.

"Freeze-dried," said Beck. "And not half bad. It's nice and dry in here, too, by the way. Come in."

"Bugs and rodents?"

"Not one."

"I'm not sure I believe you."

"I have coffee," he said, then disappeared back into the plane again.

Joelle's mouth watered at the very thought of coffee of any kind—even whatever the freeze-dried equivalent might be. And a raindrop landing on her forehead clinched the deal.

"Okay," she said. "I'm coming in. But if I get inside and find out you're lying about the coffee, there will be *serious* consequences."

She stole one more look around, wiped off one more raindrop, and at last took a cautious step forward. Her expectations were low. But she was pleasantly surprised when she made her way through the door. The interior of the plane *was* dry. Everything was on a funny angle because of the way it had crashed, but it looked pretty well untouched by the elements. The space she'd been able to see from outside—the cabin—was blocked off from the rear of the plane by an articulated metal door. It meant the air and the rain and the foliage from outside hadn't been able to make their way through much over the years. The small rear compartment was bigger than she would've thought. It featured a leather bench and a tiny table, where Beck sat. To his left was a cabinet, which was open to display a cache of silver packages. He really did have a cookie in his hand, and a few more laid out in front of him.

Joelle crossed her arms. "Coffee?"

Beck reached under the table and pulled out a can. "Yep."

"That is *not* coffee."

"On the contrary. It is."

He slid the can toward her, and she eyed it doubtfully. But he was telling the truth. The label claimed that the contents were made of the finest beans and full of flavour.

"Go ahead," said Beck. "There's only one. But you can have it."

Maintaining her air of suspicion, Joelle grabbed the can, popped the top, and took a tentative sip. It was lightly sweetened. Rich. And yes, in the current moment, definitely made of the finest beans.

"Well?" Beck prodded.

Joelle let out a contended sigh. "I've never in my life loved something more."

"Glad to be of service. There's also a jacket here that might fit you. You know. If you're still desperate to give my shirt back, that is."

"Depends on the jacket."

Mouth quirking, he put a hand behind his back and pulled out a bright pink, microfleece coat. It had a purple collar. Yellow zippers. Some kind of puffball hanging from one of the pockets. And it was incredibly appealing. Entirely more than it should've been.

Without preamble, Joelle pulled off Beck's shirt. She tossed it to him, yanked the jacket from his hands, and put it on. The immediate warmth made her aware that she'd been colder than she'd realized. A relieved shiver wracked her body.

"Wanna join me?" Beck asked. "I was thinking this might be a good place to make camp for the night."

Joelle didn't cover her surprise. "For the night? You don't think it's too early?"

"Probably. But if we keep going for another couple of hours, we're not going to find another place that's warm and dry and has *food* inside it. Unless you'd prefer another cave and some roasted squirrel."

"I have about as much interest in eating squirrels—roasted or otherwise—as I do in fighting rabid ones."

"So let's stay here. They can't track us anymore, so there's not much risk in hunkering down for a while."

She still hesitated. "You're not worried about losing time?"

"I've waited two years already," he said. "What's another few hours?"

An unexpected lightness settled over Joelle. She smiled, slid in beside him, and helped herself to a cookie.

*   *   *

Beck wasn't being entirely honest with Joelle. He now knew exactly where they were, and it was far closer to civilization than it seemed. Just a few hours of walking would bring them to a road. Another hour or two *on* that road would lead them to a rest stop. In truth, the moment he'd stepped into the small plane, the cellphone in his pocket had come to life with a single, intermittent bar. It'd been enough. He'd fired off a text to his contact on the other end of the evidence line, and they'd made arrangements to meet up the following morning at the rest stop in question.

Beck could have pushed for tonight. His contact had seemed surprised that he didn't. Hell. He'd surprised himself. It wasn't as though his urgency had eased, and he had no qualms about a middle-of-the-night rendezvous to get this nightmare over with. If he'd been alone, as he'd always assumed that he would be, there wouldn't even have been a question about doing it. But seeing Joelle relax made every extra minute worth it. He had nothing to offer her except these few hours, so if he could give her those, he would.

Not like you mind it either, said a voice in his head.

He wouldn't even try to deny it. He loved everything about being tucked away in the old airplane with Joelle. He liked that their body heat and a single emergency candle warmed it up enough that she had to take off the hideous jacket again. He enjoyed finding a pack of playing cards and challenging her to a game of Crazy 8s, and he was glad when he lost. Even the freeze-dried food was more than tolerable. What Beck liked best, though, was when the evening wound down. It meant searching out a blanket, cuddling up on the bench seat, and getting uncomfortably comfortable together. It meant having Joelle let out a contented sigh while pressing her body against his like it belonged there.

"I never did get to tell you what it would look like," he said, trailing his fingers up her arm.

"What do you mean?" she replied.

"What it would look like between us if we were normal people."

"We *are* normal people."

"Oh. So now you think all this is normal?" he asked with a chuckle.

"Well, no," she said. "But just because our circumstances aren't normal doesn't mean *we* aren't normal. You're an accountant. I'm a nurse. That sounds pretty normal to me."

"Joelle?"

"Yes?"

"Are you deliberately deflecting the conversation away from me telling you how things would be if we weren't running from our lives?"

It took her a couple of seconds to answer. "Maybe I am. Because if I admit that things aren't *normal* normal, I also have to admit that they can't be."

"Okay. I'll change the subject. You want to talk about ice cream? What's your favorite flavor?"

She laughed against his chest. "It's definitely cookies and cream." Then she sighed. "But no. You shouldn't change the subject. If you do, I'll probably spend a lot of time regretting that I asked you to."

Now it was his turn to pause. In his head, the conversation was a lighter one. Hearing her words made him sure that it wouldn't end that way. When he stayed silent, she tipped her head up to meet his gaze. Even in the waning light, the green of her irises still managed to shine. The need to talk faded to a pale shade beside the need to kiss her, and his attention dropped to her lips.

"Oh no you don't," Joelle said, pushing back from him a smidge. "I might only have known you for two days, but I recognize that look already. You are *not* going to kiss me into forgetting that you were about to give me a play-by-play of our pretend romance."

He couldn't fight a laugh. "Talking was *my* idea, remember?"

"Are you saying you weren't thinking about kissing me just then?"

"I've been thinking about kissing you ever since I saw you on that runway."

"You *have* kissed me."

"I know. And that's precisely why I can't *stop* thinking about it."

Her face was pink, but she was smiling as she shook her head at him. "No kissing. Just talking."

He raised an eyebrow. "Like . . . forever?"

"For now," she said. "Maybe if I like what I hear, I'll change my mind."

"Okay," he conceded, smoothing her hair back. "Let's break it down from the beginning. First off, there was the moment where we met. A key part of any good relationship."

"The runway? Are you sure you want that to be key? I was pretty mad when I found out you tricked me."

"Yes. The attraction was immediate," he stated.

The color in her cheeks deepened. "Was it?"

"Wasn't it?"

"Fine. I guess it was. Except there was a bit of a hitch. What with you being a convicted killer and all."

His mouth twitched. "That's because if we just liked each other, it would be too easy to make a good story. I had to start out as the bad guy."

"With a heart of gold," she said.

"Or at least gold-plated," he replied.

"Haha."

"So what next?" he asked.

"We almost died," she reminded him.

"Yes, in real life. But the more important bit is where we got to know each other. We built some trust."

"And then we almost died *again*."

Beck laughed. "Okay, I get it. It's a theme. We're not

supposed to be focused on that, though. This is about us in our normal world."

"Fine," she said with an exaggerated sigh. "We met, and we didn't almost die. Then what?"

"We kissed, obviously." He dropped his voice low and trailed a finger along her jaw. "We kissed a *lot*."

"Or at least some." Her reply had a throaty quality that made him want to groan.

"No," he said. "Definitely a lot. In fact, in *my* version of events, we can't keep our hands off each other."

Her eyes rolled. "Of course we can't."

"I can stop telling you the story if you don't like it."

"No. I'm invested now."

"Could've fooled me."

"I am. I promise. I want to be lavished with your fantasy version of events."

"Prove it," he said. "Add a detail I'm not expecting."

"Hmm," she replied, pursing her lips. "I'm pretty sure in the hypothetical normal, I'd be getting ready to leave a toothbrush at your house at this point. How's that?"

He smiled again. "Perfect. Next up, we meet each others' friends. We go on double dates, but we'd really rather be alone. We talk about the future a whole hell of a lot. We fight sometimes, because that's how passion works."

"But we always make up," she added. "Because it's worth it."

"We have our first Christmas together, and we talk about the future even more."

"We break up once, because it scares us both," she said softly.

His lips grazed her forehead. "It happens, but we realize we can't live without each other, pretty damn quickly."

"We talk about moving in together," she suggested. "Maybe we even do it."

"We probably do," he agreed. "Do we get engaged? Are you the marrying kind?"

"If this weren't a hypothetical, that'd be a pretty loaded question."

"Lucky for you, it's just a story."

She was quiet for so long that Beck started to think she might've fallen asleep. At last, though, she exhaled and spoke again.

"I'm definitely the marrying kind," she told him. "Or I would be, if I fell in love with the right man."

He stowed an urge to ask—not hypothetically—if she could see him being the right man, and instead said, "Kids? You want a million?"

"Yes. Well. No. Not a million. But at least one or two, no question."

"Good."

"Beck . . ." There was a catch in her voice, and she didn't have to add anything to make him understand that the conversation had reached the limit of its lightness.

"It sucks, sweetheart, I know," he said, the endearment feeling natural as it slipped out.

"Can we pretend it's not hypothetical, just for the next few hours?" she asked. "Is that a crazy thing to do?"

"It might be crazy," he replied, "but that doesn't take it off the table. Not for me, anyway. I can kiss you. A lot. You can go ahead and be unable to keep your hands off me. You can make me want to fight and make up and leave my toothbrush at your house. And if you want me to, I can fall in love with you for just as long as we have. Say the word."

"Yes," she said. "Do all of that, please."

And happily, he did.

Chapter Nineteen

As they undressed, there was no awkwardness. No shyness. There were a few laughs as they tried to keep their balance holding one another in the tilted plane. But even that pause didn't slow down or dampen the mood. And maybe that should've seemed strange to Joelle. Except it didn't. Instead, it felt as though it was exactly what she'd been waiting for. A missing piece.

Beck Samson.

He fit her just right. Tender and strong. Passionate. Fulfilling. Everything she didn't know she needed until she had it in that moment.

It was no surprise that she fell asleep in his arms afterwards. And when the beginnings of the sunrise tugged Joelle from a dreamless sleep and she realized that she was still cradled in his embrace, she didn't feel even a moment of disorientation. Her head rested on his bare chest, and her body was draped partially over his. One of his large hands rested on the small of her back, and the other held tightly the knee she had pressed to the top of his thigh. She couldn't remember the last time something had felt more comfortable. More normal. Like she belonged in exactly that spot at exactly that moment.

She let out a contented sigh, then stilled as Beck shifted. She didn't want to wake him. Not yet. It would spoil the lingering enjoyment, and she was going to have to let that go soon enough anyway. Her eyes found her fingers, which were splayed out on Beck's abdomen. Her skin looked even fairer than usual against his olive-toned stomach. She liked it. The contrast was aesthetically appealing for no pinpointable reason. Maybe it was just the difference itself. She let herself trace a small circle just above his bellybutton, and she smiled when goosebumps followed the motion. A toe-curling tingle crept up.

I guess there might be some benefit to waking him up, she thought.

But before she could act on the impulse, a light buzzing noise jerked her attention away, and the sound seemed so out of place that it took a few seconds to actually make the connection. *O'Toole's phone.* They had cell service.

She sat bolt upright. "Beck?"

He grunted, but he didn't wake beyond that.

Joelle bit her lip. She knew she ought to give him a gentle shake. But as she stared towards the phone, curiosity overrode sense. Pulse tapping nervously, she reached over and grabbed it. She tapped in the password—*1-2-3-4*—and saw that it was an incoming text rather than a call.

We still on for this morning? it read.

For a second, she assumed the message was for Darby. But when she tapped the screen, she saw a whole series of texts. And it only took a second more to realize the thread was to and from Beck. With her gut clenching, Joelle read through the whole thing.

> *Beck: It's me. Rendezvous is on.*
> *Unknown: Me who?*

Beck: No time for fucking around. Cell service is garbage, and I've got company.

Unknown: How can I be sure this is the right "me"?

Beck: Ask me for the password.

Unknown: What's the password?

Beck: Nancy.

Unknown: Glad to know you're not dead after all.

Beck: You and me both. Are we good?

Unknown: We're good. Better late than never, as they say. I can ping the GPS coordinates off this phone and meet you ASAP.

Beck: Do it. You might find out that I'm close, but I need the night to take care of a few things.

Unknown: Oh, really? I thought out of the two of us, you'd be the one pressing the urgency behind this.

Beck: I am. Can you see where I am yet?

Unknown: Sure can. If you keep going on the obvious trajectory, you'll hit the road before too long. Follow it south for 2km, and you'll come to a rest stop. It's defunct. Says there's a gate. I'm sure you can find a way around that.

Beck: That easy?

Unknown: That easy. But hang on. What did you mean about having company?

Beck: Nothing. Like I said, I'm going to need the night to take care of it.

Unknown: It?

Beck: I repeat . . . I said it was nothing. Tomorrow morning. I'll update you when I'm on the move.

Unknown: Roger that.

Joelle exhaled. The sign-off was the last text before the one that had just come through asking if they were still on for this morning. Something pretty damn close to fear slithered along her shoulders. She knew that her life was still in danger. Her intimacy with Beck didn't change that. But she didn't understand why he wouldn't mention the communication to her. And if they were that close to reaching their destination, why hadn't he told her that, either?

She glanced over at him. The past two days' worth of bruises and abrasions held her gaze, but his chest rose and fell evenly. If he had concerns, they weren't disturbing his sleep.

He wouldn't hurt me. The thought was firm, and her trust didn't waver, but it was still followed by a question. *So why can't I shake this feeling?*

Her gaze stayed on him as she frowned and tried to work it out. Obviously, she was "the company" in question. But it seemed like such a strange way to refer to her. And it was definitely one thing that didn't sit quite right. So was the curse Beck had typed. If there was no time for fucking around, why were they still on the mountainside? The words "take care of it" had such an ominous ring. And then there was the password. *Nancy.* Who was Nancy? Joelle looked back to the phone and reread the whole string of messages.

What does it mean?

"Joelle?"

At the sound of her name, she jerked her attention back to Beck. He was propped up on one elbow, studying her with slightly bleary eyes. Immediately, her face flamed at being caught snooping through the phone. But as quick as the embarrassment came, so did a question about whether it was warranted. The cell wasn't Beck's, after all. And she hadn't set out to read what he'd written. Not initially, anyway.

"Everything okay?" he asked, his stare growing a little sharper.

Joelle held up the phone. "You got a message."

A wariness passed over his face, but there was no complaint or accusation in his response. "Oh, yeah? From my contact? What's it say?"

"Just making sure you're still on for the meet-up."

"Did you confirm?"

"No. I wasn't sure if I should."

He met her eyes. "I can do it, if you'd rather."

She hesitated. "Sure. But Beck . . ."

"Yes?"

"Why didn't you tell me you talked to him already?"

"Come over here," he said.

"That's not an answer," she told him.

"I know. But the fact that you're sitting over there in nothing but your bra is making it hard for me to think."

Blushing and still clutching the phone, she scooted closer and let him pull her back down onto his chest. His fingers slid through her hair, the motion soothing away at least some of her tension.

"This is going to sound pretty lame, I think," he told her, "but I just wanted a bit more time with you."

There was nothing insincere in his tone or his words, but Joelle still felt a frown forming. "You could've told me anyway. I wouldn't have objected to your straightforward lameness."

He laughed. "Bold of you to think I'm secure enough to humiliate myself so readily."

"Yes. Insecurity is the first thing that comes to mind when thinking about you."

"Okay. Maybe insecurity wasn't the best word."

"Do you know him well?" she asked abruptly.

"Who?" he replied.

"Your contact."

There was a pause before he offered a neutral-sounding response. "Well enough. Why?"

"It just seemed like a casual conversation." She tried to put a shrug into her words, but she wasn't entirely sure she succeeded. "And you had his phone number memorized, obviously."

"Too old school for you?"

"No. I guess I just thought it was someone you knew rather than the guy on the other side."

"If there's something you want to ask me, Joelle, you can ask," he said, his voice just shy of stiff.

She glanced at the phone. She felt like she *did* want to ask something. She just had no idea what it was, specifically. The password? It didn't really matter. Not referring to her by name? Now that she was thinking about it, it was probably an avoidance in order to keep her safe.

Finally, she gave her head a small shake. "No. It's nothing. Everything has just been so crazy these last couple of days, and it's making me question everything, I think."

He pulled back, studied her for a second, then leaned in and brushed her mouth with a ghost of a kiss. "Regrets?"

"Oh, plenty," she said. "But about last night, specifically? Not one."

"You sure?"

"Yes. But you really could have told me."

"You're right," he agreed. "I *should* have. I'll do it now, okay?"

"Belated much?" she replied.

"I know, but I'll do it anyway." He lifted her hand—the one that didn't continue to hold onto Darby's cellphone—and touched his lips to the tips of her fingers. "The cell service came up when I stepped into the plane. I sent the messages because I saw the chance to do it. As soon as I had . . . I wished that

I hadn't, so I didn't tell you. It wasn't my intention that it feel like I was tricking you."

"I care less that you didn't tell me and more that you felt like you had to hide it after."

"I'm sorry." He kissed her palm, then her wrist.

Joelle's breath caught. "Are you trying to distract me?"

"No. I'm being distracted *by* you, I think." He bent in and nipped at her neck.

"Don't we have to answer your contact person?" she replied, swallowing as heat bloomed down her throat and into her chest.

He pulled back. "Sure. You want to do that now? I can text him. Or you can."

Her worries seemed very far away now. And they got even more distant when Beck's hand slipped under the blanket and gripped her thigh.

"Text who?" she breathed.

His grin was pleasantly lascivious, and Joelle let herself pretend that the rest of it didn't matter. And maybe it didn't, at least for right then.

*   *   *

In keeping with the past few days, the minutes before leaving the plane spanned a lifetime. Some of it was deliberate. They got dressed slowly. They took their time packing up snacks from the left-over selection of freeze-dried food. They kissed and kissed. Then kissed some more.

When Beck closed the plane door, though, the moments dragged by in a way that bordered on painful. The click of the latch felt permanent; it was an action plagued by true regret. Like a goodbye. Like something to mourn. A funeral for a relationship that existed in their heads and nowhere else. He couldn't even muster up a smile at the fact that Joelle had wrapped herself into the brightly colored jacket that clashed so sharply with her hair. The sensation grew worse as Beck typed up the text to his contact.

En route, he wrote, his fingers hovering for a few seconds before he hit send.

The words seemed inadequate. As did the almost immediate response that chimed in a moment later.

See you soon, was all it read.

He stuffed the phone into his pocket and turned to Joelle. "Ready?"

"Is that it?" she asked, the question far more loaded than its own simplicity.

He nodded. "That's it. But before we go, I guess we need to talk about what's going to happen when we meet up with my contact."

Uncertainty flickered across her pretty features. "Okay."

"You know they've got a new identity ready for me."

"Yes."

"And you know that you were identified by the men who were after me."

Her throat worked in a silent swallow. "Yes."

"I want to make sure that my contact can ensure your safety," he said. "So I think you should let me talk to him alone."

The smallest frown creased her forehead. "Why?"

"I just don't want to take any risks." He grasped one of her hands for a second. "I don't want him to think you're on the wrong side and come at you. I don't want him to think I've got anything bad planned for you and come at *me.*"

Her expression cleared. "Okay. So when we get to where we're going, I'll just do what? Wait in the wings?"

"It'll only be for a minute or two."

"Got it."

"Let's do this, then," he said.

He wanted to kiss her once more. To provide a bit of reassurance. Except it no longer felt natural. Like the moments they'd shared had been wiped away. The sweet nothings of the previous night were a part of a different world, and they started the final leg of their journey in utter silence.

For several minutes, Beck fought to find the words to say. They wouldn't come.

How the hell did we get to this point? he wondered, not daring to even steal a glance in Joelle's direction.

How had he gone from having one goal—in the most single-minded way possible—to wishing there were even the remotest possibly of something to be had outside that goal? To letting himself pretend there might be. There wasn't. There never had been. At the bottom of the mountain, there was only an ending. At least as far as the two of them were concerned. Beck couldn't even begin to think of a way to make things last any longer. Where he was going, she couldn't simply follow, even if he wanted her to.

Not to mention that it'd also be totally insane to ask a woman you barely know to run away with you.

The idea lingered anyway. Beck almost voiced it. After all, everything over the last two years had been almost beyond comprehension. He couldn't do it, though. He wouldn't ask Joelle to sacrifice the life she knew for one of complete uncertainty.

* * *

Joelle couldn't help but notice how the starkly barren landscape perfectly matched the feeling in her chest. Cold. Not quite devoid of life. But battered by the elements, with no hint that it would ever grow into something more.

Her throat burned with sadness. And even though she told herself it was irrational to feel heartbroken over losing a man she'd never really had, the sting refused to subside. She actually couldn't stand to look at the rocky terrain. Or at Beck himself. Instead, she kept her gaze on the distance. On the patch of trees ahead. On the blue horizon. At least they offered some flecks of color on their otherwise dull trajectory.

A gust of wind kicked up, and Joelle was almost thankful for the way it stung her vision. It gave her an excuse to wipe her eyes. But as she lifted her hand, she forgot both the encroaching tears and the cold wind as a flash in the distance caught her attention. And she experienced a moment of willful, hopeful déjà vu. The last flash on the horizon had yielded her a night with Beck. What was this one going to offer? It was disconcerting. It made her feet slow. Then it made them stop. And then it saved them.

Because as she stood there, blinking, a red dot appeared on the ground. It slid closer.

Not a plane! her subconscious yelled. *Not a plane at all!*

"Look out!" she screamed, grabbing Beck's hand.

He didn't argue or protest or ask for an explanation. He let her tug him to the side, and thank God for that. The ground erupted with an incoming bullet.

Someone was firing at them with a long-range weapon. Simply hitting the ground would do nothing to save them, and there was no cover in easy scurrying distance, either. Despite that, for a bizarre moment, the dominant sensation running through Joelle was relief. A slightly hysterical giddiness bubbled through her. Because sure, they were being shot at. And sure, their lives were hanging in the balance. But at least it delayed the inevitable ending of their time together. It was an outrageous sensation that should've made her question whether the situation had finally made her crack. There was no time to do it.

"Run, Joelle!"

The urgency in Beck's words snapped her into flight mode. With a burst of energy that she wouldn't have thought she'd had left—not even with the relatively good rest of the night before—she tore over the rocks. Pebbles flew up and smacked her face. She ignored the bite. She pushed through a stumble and a slight twist of her ankle. She could feel Beck beside her the whole time, but the moment of poorly placed relief had evaporated.

They reached the edge of the trees and ducked into them before she clued in that their new position created another problem. They were under cover. But their run had brought them nearer to the gunman. Joelle's fear spiked.

"Beck," she said in a hushed voice.

He knew what she meant without being told, and he answered in an equally low tone. "Being closer to him in the trees is still better than being far away and exposed to whatever the hell he's using to shoot at us."

She breathed out. "Right. Okay. I—"

Her jaw snapped shut. A burning breath pulled through her nostrils, and her eyes fixed on Beck's shoulder. A jagged gap marked the fabric of his shirt. Through it, the darkest crimson flowed.

"You got hit," she whispered. "Why didn't you say something?"

"I'm fine," he replied.

But she could see the way he grimaced as he spoke. And when he gave his shoulder a roll as if to prove that he was telling the truth, his eyes pinched and his jaw tightened.

"You need to let me look at it, Beck," she told him.

He shook his head. "No, what I need to do is to get us far-ther into the woods to find better cover."

She eyed the wound. "Fine. Let's get somewhere safer first. But I *have* to look at that."

He nodded his silent agreement, and together they resumed their trek through the foliage. Joelle divided her attention between trying to move as quietly as possible and watching Beck for a sign that he was worse off than he admitted. Thank-fully, she didn't find one. And after a couple of minutes of navigating the forested area, he slowed and then stopped.

"Wait here for a second," he murmured. "I'm just going to take a really quick look around."

She didn't want to be alone, but she didn't argue. She watched him step carefully away, then exhaled and started to lean back against a thick evergreen trunk. Her shoulders barely met the bark, though, before she froze. Just a few feet away, tucked into the greenery, was a man's body. He lay facedown on the ground. And a gaping hole in the back of his head told her that he was very, very dead.

Joelle managed to stifle the scream that built in her chest. But she couldn't stop herself from stumbling backward. Her foot immediately caught on an exposed root, sending her keeling to the side. Her hands came up to stop her fall, but there was nothing there to brace her. Her whole body went crashing into a dense thicket, and the noise echoed through the woods.

She scrambled to get to her feet and take cover. Her eyes darted around. There was zero chance that the commotion hadn't drawn attention. And sure enough, as she stabilized herself, a branch cracked somewhere nearby. Was it Beck? Or the gunman?

Joelle tensed. She didn't dare make a run for it—that would just guarantee her capture. But she pressed her body to the nearest tree and tried to make herself invisible. Of course, there was little chance of hiding while she wore the fluorescent pink jacket. A fact that might've made her laugh if she hadn't wanted to cry.

Another branch cracked, this one closer. Her eyes tried to sink shut, as if not being able to see would eliminate the threat. She made herself hold them open.

Beck, where are you?

The rush of her own heartbeat grew louder with each passing second. And when a camouflage-clad figure came into view, the sound of her blood pulsing through her body actually blocked out whatever noise might've come with his movement.

The man was short, compact, and vaguely familiar. His blond hair was cropped military short. His expression was cool. He held a long black rifle—the kind Joelle associated with sniper movies—in one hand, and he didn't look the slightest bit concerned about her presence. She was going to *have* to run, jacket or no.

She lifted a foot. But just then, Beck stepped in front of her, blocking the other man from coming any closer. He'd obviously been waiting and watching. And he'd already freed his own gun and was taking aim. Joelle readied for him to fire. Or at least for him to earn them a stand-off. Neither thing happened. Instead, their attacker simply brought his rifle up and slammed it into Beck's fresh wound.

The effect was immediate. Beck let out a wordless holler. The weapon fell. And the gunman had the advantage. He kicked Beck's gun away and moved back.

"You know, Samson," he said easily. "For a supposedly smart guy, you make some stupid choices."

"Oh yeah?" Beck's reply was spoken through clenched teeth. "How do you figure?"

"You know who I am, I'm guessing?"

"Is there anyone who doesn't know you, Corbain?"

Corbain. He was from the pair they'd seen sitting around the fire the other night. The man Beck had said was bad news, all around.

"Then you should know that I have a plan for every contingency." Corbain tilted his head. "Even if you felt like you really *had* to play the hero to Ms. Diedrich here, you could've done a better job. Hell. You might've gotten away if you hadn't stopped for the night. But I guess we all have our priorities."

He reached under his jacket then and whipped out a piece of wood. He let it fall to the ground, and Joelle's heart dropped with it. Because it was *Hope*—their makeshift boat. But the hollowed-out space where they'd secured the GPS tracker was empty. Not that it mattered anymore. Now, it just felt sad and ironic.

"My friend Kit might've been reliant on technology, but I don't have the same weakness," Corbain said.

"Speaking of Kit . . ." Beck replied.

The other man glanced toward the body on the ground and shrugged. "Had to be done sooner or later. And while we're on the topic, I appreciate the favor you did me yesterday. Killing O'Toole and his buddy was going to be a pain in the ass."

Joelle spoke up without thinking about it. "We didn't kill them. They killed each other."

Corbain turned his cold, flat gaze her way. "Well, isn't that so very convenient for all of us?"

She fought a shiver at the look in his eyes. Because he *meant* the words. He was truly thankful that the task had been taken care of for him. This man was a killer. He was an executioner. But he didn't take pleasure in it. It was just his job. And for some reason, that was worse.

"You're going to run out of friends to help you pretty damn quick here," said Beck.

"Still haven't quite caught up, have you?" replied Corbain. "No one whose name was on that flight manifest was ever getting off the plane alive. Not the ones flying it. Not the ones who thought they knew what was happening. Not you. And certainly not your pretty friend here."

Now Joelle *couldn't* fight the shiver. It wracked her entire body and made her teeth want to chatter.

"Tell me what I want to know, and I'll make it quick," Corbain said.

"Fuck you," Beck replied in a blasé tone.

"Have it your way, then."

The other man shrugged again, and Joelle expected him to lift the rifle and take aim. Instead, he dropped the gun. With blurring speed, he whipped a knife from somewhere—maybe a pocket, maybe even his sleeve—and lunged forward.

Chapter Twenty

Beck was anticipating an attack. And not just *any* attack. *This* attack, specifically.

He knew Corbain's endgame was to extract information from him. But first, the man would need to dispose of Joelle. Even before that, he'd have to incapacitate Beck and render him unable to offer her any kind of protection. The rifle was no good at close quarters. It made Beck sure that Corbain would come at him first. So he made the easiest maneuver in response. He stepped to the side—just a couple of inches—and stuck out his foot.

It worked. Corbain had clearly over-estimated the likelihood of his success. The boot knocking into his ankle was enough to send him off kilter. He fell forward, and as he landed, he let out a cry so guttural that Beck couldn't help but back up, his plan to take advantage of the situation slipping away for the moment. A glance toward Joelle told him that she'd covered her ears.

What the hell just happened?

A second later, he got his answer.

Corbain grunted and thrashed before he violently pushed

himself to his feet, then looked down at his chest. He made an incomprehensible noise before spinning on wobbly feet to face Beck and Joelle. A tree branch jutted out from under his ribcage. He looked as though he'd been shot with an arrow. Or maybe impaled by a spear. Either way, Mother Nature had thoroughly lanced him. His gaze was wide, and his expression was puzzled in a way that could've been comical under other circumstances. Right then, it was just macabre. Especially when blood dribbled over his lower lip and onto his chin. He swayed. Reached a useless hand out for some nonexistent support. Then collapsed, dead-eyed, right on top of Kit.

Beck took a small step closer. He half expected the man to rise up again. He was, after all, the last one chasing them. The final living member of the group who'd caused this whole thing and been hell-bent on stopping him from reaching his destination. To have Corbain killed by a tree branch was almost disappointing. At the very least, it was anticlimactic.

"So much for a plan for every contingency," Beck muttered darkly.

He stared for a second more. Just long enough to be one hundred percent certain that the man was dead. Then he turned to Joelle. Her face was paler than he'd seen it, and every instinct screamed at him to pull her into his arms. To run his fingers through her hair and soothe away that look in her eyes. The situation practically demanded it. But he didn't do it. He ordered himself not to. He stood extra still, the air almost burning his lungs with the effort it required *not* to move.

This is it, he thought. *This is the moment. If I don't kiss her once more now, I'll never get to do it again.*

Joelle stared back at him for a long moment—like she was waiting for him to come to that conclusion and do something about it. When Beck stayed where he was, she finally just drew a ragged breath then expelled it.

"I should still look at your gunshot wound," she said softly.

He offered a nod he knew must look curt. "Let's just get it done quickly. I don't want to be late."

She instructed him to sit down, and he made sure that he did it in a spot that didn't leave the two men's bodies in view. As Joelle got to work, it struck Beck that it was the first time she'd had to use her professional skills since the crash. It was almost absurd. Stranded in the mountains, hounded and shot at. Yet there'd been no occasion for his own personal Medical Escort to do anything medical until now. He started to make a joke about it, then stopped himself. He needed this to be done. He needed to stave off further connection.

Beck closed his eyes, disallowing the minutes to have any intimacy. Instead, he imagined himself back in the prison infirmary. In place of Joelle's delicate hands, he envisioned those of the nurse—Leon—who ran the first-aid department there. Leon was sixty-two. A couple of inches shy of six feet tall. And nearly three hundred pounds. There was nothing gentle or romantic about any care the man ever administered.

"I think that takes care of it," Joelle said. "Best I can do here, anyway."

Beck didn't even glance down to see what she'd done. His shoulder throbbed. But the pain was nothing compared to the ache in his chest.

From there, time sped up. The next couple of hours seemed to take scant minutes. Beck would even have argued that everything happened at an implausibly fast speed.

The mountainous terrain became easier to navigate. The seemingly ever-present wind tapered to a breeze, and the temperature rose by a few degrees. Joelle shed the borrowed jacket. Beck wiped sweat from his brow.

Just once, they stopped. They ate the snacks they'd brought and talked like strangers.

When they got going again, their pace increased, and they encountered nothing to slow them down—no bears, no armed men, and no inclement weather. The lack of impediment was almost surreal. Then, quite suddenly, there were signs of civilization. Powerlines visible in the not-too-far distance. The sound of something that might actually have been a car engine, and even the very faint scent of smoke. Beck wished it would slow them down. It didn't. They continued with their steady progress until there was no doubt at all that they were nearing the road. Beck might even have kept going if Joelle hadn't abruptly spoken.

"Wait," she said, her voice so soft that he was surprised he'd heard it at all.

Briefly, he considered whether he might be sorrier for turning back more than he might regret pretending he'd missed the request. He quickly sided with the latter. He paused his steps and faced her.

"Now's not the best time for a bathroom break," he replied with more lightness than he felt. "Especially considering how that last one turned out."

She didn't smile. "Trust me, I won't be running off and hiding up in a tree now. I want to go home, too."

The word *home* cut at him, but he ignored the sharp stab and offered her a raised eyebrow. "So what's the hold-up?"

"I can see the road."

"Yeah. Me, too. That's kind of the point."

She shifted from one foot to the other, then shrugged and spoke in a rush. "I just wanted to tell you that even though it means never seeing you again, I'd rather suffer through that than be worried about the LaBelles coming after you for the rest of your life."

His ribcage was suddenly two sizes too small for his lungs. He tried to draw in a breath, but the air caught halfway and wouldn't go farther. How the hell was he going to let go? She deserved more, but she also deserved a more thorough explanation. The lack of oxygen was starting to make him light-headed.

Joelle stepped forward, concern etched in her face. "Beck? What's wrong? Is your shoulder bothering you?"

"I'm fine," he managed to get out. "I just—"

A horn blared, cutting him off and nearly making him jump.

"Christ," he swore.

Joelle was looking at him like she was expecting him to say something important.

Weren't you about to?

He opened his mouth, but he was interrupted again, this time by a backfire.

"I guess that's a sign, isn't it?" she said. "We should go so you can still be on time."

He didn't like the way she separated the two of them in the last part of her statement. *They* had to go. Yet *he* was the only one who had an obligation to be somewhere. It wasn't untrue. That didn't mean he liked the way it felt to know it.

*   *   *

Joelle listened as Beck gave her the instructions. Wait in the trees. Stay safe. Hidden from sight. Sit tight until he told her it was okay to come out. She nodded her understanding. And for a few minutes after he slipped away, she did what she was supposed to. But it didn't take long for her to question why she was simply accepting the order. Being unable to *be* seen also meant being unable *to* see. She didn't like it one bit. Not having eyes on Beck made her stomach dance nervously. Knowing that he'd walked away with a stiff look on his face and just the quickest touch of her hand made her worry.

Another few minutes passed. And her feet started to move on their own. They took her from the cover of the forest to the edge of it. Then they transported her from there to the gravel shoulder on the road. She paused. Not because she had second thoughts about following Beck, but simply because she didn't want to get caught doing it.

She took a tiny breath, shot a look to either side, then darted across the road. It was a short run—two highway lanes and a wide, painted divider in the middle—but it still made her heart pound. Especially when a motorbike zipped by just moments after she came to a stop on the other side. She had to cover her mouth to muffle the yelp that escaped. Even then, she half expected Beck to somehow either hear it or just sense her presence and then come bursting back out from the turnoff that led to the rest stop. She tensed. Her eyes hung on the chipped white gate that shuddered in the breeze. She listened for the incoming holler for her to turn back around. But it didn't happen. In fact, the air was so silent that Joelle wondered if something worse had gone wrong. Automatically, she turned up her pace.

She hurried along the crushed rock, her shoes crunching lightly with her steps. She pushed through the gate, which squeaked a protest that made her wince, and she kept going. But as she reached the big sign that once upon a time had announced the few amenities at the rest stop, she slowed again. Caution reared up. Belatedly, she realized it wasn't actually Beck she needed to worry about. In her head, she heard him warn her about the potentially negative consequences of her unexpected presence.

"Dammit," she said under her breath.

She took one more step, then decided to minimize any unneeded risk. Or any *further* unneeded risk, anyway.

With a quick glance past the sign—there was nothing to see but the curve in the unpaved road—she slid back out of view. She ducked into the tree cover once more. Now on silent feet, she picked her way through the overgrown bush to the designated meeting spot. There, she crouched down and peered out. And she blinked.

She didn't know what, exactly, she'd thought she might find. But she did know that it wasn't what she saw in front of her now.

Beck was alone. He sat on a large, flat rock at the edge of the parking lot. His elbows rested on his knees, and his gaze was pointed down at the ground between his feet. There was no sign of anyone else. No sign that there *had* been anyone else. The dirt on the ground was undisturbed. Marked with bits of grass, but with zero indication that any tires had crossed it any time in the recent past.

What happened? Joelle thought.

The answer was obvious, of course. He was still waiting because his contact hadn't turned up yet. But for a strange moment, it wasn't the explanation that filled Joelle's mind. Instead, it occurred to her that things weren't quite what they seemed. Or at least they weren't the way Beck had *made* them seem. She had no real reason to think so, no evidence to back up the feeling. But apprehension settled in her stomach anyway.

She took a small step forward, then froze as the sound of tires on gravel carried through the air. It wasn't the noise that gave her pause, though. It was the fact that Beck jerked his head up and the abrupt stiffness in his body. And how, when he pushed to his feet, a flash of some strong emotion overtook his face.

Joelle's throat tightened. She took another step. But the roll of approaching tires got louder, and she stopped again. She knew she only had a few seconds to make a choice between moving forward and turning back. She eyed Beck. She watched him straighten his shoulders. His eyes closed. And when they opened again, his expression had evened into an unreadable one. An in-control one. His attention fixed on the road, and Joelle was sure that he wouldn't appreciate it if she suddenly dived out in front of him, demanding an explanation for some imagined inconsistency.

Right, said her subconscious as she ducked into the greenery once more. *You know that because he* told *you to stay hidden.*

But her internal sarcasm fell to the wayside as not one, but *two* vehicles rolled into the parking lot. Unease prickled. The first vehicle was a sedan. Dark. Unmarked. The exact type of car Joelle would anticipate finding with a police officer behind its wheel. The other was a little different. Still dark, still unmarked. But it was an SUV. Not flashy, and no bells or whistles aside from the tinted rear windows. It was the kind Joelle associated with suburban moms who wanted to steer clear of minivans.

The sedan cruised to a halt just a couple of feet from Beck. The SUV driver—whom Joelle didn't get a look at—pulled the vehicle to a halt straight across the road, effectively blocking the way in or out.

The discomfiture heightened.

Joelle sought Beck and his reaction. His body language didn't scream of surprise. His face was still clear, those earlier signs of emotion still under wraps. Was it because he was expecting both vehicles, or was he just wearing a really well-crafted mask? She couldn't have said. His eyes did flick to the SUV and hang there for an extra, inexplicable second. But that was the only hint that something more was going on in Beck's head.

What did it mean? Joelle didn't know, but her attention was pulled from him to the sedan as its door swung open. The motion was silent in a way that suited both the car and the moment, and Joelle's heart jumped with nerves.

A moment later, a man's gray-clad leg appeared. The black dress shoe attached to it hit the ground. And in a movement that seemed rife with exaggerated slowness, the rest of the body followed. An arm, which was wrapped in the sleeve of a gray suit jacket. A narrow set of hips, and an equally slender torso. At last, a head. Light brown hair, longish but styled. Angular jaw. A close-cropped beard. Nothing too distinct. Except for the empty holster at his side and the way he positioned himself as soon as he'd fully exited the car. Hands on his head. Widened stance. Stock still. It was a prisoner's pose. No doubt about that.

Why?

The question was quickly answered. A second man climbed from the car. This one came from the backseat. He was an enormous beast, dressed casually in jeans and a thick jacket, his dark hair secured in a ponytail. But the nuances of his physical appearance were insignificant compared to one very important detail. He was armed with a handgun, and he held it pointed straight at the first man's head.

Joelle's mind raced alongside her pulse. Her eyes found Beck again, but he still seemed unperturbed. He barely glanced at the man who had his hands on his head. All of his attention was on the one with the gun.

Understandable.

But it wasn't. Not the *way* Beck was looking at the armed man. Calmly. A touch wary, but unsurprised. Like Beck not only knew him but was *expecting* him. Joelle couldn't fathom what it meant. She also wasn't sure she wanted to posit a theory. So she was relieved when the two men started speaking because it saved her from having to think on it too hard.

"Morning, Maurice," Beck greeted.

"Morning, Samson," said the other man.

Neither of them acknowledged the guy standing between them, and there was no movement from the other vehicle, either.

"Been a long time," Maurice added.

Beck's reply was dry. "Might have something to do with me spending a couple of years behind bars."

"Guess it might."

"Thanks for that, by the way."

"Nothing personal." Maurice gave him an up-and-down look. "You've got a weapon?"

Beck responded with a curt nod.

"Wanna hand it over?" the man asked.

There was a pause, and Joelle waited for Beck to pull some tricky move and regain the upper hand. But he didn't. He just reached for the gun at his waistband and held it out, handle first.

"Good," said Maurice, taking the weapon and deftly making it disappear into his coat. "Now. Onto business. You know what I want."

"I do," Beck replied.

"Can I assume you're ready to hand that over, too?"

"It's not really a handover thing, actually."

"How do you mean?"

For the first time, Beck glanced toward the man being held hostage. "You want him to hear this?"

Maurice considered it for a second. "He's not coming out of this alive. You know that, right, Samson?"

Joelle's skin prickled. Her gaze went to Beck. The flex of one of his hands was the only indication that the other man's words affected him at all.

"Without him, I wouldn't have been on that plane," he said. "He's the one who made the arrangements with Dr. Karim."

Relief started to make its way under the prickle. Beck was defending the captured man. Maybe it would do some good. But then Maurice spoke again, and the relief was dashed.

"He was a means to an end," he stated. "You got a plane ticket outta prison, we get the goods."

Finally, the man whose life was in question addressed Beck. "You don't want to give in to his demands, Samson. If you do, you'll lose your only bit of leverage, and he'll just kill you, too."

Beck turned a mild look at the gunman. "Is that true, Maurice?"

The other man shrugged. "More likely to kill you if you don't give me what I need, to be honest. But you can go ahead and trust the detective if you'd prefer."

"Maybe I won't take the risk," Beck replied. "I'm going to send you a text. It's going to be a link to a set of GPS coordinates. You should be able to call them in and verify what you need to verify, pretty damn quickly."

Joelle's puzzlement grew. So did her worry. She couldn't make proper sense of the conversation at all. The man in the suit was a detective. That much fit. He had to be Beck's contact. But who was Maurice? The most logical explanation was that he was connected to the LaBelles. Which should've made Beck more upset. And Joelle might've passed off his indifference as an act, but if that were the case, why did he already have the man's number? Her thoughts churned. She studied him, trying to find a greater sign that he was worried about the situation. Or that he had some reason not to be concerned. She found none.

Come on, Beck, she willed silently. *What's in your head?*

Her own palms were sweaty as she watched him pull out O'Toole's phone and tap his fingers across the screen. She was so tense that she let out a gasp when Maurice's cell chimed loudly with the incoming text. Cursing her own carelessness, she bit her lip and held her breath. But none of the men looked her way. The detective was glaring at Beck, while Beck watched Maurice, who was dragging his phone from his jeans pocket.

Joelle started to exhale, but she stopped with the breath only halfway out. Because Maurice had repositioned himself just the slightest bit. As a result, his gun sagged. And Joelle spied an opening. A slim one. Maybe only a *quarter* of a slim one. But she didn't have time to stop and think it through. She blew out the rest of the air, drew in a fresh lungful, and went flying toward the gunman.

Chapter Twenty-One

All Beck saw at first was a red blur. It caught him just off guard enough that he didn't clue in to what was happening until it was too late.

Joelle.

What in God's name was she doing? Her trajectory sent her into Maurice's legs, and clearly the other man was even more startled than Beck, because despite his size, he folded in half and hit the ground. The gun flew free. Of course, Detective Orion took immediate advantage. He sprung forward and dived after the weapon.

Beck was momentarily immobilized by a mix of residual surprise and indecision. He knew only a second or two passed, but as quickly as his brain had to be spinning, his thoughts seemed to be coming in slow motion. He wanted to go after the gun. Being armed seemed imperative, and he needed the weapon to protect Joelle. But there was too much physical space between himself and the gun. Following the detective to the ground meant abandoning Joelle to whatever impulsive retaliation Maurice took in those moments. Beck couldn't take that chance.

Speaking of which . . .

He spun in Maurice's direction. Already, the other man had

Joelle's bright hair grasped in his meaty fingers, pulling her to her feet as he stood up with a furious look on his face.

"Don't!" The word came out as a gasp, but Beck didn't care.

Maurice lifted his head and met his eyes. "You want to explain what the hell is—"

The gun cracked, cutting him off. The detective had fired wide, though, and the ground beside Maurice exploded. The big man's grip on Joelle faltered, and she collapsed forward. This time, Beck's reaction was automatic. He rushed toward her. He dropped to his knees just as Orion fired off another round. Again, the bullet smashed into the gravel, and again, a spray of debris sailed up.

Beck used his body to shield Joelle. He had no idea whether the detective was truly a terrible shot, or if dumb luck was just going their way. If it was the latter, he didn't want to push it. He moved to pull Joelle out of range. Before he could do it, though, a third pop sounded. Except this one didn't come from Orion. It came from Maurice, which reminded Beck that the other man had confiscated his weapon. He was thankful, at least, that the two men were distracted by their own battle. It gave him time to resume his attempt to guide Joelle to safety.

Grabbing her hand, he pulled her toward the sedan and opened the door. "Get in."

Her green eyes were wide. "What are you going—"

"What I need to do!" His tone was hard, but he couldn't muster up an apology under the present circumstances. "You weren't supposed to follow me."

"I know, but—"

"Get in the car."

"Beck."

"Get. In. *Now.*"

She inhaled sharply, but this time she did as he'd ordered.

He met her gaze, hoping that she could read what he felt under his frustration—fear for her life—and then slammed the door and spun to face the ongoing fight. With his back pressed to the exterior of the sedan, he took a quick inventory.

Orion was lying down behind the same large rock that Beck had used as a seat while he waited for the meeting. The detective had his weapon on top of the flat surface, pointed nowhere in particular, and it was easy to see why the man's aim was so off. He'd suffered a head injury, likely in his wild dive to retrieve the gun. A thick stream of blood ran from his temple to his left eye, obscuring it.

Beck swiveled his head in search of Maurice. For a second, he couldn't get a visual on the ponytailed man, and his pulse sped up. Where had he disappeared to? Another turn of his head, and Beck spied him. He'd taken up a position a couple dozen feet away, his large frame not at all covered by the tree where he stood. He did have an advantage, though—zero blood in his eyes. As was evidenced in the way he lifted his gun, took a shot, and split the rock where Orion was trying to hide.

Beck flung a final look at Joelle and then threw himself into the fray.

*   *   *

Joelle had no clue what Beck was planning. And even if he'd had time to explain, she couldn't blame him for not wanting to share his endgame. She was the one who'd put them in this position. With her heart in her throat, she resolved not to do any further damage. She followed his movements with her eyes rather than with her feet, watching as he crossed the parking lot at a sprint. He made it only halfway before Maurice let another bullet fly. Immediately, Beck hit the ground, arms out, stomach flattened. And for a moment, Joelle feared the worst.

But a heartbeat later, he rolled over in the gravel, then came to his feet again, dust flying. She wanted to be relieved, but she didn't dare let herself feel it.

Her attention stuck to Beck as he continued on his route, and she still didn't let herself breathe—not even when he made it to Detective Orion's hiding place unscathed. There, he hit the ground once again. But this time, it was clearly on purpose. And finally, Joelle inhaled and exhaled several times in quick succession.

Not hyperventilating, she told herself.

She held still, ready for Beck to make his next move. To do something that would give the detective an advantage and put Maurice back in whatever place he ought to have been to start with. But that wasn't what happened. Several seconds passed. Then Beck reappeared. And he held the policeman by the back of his suit with one hand, while he gripped the gun in the other.

Joelle blinked, wondering if she was seeing things in the wrong way. She had to be misinterpreting the situation. *Had* to be. Because from her perspective, it looked like Beck was holding the detective captive. Like he was walking the man toward Maurice.

It might be a trick, she thought. *Like when he grabbed you for the first time after the plane crash.*

She waited for the idea to come to fruition. Instead, Beck gave the detective a shove so hard that the man fell to his knees. Then Beck opened his mouth, and even though Joelle couldn't actually hear him she was sure of what he called out.

Maurice.

She wanted to be wrong about where his true loyalties lay. So desperately that it hurt. But if there was any doubt, it was sapped away when he turned a brief glance in her direction. There was guilt there. So much guilt. And as he looked away again, the truth solidified in Joelle's mind. The detective wasn't his contact. Maurice was. And everything Beck had told her was a lie.

Chapter Twenty-Two

Joelle had to get away. Even though her head was spinning, she knew that much. No matter how sorry Beck might appear, she couldn't stay there with him. With Maurice. With whatever the plot was that held the two men together and put a law enforcement official down at their feet.

But how do I do it?

A solution cropped up immediately in the form of a set of keys jangling from the ignition. She very nearly leapt over the seatback right that second. But a voice in her head urged her to move cautiously. She fixed her gaze on the three men outside. The police officer was still down, though he'd rolled to his back. Beck stood over him, the gun adding more than a hint of menace. And Maurice was tucking away his weapon and striding over to them. None of them were looking her way. But the moment she caused a commotion, she'd draw their attention.

Her eyes went to the keys again. Could she get to the front seat without being noticed? Probably not. At least not from within the car. There was nothing subtle about a grown woman clambering from the back of a vehicle to the front of it. But she thought she stood a chance if she tried it from the outside.

She brought her attention back to the men in the parking lot, and she kept it locked there as she reached for the door handle. Slowly—oh so slowly—she pulled. The latch gave the smallest click, and Joelle paused, waiting to see if the noise attracted any scrutiny. But Beck and Maurice were involved in a discussion, and the latter of the two men had his booted foot pressed to the detective's chest.

"Okay," Joelle whispered. "I can do this."

Carefully, she gave the door a nudge, opening it just an inch. Again, she waited. Again, no one looked her way. Maurice was pulling his phone out while Beck said something to the man on the ground, who shook his head.

Joelle pressed on. She pushed the door until it was just wide enough to slip through, then moved into position. She took a breath, slithered out in silence, and sank down to the ground. Not having a visual on the men made her nervous, but she shoved aside the flutters in her stomach and didn't waste precious time.

She gently pressed the rear door shut.

She got to her knees and grabbed hold of the driver's side handle.

She pulled.

She moved noiselessly from the gravel into the car.

And then she sped up.

She closed the door behind herself, put her hand on the keys, and she turned. The engine came to life, and the secret nature of her movements dissipated. All eyes shifted to her. Even the detective on the ground turned his head toward Joelle.

The detective. As she shifted into Drive, she realized she had to make an effort to save him as well as herself. *But how?*

She eyed Beck. He looked like he was readying himself to stalk in her direction.

That's it, she thought. *I need him to come this way. Maurice, too.*

If she could pull both men away from the policeman, she'd have a better chance of succeeding in her rescue attempt.

Taking a steadying breath, she dropped from Drive into Reverse. She hit the gas and pulled back a few feet. Beck took a step. Joelle reversed again. Beck said something to Maurice, then took another step. Joelle met his eyes, and he waved his arms and spoke again, this time to her. But she couldn't hear him, and she didn't want to. She shifted back into Drive, spun the wheel, and hit the gas. Beck's brow furrowed furiously.

"Good," said Joelle under her breath. "You just go right ahead and be pissed off. That'll make two of us."

She pushed down on the gas once more, then the brakes, then the gas again, intentionally making the car jerk. At last, she got a proper amount of Maurice's attention. He lifted his foot off the detective and shifted so that he was facing her.

"C'mon, you son of a bitch," she said. "Do it. Come at me."

But he didn't have to. From the ground, the policeman shot out a hand and grabbed Maurice's calf. It was a bold move, all things considered. But surprise worked in the detective's favor. Instead of relying on the weapon he still held, Maurice tried to pull his leg away. It was the wrong choice. It gave the cop an opportunity. He swung up a foot and smashed it into Maurice's crotch, dropping the other man. The upheaval drew Beck's attention away from Joelle. And that was *her* opportunity. She slammed her foot onto the gas and let the tires spin as she took off toward him. She knew the satisfaction she got from seeing him jump out of the way was a little over the top, but she tempered it with the fact that she wouldn't *actually* have hit him. Not on purpose. But it didn't matter. Her aggressive maneuver accomplished what she needed it to do. Maybe it even exceeded her expectations. Beck's evasion threw him completely off balance. He struggled to regain his footing, and when he stumbled to one side, he tripped over Maurice, who hadn't yet recovered from his own fall.

Joelle stared for only a second more before she gathered enough sense to pull the car around to the spot where the detective now stood. The suit-clad man glanced back toward Beck and Maurice, then reached out for the door handle.

"Hurry!" Joelle called.

But it was too late. Beck was back in control. The policeman barely got the door open before he was tackled. Together, he and Beck hit the ground. Joelle watched them tussle, her heart in her throat. She was going to have to make a choice. Leave on her own and abandon the detective. Or do the unthinkable and try to take out Beck and Maurice with the car. The former would be more likely to ensure that she survived. But she wasn't sure if either decision was one that she could live with. Be directly responsible for the loss of two bad men's lives? Or be indirectly responsible for the loss of one good man's life?

Still uncommitted to one direction or the other, she put her hand on the gear shifter and started to lift her foot from the brake pedal. As she did, she took an automatic look around. And she realized that it didn't matter which choice she made; the second vehicle—the SUV with the tinted windows—was blocking her in. In the midst of the chaos, it'd slipped her mind. And now she wondered what its purpose was. Yes, it was acting as a barricade. But presumably the driver was there as backup. So why hadn't he gotten out to help?

Her eyes hung on the vehicle for a little too long. Joelle felt the car shake with a sudden, unexpected impact, and she tore her gaze away from the SUV just in time to see the detective's body fall away from her passenger-side window. It only took a second to process the fact that he'd been thrown against the car. And in that second, Beck reappeared. He tore the door open, climbed into the seat beside Joelle, and turned her way.

Her reaction was instinctive. She spun toward her own door, fully intent upon making an undignified escape. Beck was too quick. His hand found the back of her shirt and tugged. Joelle couldn't pull free, and flight turned to fight. She rounded on him, fist clenched, and arm raised. But he was still faster. His hand came up and closed on her wrist, immobilizing her.

"Joelle," he said.

She pretended that the sound of his voice didn't send a sharp stab of hurt into her heart.

"Fuck off, Beck!" she spat. "Let me go."

She lifted her other hand and aimed for an open-palmed hit. And as much as it frustrated her, it didn't surprise her when *his* other hand came up and stopped the blow.

"I need you to listen to me," he said.

"What will you do if I don't? Punch me? Shoot me? Kill me and throw me in the back of—"

He dropped her arms, and the sudden freedom startled her so much that she stopped speaking and went still.

"I'm not going to hurt you." He somehow managed to sound wounded by the implication.

Joelle didn't let it prick at her; he didn't deserve any kind of understanding. "You've already hurt me."

"Give me a minute to explain," he replied. "Please."

His gaze was plaintive. It made her *want* to listen. But she didn't *want* to want to. And she was glad there was some movement outside the car just then because it gave her an excuse to look away. Exhaling, she glanced over Beck's shoulder. It was Maurice. He'd finally gotten to his feet, and he was clearly looking for someone to blame for his fall. And if he picked her, then Beck would be her only hope for any kind of protection. Assuming he cared enough to give even a bit of it.

Joelle brought her attention back to him. "What can you possibly have to say to me that I might want to hear?"

His shoulders sagged just marginally. "Everything I told you is true."

"Except for the part where you aren't turning over evidence to the police."

"Except that."

"That's the whole thing, Beck! The whole reason you were getting off the mountain. The whole reason I trusted you, and the whole reason I—" She managed to stop before she embarrassed herself by reminding him of exactly what they'd done the previous evening.

"And it's the whole reason I didn't tell you the entire truth," he replied.

"What *is* the entire truth, then? That you're a criminal? That you really do work for the LaBelles?"

"No. I told you the truth about everything, Joelle, short of one small detail. The evidence I collected was never for the police. It was always for the LaBelles."

"You call that a small detail?" she asked. "If it's true that they killed your friend and framed you for it, then why would you give them anything? And if the LaBelles haven't been the ones trying to kill us, then who has?"

"A rival gang," he told her. "And Ward wasn't my friend. He was my business partner. But I'm not going to make excuses for what they did to him or pretend that I haven't spent two years raging against what they did to me, or the injustice of it all." He sighed and put his hand on the back of his neck. "I had no choice."

"I don't understand any of this."

"I know. Just let Maurice do his thing. He'll verify that the evidence is where I say it is, and I'll talk to him."

Automatically, Joelle sought a visual of the man in question. Then she wished she hadn't. Maurice had found a target for his anger—the detective. He had the other man by the arm, and he was dragging him across the gravel.

His thing, she thought, her skin crawling.

She redirected her attention back to Beck. "What will you talk to him about? The possibility of not killing me?"

He met her eyes, and what she saw there made her shiver.

"It has to happen like this," he said softly. "You can't win a fight against the LaBelles."

"You can at least *try.*"

"I did try. For fifteen years."

Her confusion reached an all-time high. "I don't—"

"Understand," he interjected, scrubbing his palm over his chin. "Give me five more minutes. Please."

Joelle wanted to put her head down on the steering wheel and cry. Beck had no right to ask her for five *seconds*, let alone five minutes.

But you're going to give it to him anyway, aren't you?

"I swear to God . . ." She trailed off and shook her head. She couldn't finish. She wasn't even sure what she was trying to say, and there was certainly no real threat in anything she might manage to get out. But Beck seemed satisfied nonetheless.

He held out his hand. "The keys?"

That, at least, she could respond to. "You're kidding, right? You want me to hand over the one way I have of escaping?"

"My argument with Maurice won't carry quite as much weight if he thinks you're a flight risk."

"I disagree. If you leave the keys with me, then he knows I'm staying by choice."

"You're blocked in anyway." He gestured toward the SUV.

"I'll find a way around it if I have to," she replied.

"Joelle."

She shook her head again. "No. You don't get to say my name like that."

"J—" He stopped and ground his teeth together. "Please. You have to trust me on this."

"Right." She bit off the word, then yanked the keys from the ignition and held them out.

She did it in anger. Except as soon as his fingers brushed hers, she regretted it. Partly because it really did mean giving up the hope of freedom. Mostly, though, because the tingle where his skin met hers was immediate. Unwanted. But undeniable at the same time. He must've felt it, too. His eyes came up to meet her gaze, and despite everything, the want there was transparent. His mouth opened.

"Just go," Joelle said quickly.

His lips pressed together. Several heartbeats passed. Then he nodded and slipped out, his attention on Maurice.

* * *

Beck would have far preferred to stay in the car with Joelle. There wasn't much he wouldn't have given to do it. It wasn't an option, though. Just like not giving Maurice the evidence wasn't an option.

He slammed the door behind himself and forced an exterior calm that didn't at all reflect the roil of his gut on the inside.

This has to work.

"Maurice," he called out. "I think Detective Orion gets it."

The other man drew back his fist one more time anyway, and he slammed it into the policeman's stomach before letting him go. Orion sagged to the ground, and Maurice turned to Beck.

"I'm not entirely sure he does," he said with a blood-stained, dirt-smudged smile.

Beck shrugged. "Can we wait until after to figure that out?"

"I suppose. Remind me where I was on that front?"

"You were about to call and verify the location of the evidence."

"Ah, yes. Keep an eye on our friend here while I finish that up." Maurice started to turn away but paused to flick a look toward the car where Joelle sat waiting. "Should we be expecting a few more girlfriends of yours to come flying out of the woods?"

Beck made sure not to follow the other man's glance. "I'm a one-woman man, Maurice. You know that."

"Yes, I do. Which I guess begs the question of whether this one might attack me again, just for fun?"

"She won't."

"She wasn't a part of this deal."

"I know."

Maurice narrowed his eyes at Beck for another second, then stepped past the fallen detective to retrieve his phone from the ground. Beck waited with as much patience as he could muster. He would've liked to spend the minutes talking to Joelle, but damned if he was going to ask permission from the behemoth of a man who already wielded entirely too much power. And it *did* take minutes. A good ten of them. At last, though, the other man signed off on the call and moved nearer again.

"Tricky bastard, aren't you?" he said.

This time, Beck's responding shrug was genuine. "I try."

Maurice waggled a finger at him. "I think you know that you succeed. Care to share the secret of how you managed to hide a thumb drive under the boss's bed? From inside a federal prison, no less."

"I don't think anyone would win if I disclosed that," Beck replied.

He let himself smile, though. It *had* taken some ingenuity. Also a little familiarity with the most-senior LaBelle's preferred escort agency, a stack of cash, and some handy accounting tricks that would save the owner of the agency even more money over the coming years.

Maurice smiled back. "Guess I can respect you wanting to keep your sources tight. Not sure about the boss, though."

"My deal with him was no questions asked," Beck said evenly. "He's a man who keeps his word, and so am I. Speaking of which . . . I'm ready to collect on my half of this bargain."

"I bet you are."

The other man just stood there, and there was a moment—a long one—where Beck thought he might try to renege. At last, though, Maurice brought his attention to the SUV that blocked the road. He lifted a hand and flicked it in a "come here" gesture. Beck held his breath.

In seeming slow motion, the side door of the vehicle swung open. A head of dark, braided hair appeared. A face—girlish and not yet rid of the sweetness of childhood—followed it. There was another still moment. Blue eyes met blue eyes. Then came a rush. An all-arms-and-legs body jumped from the SUV and came running toward Beck. *At* Beck. Automatically, he bent a knee to receive the incoming embrace more easily. Spindly arms wrapped around his neck. The scent of fruity shampoo filled his nose. And then her voice carried to his ear, sending two years of separation completely away.

"Dad!" she said. "Did you get old, or are you just tired?"

A laugh burst out, and Beck was thankful for it because it

was a hell of a lot less embarrassing than the tears that wanted to come.

"I missed you, too, Ladybug," he replied, letting her go and stepping back to take a better look at her. "I don't think you got any older, though. Maybe you shrunk?"

She made a face. "I'm almost eleven. I grew *inches*. And I'm too old to be called Ladybug."

Beck fought a grin. "Princess Nancy?"

"Dad. Just Nancy."

"Okay, then. Just Nancy. Give me another hug."

She reached in and threw her arms around his neck again. Beck held on for an extended moment before releasing her once more. The driver of the SUV—a sour-faced, light-haired woman who had the same slim build as Nancy—had made her way out of the vehicle and was standing a few feet away with a thick, business-sized envelope in her hands.

Beck greeted her with a curt nod. "Elrissa."

"Beck," she said, her voice cool. "Happy and healthy, as promised."

He resisted a compulsion to ask her sarcastically what*ever* he could do to repay her and just nodded a second time. "We both appreciate that."

"Not both of us," his daughter said with more than a hint of resentment.

He gave her shoulder a squeeze in silent solidarity. "She did her best, I'm sure."

"I had a nanny."

"I know."

"I didn't get to go to real school."

"I know that, too."

Elrissa didn't respond to the exchange. She just swept an indifferent look over the parking lot, reminding Beck that there was a distinctly non-PG scene on display. He adjusted his position to block Nancy's view and waited for Elrissa to finish her onceover and shift her focus to Maurice.

"You can put the detective in your trunk," she said to him. "While you do that, I'll give Beck his new identification and the keys for the SUV."

"What about the woman?" Maurice replied.

Now Elrissa brought her eyes to the car, and Beck couldn't stop himself from following her gaze. His defensive instincts were already alight. He had no idea what to expect. His plan had hinged on a careful conversation that hadn't involved a gunfight. Or in Joelle being there to witness it.

"She doesn't know anything," he said quietly. "Not about your business and not about the evidence."

"She knows about *you*," Elrissa replied. "She can identify Maurice and the cop, and I'm sure you know without being told that average citizens don't have any interest in protecting people like us. What's she going to tell people when she gets back to civilization? That she walked away from the crash on her own?"

Beck ordered himself to stay calm. "Give me ten minutes with her, and she'll say what needs to be said. I'll make sure of it."

"Who is she?" Nancy asked, tugging on his hand.

The question made his heart squeeze, and he didn't dare look down as he answered. "A friend, Ladybug."

His statement was met with silence, all around. It made him want to speak up. To tell them he had a backup. A failsafe. Except it wasn't true. He hadn't planned on needing another bargaining chip. His only option was the truth.

He let out a measured breath. "I gave you the evidence when I could've held out and asked you to find a solution to my friend's presence. You would've negotiated, but I didn't ask you to."

Elrissa looked truly interested for the first time. "So now you *are* asking, but on the basis of good faith?"

"Yes."

"Intriguing proposal."

"How intriguing?"

"Just enough, I think." She tipped another look at Joelle. "She's pretty. If you like that whole redhead look."

Beck neither agreed nor disagreed. He just waited.

"All right," said Elrissa. "We're starting to run short on time, anyway. It might be more of a mess to try and clean her up than to let her go. Talk to her. If she agrees, I'll happily drive her into town myself."

"She'd probably prefer to walk."

"I'm sure she would. But where would the fun be in that?" She flashed a cold smile. "Getting a ride with me is my condition. And you can leave Nancy here with me while you have your heart-to-heart. I don't want you getting any ideas about taking off."

"Fine." He bent down to his daughter. He was loath to leave her again after the too-brief, long-awaited reunion. He had little choice, though, if he wanted everyone that he cared about to stay alive. "I'll be right back, Ladybug."

"Promise?" The doubt in her voice broke his heart.

"Promise," he said firmly.

He straightened up and swung toward the car, the pressure in his chest easing just the slightest bit as he met Joelle's eyes through the window. It was going to work out. It had to.

Chapter Twenty-Three

All of the thoughts that had been swirling around in Joelle's head for the last couple of minutes came to a full-stop as Beck stepped toward her and fixed her with a hope-filled look. What was he coming over to say? What *could* he say that would explain all of this? Automatically, her attention shifted from him to the young girl, then back again.

His daughter.

She hadn't been able to hear the conversation, but there was no denying who the girl was—aside from the fact that she was far more willowy than Beck could ever have been, she looked exactly like him.

Like him . . . and like that woman.

A pang of unreasonable jealousy struck Joelle. She had no claim on Beck. She shouldn't even *want* to have a claim on him, all things considered. But being hit with the fact that he had a daughter, and that the daughter had a mother . . . it was an unexpected blow. Or at least the latter piece was.

He wouldn't have been with you if they were still a couple, she told herself.

But she didn't know for sure if that was true. Every single thing seemed uncertain as she watched Beck finish circling around the car to the passenger side. But when he politely tapped on the window as though he needed permission to enter, a bubble of amusement did manage to surface. And despite the absurdity of it, he didn't open the door until Joelle had gestured for him to come in.

"So," he said when he'd settled into the seat beside her and closed the door.

"So," she echoed.

He inclined his head toward the group outside. "They gave me a few minutes to talk to you. If you're willing to listen."

There was something about the way he said it that made her swallow. "And if I'm *not* willing?"

"I'd rather that not be a thing."

"Okay. Then I guess I don't have much choice but to listen, do I?"

Except for a briefly pained look, he didn't react to her snippy tone, and she immediately felt bad.

"I'm sorry," she said. "I do want to hear what you have to say. Please."

He grabbed the back of his neck and squeezed, then dropped his hand and glanced toward his daughter, who was clearly trying to pretend not to have any interest in them.

"Things are a little more complicated than I let on," he said with a sigh.

"She looks like you," Joelle replied.

"Even more than she did two years ago when I last saw her in person," he agreed.

Her heart twinged. "What's her name?"

"Nancy," he said. "She'll be eleven next month."

Nancy. The password.

Joelle looked out at the girl again. "Why didn't you just tell me about her? I would've understood."

"I know you would've. But I couldn't do it. Not if I ever wanted to see her again." His eyes closed, and his hands flexed for a second before he lifted his lids and met her gaze again. "Two years ago—on the same day they framed me for Ward's murder—the LaBelles made my daughter disappear, and I don't mean just physically."

"I don't understand."

"Trust me. Neither did I. But don't get me wrong. The authorities literally couldn't locate her. Except it wasn't just that. When the arresting officer read me my rights, the first thing I asked was for them to look after Nancy. I *begged* them to make sure she was okay. They agreed. They took the info about her school, and I said I'd answer their questions as soon as I knew she was alive and well. But then some social worker showed up and told me she wasn't at school. Not only that, but the school had no record of her existence." His mouth twisted. "Allegedly."

"But they were lying, obviously," Joelle said.

"Yeah, no shit."

"Someone wasn't able to figure that out?"

"You'd think, right? Except no one did."

They were both silent for a minute. Outside the car, Maurice was dragging the detective unceremoniously across the ground. Thankfully, Nancy's eyes were still on them. The woman beside her was staring down at her phone as though nothing was wrong at all.

Joelle looked back to Beck. "What about her mom?"

"Not a factor. And you have to keep in mind that I was locked in an interrogation room with no way to prove myself, and all that stuff I said about the LaBelles having people every-where was as true then as it is now. Corrupt police. Crooked judges. Falsified evidence. I didn't even know if I could trust my own lawyer." He paused. "No, scratch that. I knew I couldn't, regardless of how much I was paying him. It all sounds crazy, right? Impossible, even?"

She nodded. "A little."

"More than a little," Beck said. "It's okay to say so."

"Okay. A lot."

He gave her the smallest smile. "The truth is, I thought maybe *I* was going crazy. I couldn't form a coherent sentence that didn't involve my kid. I couldn't answer any of the police's damn questions. How could I? I kept sending them to different places where Nancy had to be—friends, the dance school, her babysitter's—and they kept telling me she wasn't there. She wasn't *any*where."

The pain of reliving it made his face pinch, and Joelle put her hand on his arm. She gave his wrist a reassuring squeeze and wondered if it was strange that she was the one about to offer some comfort. But her verbal response stopped before it even started because the rear of the car suddenly sagged down as though some weight had been dropped on it. Startled, she swung her attention over her shoulder. Through the rear wind-shield, she could see that the trunk had been opened in silence. A heartbeat passed, and the lid slammed shut again, revealing Maurice's oversized form. He fired them a dark grin and a salute, then headed back toward Elrissa and Nancy.

The air cut out of Joelle's lungs. "Did he just . . ."

"Yes, I think he did." Beck's tone was grim.

A silent moment passed. Joelle tried not to imagine the detective's body folded up just a few feet away. It was almost impossible.

Focus on what Beck was telling you. What were you about to say to him?

Feeling slightly dizzy, she followed her self-directed command and addressed him in what she hoped was a calm voice. "I understand if you don't want to explain the rest of what happened."

He shook his head. "No. I genuinely want you to know all of it. The extent of it." He stopped and breathed in and out a few times, then went on. "The LaBelles erased the history of her *existence*, and after a full day of trying to convince people my daughter was missing, it made me feel like I was losing my mind. The police had an EMT come in and sedate me. I woke up chained to a bed in a psych ward. I kept asking how it was possible that no one could *find* her. We kept a low profile, but we had friends. She took ballet. But everything I tried to tell them just made me seem like I'd fallen even farther over the edge. And the clincher? They went to my house, and they said they found no evidence that I had a daughter."

"But . . . *how?*"

"I don't know. Not exactly. Some of it could've been lies. Some of it could've been an elaborate game. The LaBelles have a far, far reach. Far bigger than they want anyone to know. I'm sure I lost my mind for real, at least for a while."

Joelle felt sick. "How long did they force you to live like that, Beck?"

"Long enough to be charged with murder," he replied. "Long enough to let my lawyer convince me to take a plea deal even though I'd done nothing wrong. Long enough for them to make sure that I knew they were in charge."

"I'm so sorry."

"Yeah. Me, too."

"How did you find out what had actually happened?" she wanted to know.

"When Elrissa showed up at the psych hospital," he explained, dipping his head toward the window again, indicating that he meant the woman standing beside his daughter. "She said they had her. That they'd had her all along. She showed me a fucking video. Nancy was fine. Doing schoolwork in some home office. They'd told her I was on an emergency business trip. She believed them. Why wouldn't she? And if I refused to search for the evidence—the proof of the LaBelles' cooked books—that Ward had hidden away, they'd simply keep her."

"So you agreed," she said softly.

"I did," he replied. "There was no way I was getting out on my own. My only hope for getting my daughter back was cleaning up my mind and finding a way to do what Elrissa wanted. And here we are."

Joelle's eyes drifted to the assembly in the parking lot. Elrissa, Maurice, and Nancy. The detective was no longer in sight, of course. But knowing that he'd been tucked away into the trunk of his own car—the car where they sat—did nothing to ease her mind.

Her stomach flopped. She looked at Nancy, half using the girl as an anchor. She didn't have a child of her own. But she could feel Beck's love and desperation, and she couldn't blame him for doing everything in his power to get his daughter back. Even if that meant breaking the law.

Even standing by while a police officer is executed? asked a little voice in her head.

Just the thought of trying to answer the question made her eyes sting.

"Beck . . . I don't know what to say."

"Say that you'll let it go."

She jerked her attention back to him. "What?"

"Say that you'll let Elrissa drive you into town. That you won't tell the police anything about a single thing that happened here."

"I . . ."

He closed both of his hands over hers. "Please. It's more or less what you were going to do anyway before you knew the rest of it. And they've agreed to let you go. All you have to do is pretend that you were the only survivor."

She blinked. "They'll recover the bodies."

"The LaBelles will take care of it."

She believed him. After what they'd done to him. Knowing what they were capable of where his daughter was concerned. But she still felt like she wasn't seeing the whole picture.

"Just so we're clear," she said. "You want me to go with Elrissa. You're going to take Nancy, and the two of you are going to start a life completely separate from her."

A tiny frown creased his forehead—like she was the one saying something odd. "Yes."

"And Elrissa doesn't care?"

"Why would she care?"

Now *she* frowned. "How could she not? If it were my kid, I'd—"

"Hang on," said Beck. "Did you think Elrissa was Nancy's mother?"

"Isn't she?"

"God, no. I know there's a family resemblance, but she's just a cousin. Third removed? Fourth?"

Joelle looked at the phone-immersed woman once more. She was relieved that Elrissa wasn't the girl's mother after all. Partly because she appeared to be so indifferent to Nancy, and partly because of that unwarranted jealousy.

"Nancy's mother passed away when Nancy was two," Beck said.

For what seemed to be the millionth time, Joelle's heart tightened. "I'm sorry."

"We were already separated at the time, but it was still tough," Beck admitted. "Nancy doesn't remember her at all, so she was spared that, at least."

Joelle suddenly felt like she had a hundred things to say. A hundred questions to ask. But she was also acutely aware that they were on limited time. Elrissa had finally lifted her eyes from her phone and was staring at the car with an impatient look on her face. And Beck's fingers drummed a quick beat on his knee.

"We have to go, don't we?" Joelle said, her voice doing its best to crack.

"Does that mean you'll do it?" he replied.

"It's not really a choice, is it? Not if I want to live."

"No. I guess not."

"I do have one more question, though," she said.

"What's that?" he asked.

"How can you be sure they'll keep their word?"

"I vouched for you. They know I wouldn't do that if there was a question about your integrity."

"I don't just mean their word about *me*," she replied. "What about you and Nancy? They took her once already. They framed you for murder. Why would you assume they're not just going to turn around and kill you when it suits them?"

"For one, they probably think I have some kind of failsafe set up in the event of my sudden death. And for two . . ." He paused, looked down at his hands, then lifted his eyes to meet hers. "They don't kill their own."

Joelle's brain processed his words. Her stomach dropped.

But she didn't get a chance to comment on the revelation or to ask if he really meant what she thought he meant. Because just then, a shot rang out, sending all other concerns to the wayside.

*   *   *

The stillness after the bang only dominated for a millisecond before Beck reacted. All instinct and no self-preservation, he flung open the car door and scrambled out. *Nancy.* Her name echoed through his head with far more force than the gunshot. He looked forward. *There.* She stood, motionless except for her quick breaths, right where he'd left her. Her eyes were wide with fear.

Beck didn't hesitate. He barely noted that Maurice and Elrissa had automatically hit the ground with no attendance to his daughter's safety. He simply threw himself toward her, turning his body into a shield. His attention, though, was up. His gaze darted around while his body remained a potential target.

Where had the shot come from? Was another one on its way? Then he spied the answer to both questions. The trunk to Detective Orion's sedan was open. The man himself was leaned awkwardly over the lip. He had one hand on his head, and in the other he held a gun. It was impossible to say which one or how he'd gained possession of the weapon. It didn't matter anyway. What was important was the fact that there was going to be very little time to get Nancy to safety.

Very little? he thought as the other man took wobbly aim at him. *How about none?*

Teeth gritted, he scooped his daughter from the ground, turned his back to the policeman, and braced for a bullet. Instead, a scream burst through the air.

Joelle.

Now it was her name that echoed through his head. He whipped toward the car, still clutching Nancy tightly. Joelle stood just outside the driver's side of the vehicle. Her mouth was open, and her fists were clenched, but her expression was as calm and even as could be under the circumstances. She was unharmed. And she let out another scream.

It's a distraction. Beck glanced back at Orion, whose gunhand was limp as he stared in the direction of the noise. *It's a distraction . . . and it worked. So take advantage of it!*

Except he didn't have to. Maurice had recovered, and he was already rushing toward the detective. For a moment, Beck was relieved. Glad to let the other man draw the attention. It only lasted as long as it took to realize that Joelle was still dangerously close to the line of fire—steps away from two men who were about to try to kill each other.

"Hold on tight," he said into Nancy's ear.

Clutching her close to his chest, he booked it back toward the car. Toward the two armed men. But mostly importantly, toward Joelle.

He reached her at the same second that Maurice reached Orion. Vaguely, he was aware that the former was yanking the latter from the trunk and throwing him to the ground. He caught a flash as Elrissa made a move of some kind, too— taking off, it looked like—and another explosive bang made him flinch. He didn't let any of it stop him. He grabbed hold of Joelle's hand, pulled her into the relative shelter at the front of the car, and set Nancy on the ground. Together, they crouched down.

"You two okay?" he asked, his voice just loud enough to carry over the ongoing fight.

"I scraped my knee," the girl replied.

"We'll bandage that up as soon as we can, Ladybug. My

friend here is a very good nurse," Beck said, then looked over at Joelle. "What about you, sweetheart? You okay, too?"

"I hate to say I've been worse, but maybe I have been. At least a couple of times over the last few days." Joelle wiped some errant dirt from her mouth. "Are *you* all right?"

He stole a quick glance at his daughter, and his heart immediately expanded. "So much better than I should be, probably."

As if to emphasize the comment, an unidentified smash of some kind carried through the air.

"I'm Nancy," his daughter announced, seemingly content to ignore the jarring sound. "Not Ladybug. Just in case my dad forgets to say so."

Joelle smiled a real smile that made her green eyes brighter. "I'm Joelle."

"And now that we're done with the introductions . . ." Beck tipped his head toward the SUV. "We need to make getting *there* our priority."

"Are we making a run for it, Dad?" asked Nancy.

"Guess we're going to have to, Ladybug," he replied. "You think you can stick really close to me?"

"Stick close *between* us," Joelle corrected in a light tone that didn't match the serious look that overtook her face.

Beck met her eyes. "Between us, then."

"Sure," said Nancy. "Will we count to three?"

"We will," Beck agreed. "I'll start. One." He nodded at Nancy.

"Two," she said, then tipped a raised eyebrow—a perfect copycat of the ones he knew damn well he had a habit of throwing around—at Joelle.

Joelle's lips turned up again as she started to finish their count. "Th—"

A bang echoed, and this one was different, because a man's

guttural, pain-filled cry followed it. The moment seemed to freeze. Silence dominated. Moments ticked by. Then Detective Orion started hollering.

"All right! Listen up. I have had *enough* of this fuckery. Every single one of you needs to stay exactly where you are," he said, his voice full of the authority that came with a badge. "An inch of movement without my express command, and I *will* respond with deadly force. And I'm sure none of you want to wind up like your friend Maurice."

Maurice. Shit.

Beck experienced an unusual pang of regret. He didn't like the man in the slightest. But he'd been a big, solid, dangerous force—one that stood between them and the policeman. Now he was dead. It felt like an omen.

Don't let it be.

"All right," the cop said after another moment. "Ms. Elrissa LaBelle, I can see you behind that tree. I know you're unarmed, so you can go ahead and come out first." There was a pause in his speech, and it was punctuated by the sound of heeled boots on the gravel. "That's good. Stop right there, and I thank you oh-so much for your cooperation."

There was another pause. Then another noise, this one far more disturbing than feet hitting dirt. It was the deadly crack of a gun, followed by a thud.

Beside Beck, Nancy quivered. A glance told him that her eyes were squeezed shut, while Joelle's were wide open with shock.

The detective's voice lifted over the residual echo. "And that's what happens when you try to run and hide. But you won't be making that mistake, will you, Mr. Samson? Because you're up next, and I think we'd all be sad to see you throw away your life like Ms. LaBelle. So what I want you to do is to come out from behind the car and step toward me."

"Daddy," Nancy whispered, sounding very scared and very young.

"It's going to be okay," Beck whispered back, silently promising to make sure it became the truth. "Right now, Joelle's going to take care of you for just a minute."

"The clock's ticking!" the detective called.

"Relax, Orion," said Beck. "I'm coming."

As he slowly stood up, he braced for the worst, but he got all the way to his feet without being challenged or fired at. He was able to take a small amount of consolation in seeing Nancy's hand slide into Joelle's—at least they would have each other while he dealt with Orion. The momentary buoyancy faded quickly, though, when he caught his daughter's voice once more.

"I don't want you to go out there," she whispered.

It required nearly all of Beck's willpower to keep his feet moving forward. It also took a serious amount of restraint not to simply rush at the detective. He needed to play this carefully. He had to consider the only advantages he might have, and he had to exploit them at the right moment. But he needed to be sure.

"Hands on your head," the police officer ordered. "Feet wide."

Calmly—wordlessly—Beck did as he was told, surveying the scene at the same time. Maurice was in a motionless heap a few feet away. Elrissa's body was closer, her face somehow managing to be sour despite the crimson on her chest and the slackness of her jaw. It was Orion, though, who warranted the most assessment. To say his state was bedraggled would've been a gross understatement. His clothes were torn in more places than not. The blood that had been on his face before had morphed into a congealed mess. His eyes were bloodshot to the point that they bordered on being hemorrhaged. He looked broken. Out of control. The only intimidating thing about him was the fact that he was armed.

"Hello there, Samson. Nice of you to join us." The other man smiled smugly, revealing a missing canine tooth. "And I'm glad to see you *can* follow instructions, even if it's a little later than it should've been. That means we can keep this going. Up on the agenda now is your daughter. Call her."

Beck replied in an even tone. "You don't need her."

"Oh, but I do. She, apparently, is the real key to getting the information you've hidden away." Orion cocked his head. "Funny how I thought it was your moral compass."

"My moral compass tells me that using a child to get what you want is wrong."

"Why don't you tell that to your family?"

"Believe me, Orion," said Beck, "I did. Repeatedly."

"And yet, you gave *them* the evidence that you should've given to me," the detective replied.

"Just leave Nancy out of it."

"Too late for that. Tell her to come out, or I'll make this unpleasant."

Spikes of ice jabbed at Beck's spine. "If you hurt her, I'll kill you, I swear to God."

Orion clicked his tongue in a *tsk-tsk* noise. "You do know that this isn't a negotiation, or even a discussion, don't you? I give the orders. You obey them."

"I'm just offering you fair warning."

"Right. Okay. Warning received. You'll kill me. I heard you." The cop rolled his eyes and jerked the weapon toward the sedan. "Now tell her to come out."

"Ladybug?" Beck called, making sure to keep his gaze level with Orion's as he spoke. "I need you to come out here and see me."

For a second, there was no response. He pictured Nancy's fingers tightening around Joelle's palm as she fought to stay where she was. In his head, he heard Joelle offering some falsely cheerful reassurance just as he'd done. Dreading it, he opened his mouth to call out again. He didn't have to. Nancy appeared at the end of the car, her thin shoulders rigidly straight as she marched out to join him. Under other circumstances, Beck might've been proud. Right then, he was just straight-up pissed off.

He narrowed his eyes at the policeman, unable to stop himself from speaking. "You want me to call for Joelle, too, or can you do your own dirty work where grownups are concerned?"

In response, Orion raised his voice. "Okay, next up is the lovely redhead. Time to join the party. Get to your feet—slowly—and come out here and stand beside your boyfriend."

"Boyfriend?" Nancy whispered right away.

Beck gave her the smallest nudge with his hip. "Not right now, okay?"

He lifted his eyes to the car, his anger rising up as Joelle stepped into the open with her hands raised. She was moving slowly, as asked. It pained him to know that this was all because of him. He had to make it right. He *would* make it right. He brought his gaze back to Orion. Then to the gun. And it struck him that he might actually know how.

Chapter Twenty-Four

Joelle paused for the briefest moment, her eyes running over Beck and his daughter. Beck, of course, appeared to be doing his best to hide an understandable fury. But it was Nancy that made Joelle's heart hurt. She looked as though she was trying not to cry, and her wide blue gaze kept slipping over to her father. It was heartbreaking. And anger-inducing. There were two dead bodies just feet away. An armed man staring them down. And the little girl had done nothing to deserve any of this.

Nothing but being born into the wrong family.

Joelle pushed off the thought. She hadn't yet had time to process that piece yet. And now wasn't the time to start trying.

She stole a look at the detective. It bothered her a lot that the man making all of this happen was the one who not only held the power, but also the one who sat on the right side of the law. She wanted to rail against it. All of it just felt so very wrong.

"Any time, Ms. Diedrich," said Orion.

Realizing she'd completely stalled, Joelle picked up her feet and finished walking over to join the trio and await their shared fate. She positioned herself beside Beck, and she probably stood a tiny bit nearer than necessary. But it was worth it when she felt the reassuring heat of his body. At the very least, it made her breathing easier. It allowed her to focus. She wondered what the policeman was going to do. His current antics seemed like overkill. But then again, he'd just freed himself from a trunk and shot a man and a woman dead. Would he read them their rights? Arrest them? Was she going to be lumped in with the LaBelle family and their criminal undertakings? At the very least, she thought he would have to find a way to separate Nancy from all of it. If it'd been Joelle, she would've done that already. But Orion's eyes just hung on Beck.

"Where is it?" he said.

"Gone by now," Beck replied, his tone surprisingly combative.

"Bullshit," the detective snapped.

"You were *here*, Orion, when I gave Maurice the info. He gave the location to his boss. Do you really think they're stupid enough to leave it where it was for a single minute more?"

Anxiety made Joelle's pulse jump. Why did he sound like he was picking a fight with the policeman? As much as his family association might make them natural enemies, he had to know that playing nice—even if that meant lying—was the only way to save his daughter's life.

But he persisted. "It doesn't matter anymore. Not to you. It's done. And even if I *had* given you the location first, you would never have been able to get to it."

"You have no idea what I'm capable of," replied the policeman.

"No, but I have some idea of what you're *in*capable of."

"Fuck you, Samson."

"I'm not wrong, Detective. Might as well admit it."

"What you *are* is walking a thin line," said Orion.

"I'm not walking any line at all. This is over. You lost."

The cop's bloodshot eyes blazed even more. "I'm only going to give you so many chances. Where's the evidence, Samson?"

"I think you mean where *was* the evidence," said Beck.

"Semantics."

"Facts."

Abruptly, the policeman raised his gun and aimed it at Nancy. "Where the fuck did you put it?"

Joelle inhaled sharply. What in God's name was he doing now? Her heart tried to beat its way through her ribcage. Had the detective lost his mind? He'd already practically executed Elrissa.

Beck, though, somehow managed to sound calm. "It *was* at Henri LaBelle's house, in his bedroom, taped to the underside of his bed. Or at least that's where it *was* an hour ago."

"Fuck," growled the other man.

He pulled back the gun and scratched his chin with it. He took a step, looking like he was preparing to pace the ground in front of their three-person lineup. But his second step ended in a limp, and he grimaced and spun back to them without moving any farther.

"You just sealed the fate of everyone here, Samson," he said. "You realize that, right?"

"Me?" Beck replied. "I'm not the one hiding behind my badge while pointing a gun at an innocent child."

"Beck," Joelle whispered. "Please stop."

He tipped a look her way and answered her far more loudly than necessary. "Stop what? Calling it like it is?"

"You might want to listen to her," the policeman said.

"I've been listening to her for days, Orion," Beck stated. "Now I'm listening to *you*, like you asked. Unless you want me to stop doing that."

"Shut up."

"Right back at you."

"Beck!" Joelle gasped.

Beck let out a laugh, and Joelle wondered if he was falling off the deep end. He was going to get himself killed. He was going to get *all* of them killed.

Killed by someone whose job it is to uphold the law, a voice in her head reminded her.

Except it didn't matter. She wanted him to live. She wanted him to have the time with his daughter that he deserved.

He spoke up again. "You said something about fate, Detective. Why don't you tell me what it was supposed to be, before all this? Because I sure as hell can't figure it out."

The other man swiped his hand over his face, and the motion left a smear of blood in its wake. "For starters, you were never supposed to figure out what was going on."

"Then you and your friends should've done your due diligence."

Something in Joelle's brain clicked. *His friends. The gun pointed at Nancy. His aggressive pursuit of the evidence.* It was all connected, and it had nothing to with Orion's status as a cop. Yes, he was a detective. But not a good one. He had to be working with the rival gang Beck had told her about. The same men who'd been chasing them the whole time. Relief—which seemed contradictory in some ways—floated up as the conversation carried on.

"No amount of due diligence would've led us to your daughter," Orion said.

"No," Beck agreed, his expression slightly pained. "My extended family made sure of that, didn't they? But with some extra effort, you might've figured out that I was already searching for the thing your bosses wanted. At the very least, it might've saved you the hassle of creating this elaborate ruse. You could've sat back and waited."

"Why the fuck would any of us think you'd choose the people who killed your business partner and framed you for it over the goddamn police?" the other man countered.

"Again . . . due diligence."

The detective's eyes narrowed in irritation, and Joelle belatedly realized one more thing. Beck wasn't just being flippant or careless with his words. He was goading the other man on purpose. He had a plan of some kind, and whatever it was, it involved distracting the detective. Maybe even pissing him off. Her relief grew. And a bit of anticipation joined it.

"What was next?" Beck added. "If you hadn't been intercepted by the LaBelles, what would you have done? You weren't going to give me that new identity you promised me because you didn't *have* a new identity to give me. There's no witness protection offered on behalf of corrupt cops."

"Did I imply that *your* fate wasn't previously sealed, Samson?" Orion shook his head. "I was only talking about them. You were always going to die."

Nancy burst into tears. Beck flicked a look down at her, and Joelle could easily read his expression—whatever he was about to say, he would rather she didn't hear it.

"So why are you holding back?" he asked. "Go ahead. Kill me now. You can't get your evidence. You're going to have to go back to your bosses and tell them how you failed. How you got bested before you even got going. How you were *had*. Might as well make yourself good for something."

"Don't tempt me, Samson."

"I'm not tempting you, asshole. I'm not swinging my hips and sending you a wink. I'm *daring* you. Calling your bluff. But

I'm guessing you won't follow through. Far too chicken shit to even *try* to make a decision on your own, aren't you?"

Joelle wasn't expecting the cop to take the bait. She wasn't even sure what the bait was intended to do. So when he lifted his weapon, pointed it at Beck, and squeezed the trigger, all she could do was stand rooted to the spot in shock.

*   *   *

Nothing happened. No flying bullet. No bang. Just the barely audible click of an empty gun. Then silence.

Beck wanted to smile. Especially when Orion tried again, and a stunned look made its way across his face. Maybe Beck *did* smile, just a little. He also didn't waste any time. He surged forward at full speed and threw his body weight at the detective.

The smaller man fell easily. His body folded, and he landed on the gravel with a noise that might as well have been a squeak. That might've made Beck smile, too, if not for the fact that it wasn't a sign of defeat. The detective fought back. He bucked up his hips and thrashed. He threw his head forward in an attempt to hit Beck's face. It was the spitting, though, that gave him his break. When the blood and saliva spattered, Beck couldn't stop himself from pulling away. It was a mistake.

One of the detective's fists came up right away, catching Beck in the kidney, and the pain was sharp enough to make his eyes water. A second and third rapid punch in the same spot increased the stab to intolerable. Which, of course, was Orion's plan. Beck had no choice but to try to catch his breath, and it gave the policeman just enough time and space that he managed to wriggle free. With an agility that belied his visible injuries, the cop sprung to his feet. With the expertise of someone trained to do it, he drew back his palm and drove the heel of his hand into Beck's chin. Beck wished he could say his size and strength saved him. They didn't. He stumbled then fell.

Blinking against the spots that danced over his vision, he braced for a renewal of the attack. But the detective was too wily to simply come at him again. Instead, the other man redirected himself. He was moving at a sprint, and it only took a moment to figure out his goal. He was after the only thing that would give him any kind of upper hand. Nancy.

Beck started to push himself up, but dizziness hit hard, impeding his progress. Thankfully, though, Joelle was closer and faster. In a breath, she was reacting to the man headed their way. She pulled Nancy in close and backed quickly out of Orion's reach. Relief was brief. Joelle's rescue maneuver threw her off balance. As she tried to stay upright, her foot caught a rock, and she slipped, taking Beck's daughter with her as she landed ass-first on the gravel.

Shit.

Beck scrambled to finish getting up. As he stood, the world blurred, then came into focus. He could see that he was too late. Joelle was still on the ground, but in that moment, it was secondary. Because Orion had Nancy. He *had* Beck's daughter. The other man's hands were on her. His fingers gripping her shoulders and pressing into her clavicles.

Everything else around Beck ceased to matter.

"Give her to me," he said.

The detective's reddened eyes glittered. There was a knowing look there. Something dark. Not a smile. Worse, somehow.

"I don't think so," the other man replied.

With his focus on Beck, he lifted Nancy from the ground. She screamed. She twisted in his arms, and she clawed at his face. He held her back. Like she was a gnat. An irritation.

An awful realization filled Beck's mind, and it was the worst thing he'd ever considered—the idea that Orion could kill Nancy with his bare hands. He had to stop it. He had to cut it off before it became something more than a thought. With his heart in his throat, he surged forward. It was clearly a move that the other man wasn't expecting. He didn't just lose his grip on Nancy and release her; he tossed her from his hands and turned to stagger in the other direction.

Beck had to go after him. He knew he did. But Nancy was on the ground. She was crying, and her lip was split. The agony of choosing between comforting her in the moment and saving her for good—and the latter was definitely the priority—gave Beck a moment of paralyzing indecision. It was just long enough for the choice to be taken away from him.

A sharp bang sounded. Orion fell, clutching his neck as blood flowed out between his fingers.

Beck was clueless as to where the shot had come from for only a second. Then his eyes fixed on Maurice. The big man was no longer crumpled up. Instead, he was on his side with his gun in his hand and his arm outstretched. Beck stared for one more heartbeat, then scooped Nancy into his arms and pulled her small, sobbing body against his chest.

* * *

Shock at the quick unfolding of events held Joelle pinned to the spot for several moments. A dead man had come to life. He'd fired his gun. And he'd quite possibly kept them from being killed.

Then her subconscious roared up, hollering out the obvious. *He's not dead, you idiot!*

It was enough to yank her from her motionless state. Her training kicked in, and she rushed over to Maurice's side. She didn't like the man—or anything he stood for—but he was in need of medical attention, and she could give it. Joelle dropped to her knees, determined to save him the way he'd just saved them. But the moment she put her hand on his shoulder and rolled him to his back, she knew it couldn't be done. He had a gaping hole in his stomach. He shouldn't have been able to move at all, let alone fire off a shot.

"I'm sorry," she said, meaning it.

He blinked once, then went still in the way that only the dead can. Joelle pressed his eyes closed, silently thanked him for what he'd done with his final moments, then pushed to her feet. With the intention of seeking out Beck and his daughter, she turned. But instead of finding the two of them, her attention landed on Orion. He was splayed out. Unmoving. Dead, surely. But Joelle wasn't taking any chances this time. She'd thought he was dead in the back of the sedan. She'd thought Maurice was dead on the ground. So she had to be sure. She stepped to the detective's body, knelt down, and—even though his eyes were open and vacant and fixed up at the sky—she put her fingers on his bloody throat. There was no pulse. She moved her fingers to his wrist. No sign of life there either.

She exhaled, then stood up and walked over to Elrissa. Throat, no pulse. Wrist, no pulse. When she was sure that the thin woman was also gone for good, she looked back at Orion, wondering if she ought to check once more, no matter how crazy it seemed. She straightened up and started to move. But Beck's voice stopped her.

"Joelle?" His tone was gentle—like he was worried about her mental state.

She spun. And when her eyes landed on him, and she took in his appearance, a sudden anger fizzled up. He had the beginning of a black eye. His shirt was torn from the neck to a point halfway down his chest. The gunshot wound that she'd patched up earlier had opened and was oozing a little. And for some reason, he had one of his boots in his hand. He was a mess.

"Joelle?" he said again, her name sounding different this time.

She tossed her hair and crossed her arms. "Where's Nancy?"

"I put her in the back of the SUV while you were checking the bodies. We have to think about going, and she needed to sit down anyway."

"Good."

"What?"

"You're a jerk," she said. "And your daughter doesn't need to hear about it."

Confusion marked his face. "Are you *mad* at me?"

"Extremely."

"Forgive me for saying this, but I don't understand."

"Please just tell me you knew the gun was empty," she said. "Even if it's a lie."

His expression cleared, and he dropped his boot to the ground, then wiggled his foot into it before taking a couple of steps closer. Joelle didn't budge, but she did give him a look that made him slow his approach.

"I knew, sweetheart," he said. "I would never have gambled on my daughter's life. Or on yours."

"What about your own?" she retorted. "Were you totally happy to sacrifice yourself in some form of martyrdom?"

For a second, she thought he might deny it, even though his face gave away the truth. But he just sighed.

"I would most definitely sacrifice myself, if it came down to it," he admitted. "In this case, though, I didn't have to. As soon as I saw the gun, I realized I knew the bullets were all gone."

"Then why'd you waste time riling him up?" she asked.

"I wanted him to admit that he was a self-serving scumbag while he thought he was still in charge."

"Swear that it's true," she replied.

"I swear. I wouldn't be able to enjoy the annoyed look on your face if I were dead, would I?"

"You scared the shit out of me."

He chuckled. "I think that's the first time I've heard you swear."

Heat crept up her cheeks. "No, it's not. I definitely told you to fuck off a few minutes ago."

"Second time then," he amended. "Third if I count the extra one you just dropped."

"Yeah, well. It's a bad habit."

"I picked it up in prison." He glanced toward the SUV. "But I guess I'm going to have to let it go now."

"I guess you will." She still wasn't quite done being mad, and she lifted her chin and narrowed her eyes. "Is your name even Beck Samson, or is it Beck LaBelle? Is your first name different, too?"

"My name really is Beck Samson. Beck Henry Samson, actually."

"Are you, or are you *not* a member of the LaBelle crime family?"

"I'm not a member of the LaBelle crime family. But my mother *was* born a LaBelle."

"So . . . what? You just decided not to join the family business? To not become a *LaBelle* LaBelle?"

"Not me. Though I like to think I would've made the same choice. It was my mom who left it behind when she met my father," he said. "She stopped being a *LaBelle* LaBelle the moment she fell in love with him. When I was old enough, she explained to me where she'd come from and what the break from them meant."

Some of Joelle's taut anger eased. But not all of it.

"If that's true, then why would they ask you to do their dirty bookwork?" she asked.

"Because they knew who I was and what I did for a living, and they like to keep things in the family," he explained. "They wanted to give me first crack at what they considered to be a good opportunity."

"And what about your wife? Your business partner?"

"I was at the beginning of my career and just paying back my student loans. She thought I should take their offer. I disagreed. Heartily. And from that . . . I learned a few things about her and her priorities. About the real reason she'd married me."

Even more tension lifted.

"She wanted money," Joelle said.

Beck nodded. "She did. She'd had a hard life—one no one should endure, really—and she didn't understand why we couldn't take the so-called easy route."

"You wouldn't do it. And that's why she went to your business partner."

"Yes. On both accounts."

Joelle hesitated, then decided she might as well get all her questions out of the way. "Is it okay if I ask how she died?"

He nodded again. "Of course you can. Tonya and Ward had the affair I told you about before. She convinced him that signing on with the LaBelles was a winning situation. He bought the deal. Kept going with it until he thought betraying them was worth more. But thankfully, Tonya's death was unrelated to me or my family or any of her involvement with my former business partner. She got sick. It was mercifully short and indescribably sad. My daughter lost her mother. I lost the mother *of* my daughter."

Joelle's heart twinged. "I know I said it before, but I'm so sorry, Beck. And that's more than a platitude."

He moved forward, and she finally let him finish closing the gap between them. When he reached out and touched her face with the tips of his fingers, she leaned into the caress.

"You know what it's like to lose someone," he said. "I wouldn't take your words as anything but sincere."

She nodded, her throat thick with emotion. "What happens now?"

"Nothing's changed. Not for me. I have Nancy. We have our new identities. We have the SUV and the cash to make a fresh start. And that's all I set out for in the first place."

Joelle cast a look at the devastation around them. "What about the rest of it? Do you think the LaBelles will still be able to cover this up? There's a dead policeman now."

"Yes, but the man who killed him is dead, too."

"True. But he's one of theirs, right? Maurice was a LaBelle?" she asked.

Beck shook his head. "Not quite. Maurice was hired muscle."

"Elrissa?" she replied.

"Yes." He said it softly as he glanced toward the thin woman's still form. "She's a member of the family, and they won't be too happy to have lost her. But it'll be a closed loop for them. Elrissa will be found to have had some kind of business with Orion. She'll have brought Maurice along as protection. And then it will have just ended badly for everyone."

"I guess I don't need to ask whether the reason for the meeting will magically appear."

"No."

"And they won't be looking for someone else to blame?" Joelle said.

"Someone like me, you mean?" he replied.

"Yes."

"No, they won't come after me."

"They did before," she pointed out.

"Only because their whole enterprise was threatened," he said. "Now that threat is gone."

"Until next time."

"I'm going to operate on the assumption that I'll never be in this position again."

Joelle nodded. She understood. It was the only way he *could* operate.

"And me?" she asked.

"That's up to you," he said. "I can drive you close to town. Or you can hike the few miles and clear your head. Or even take Orion's car, if you want. Although I think that might add more questions than you want to answer."

"Probably," she agreed, her throat growing scratchy again.

"There is one other option."

"What is it?"

He brought his hand to the back of his neck and awkwardly cleared his throat. "I could call in one final favor, and you could come with me."

"You mean, *with you* with you?" she replied.

"Yes. *With me* with me. And Nancy, too." He paused. "I'm sorry. It's an asinine suggestion, and I know it."

"No, it's not that. It's . . ." She trailed off.

It was what? She didn't know. She really didn't.

"Dad?" called Nancy, her small voice making them both turn to face the SUV.

Her face peeked out from one of the rear windows.

"I'll be right there, Ladybug," Beck replied.

"And Joelle?"

"Maybe. One more minute okay?"

"I'll start counting," said Nancy, rolling the window back up.

Beck laughed, and the sound made Joelle simultaneously

want to throw herself into his arms and burst into tears. His smile softened, then went sad, and she wondered if he was feeling the same thing. A sense of loss and need and something bigger than both of them. She thought he must, because he reached out and touched her face again, then leaned in and brush his lips over hers.

"It was just a crazy thought after some crazy days," he said against her mouth. "I'll be in the car. I won't leave until you decide, but I suspect I should err on the side of speed."

Joelle nodded because she didn't trust herself to speak. She watched Beck pick up the discarded envelope—the one that Elrissa had brought him—then walk over to the SUV and climb in. She took one step toward it, too. Then she stopped. What was she doing?

Maybe I'm just getting a ride close to town like he suggested, she said to herself.

Except she knew it wasn't true. The moment she put herself into the vehicle would be the same moment she admitted that there was no part of her heart that objected to turning her back on everything she knew and starting over. An entirely unreasonable thing to do. Crazy, just like Beck had said. People didn't just erase their pasts. They didn't leave behind their job and the people they knew. Not without some kind of explanation. Not without someone trying to figure out why they'd just disappeared off the face of the earth. Yet her feet brought her nearer to the SUV again. And belatedly, she noted that the passenger side door hung open. A clear invitation. As Joelle stared at it, the radio came to life with a male announcer's booming voice that carried out of the vehicle and into the air.

"And now, folks," said the man, *"we've got the final update on that tragic plane crash we've been reporting on for the last few days. A formal statement from the airline confirms what we've*

suspected to be true all along. No survivors. Our deepest and most sincere condolences go out to the loved ones of the victims. Now over to Janice for the latest on traffic."

Joelle tuned the next bit out. Her mind hung on the fact that she'd been declared dead. It should've made her shiver. Or at least been a little off-putting. But all she felt was an unburdening. For so many months, she'd felt alone. Guilty. Incomplete. But over the last three days, that had eased. She'd been in an actual plane crash. Shot at. Knocked unconscious. And yet, without all of that hardship, she wouldn't have met Beck. She wouldn't have at last let go of the burden of responsibility for her mother's death. She wouldn't be seeing something other than her own grief. And she realized something. She might be dead in one world. But she was being given a chance to be reborn into another. And what would be *crazy* crazy would be not to take the leap.

Wiping the tears from her cheeks, Joelle smiled. Then she straightened her shoulders and made her way toward that open, welcoming door.

Epilogue

Six months later . . .

"Ms. Channing to the office, please. That's Ms. Channing to the office."

It took Joelle a second to remember that the person being paged over the school intercom was her. In fact, it wasn't until the kid walking beside her gave her a funny look that she clued in. She was actually starting to wonder if she would ever get used to it.

"Okay, Evan," she said to the kid. "I am completely sure that your arm *isn't* broken. Not this time, anyway. Just be a bit more careful when you're using the stairs for stunt moves, okay?"

The boy—a chronic faller—gave her a solemn nod, then took off right as the announcement came again.

"Ms. Channing, you're needed at the office."

"I'm coming, I'm coming," Joelle muttered.

She picked up her pace and silently hoped that whatever the emergency was, it wouldn't take too long. She loved her position as the school nurse at the middle school. Truly. Even though half a year had gone by, she could still hardly believe that the LaBelles were powerful enough to have set this up. And yet . . . they were. Her falsified identity had passed the required background checks with flying colors. The school-board had accepted her far more easily than she'd accepted herself. And as much as she hated feeling any gratitude toward the crime family, she had to acknowledge that she was thankful for her new life. Often, she felt like this job was the calling she'd been missing. But tonight, she and Beck and Nancy had dinner plans that'd already been rescheduled three times, and they were overdue for some family time.

Family time.

The phrase made her smile. It was another thing that she couldn't quite wrap her head around. But in the best way possible, of course.

She reached the office door and pushed it open, speaking as she stepped into the space. "What's the—oh!"

She nearly stumbled as she caught sight of the group crowded around the reception desk. The office staff was present. So were the two administrators. Every teacher was in attendance, too. All fourteen of them. Including Beck, who taught the older kids woodworking. Even Nancy stood nearby.

Joelle tried again to speak. "What—"

This time, she was cut off by Beck dropping to his knee. When he did, the entire room went quiet. So did Joelle. She held her breath, her heart burning with surprised anticipation.

* * *

Vaguely, Beck was aware that everyone else—all their new friends, whom he'd invited to witness his plan—were still there. His eyes, though, were on Joelle. On the crimson wave of her hair. On those entrancing green eyes and on that soft mouth that was so often full of sass.

It was hard to believe that it'd only been six months since the two of them had crash-landed into their new life together.

The transition from not knowing each other at all to this intertwined existence had been seamless. Looking at her now, it was like she'd always been a part of him. And yet there was still one small move to make. A token of permanence that would cement them together all the more.

So what are you waiting for, Samson?

Beck cleared his throat, squeezed the velvet box in his hand, then opened his fingers. "Jo . . ."

He had a speech prepared. Really. Except he couldn't remember a word of it.

"I love you," he said lamely.

"I love *you*," she replied softly.

"Do you want to . . ." Again, he trailed off. His throat was scratchy with emotion. But thankfully, he didn't have to explain.

"Yes," said Joelle. "Yes, please."

Quickly, Beck freed the ring and slid it onto her finger. A general cheer erupted, and someone in the small crowd popped open some bubbly. Nancy pushed her way past him to throw her arms around Joelle, and he heard her whisper.

"Maybe it will be easier to remember your new last name if it's the same as ours," his daughter said to the woman who would soon be his wife.

HEADLINE
ETERNAL

FIND YOUR HEART'S DESIRE...

VISIT OUR WEBSITE: www.headlineeternal.com
FIND US ON FACEBOOK: facebook.com/eternalromance
CONNECT WITH US ON TWITTER: @eternal_books
FOLLOW US ON INSTAGRAM: @headlineeternal
EMAIL US: eternalromance@headline.co.uk